"What are you doing?"

she demanded on a shrill note of panic.

"Up until this second," he admitted with a more honest and less fierce sigh, "I hadn't really made up my mind. But I'm going over to that broken window, Miz. S. MacLean. I'm going to climb through it, which means that you must climb through it, too. I am, as I believe you legal people put it, going to leave the scene."

Lifting his foot, he karate-kicked the worst slivers of glass to the ground outside, and then, while both of them bent into contortions that they would have found enormously funny under different circumstances, he crawled through.

When only their cuffed hands spanned the breach over the glass, he gave her a surprisingly endearing grimace. "Please do be careful, counselor. All I need is a bleeding albatross around my wrist."

Dear Reader,

Spellbinders! That's what we're striving for. The editors at Silhouette are determined to capture your imagination and win your heart with every single book we publish. Each month, six Special Editions are chosen with *you* in mind.

Our authors are our inspiration. Writers such as Nora Roberts, Tracy Sinclair, Kathleen Eagle, Carole Halston and Linda Howard—to name but a few—are masters at creating endearing characters and heart-rending love stories. Their characters are everyday people—just like you and me—whose lives have been touched by love, whose dream and desire suddenly comes true!

So find a cozy, quiet place to read, and create your own special moment with a Silhouette Special Edition.

Sincerely,

Rosalind Noonan
Senior Editor
SILHOUETTE BOOKS

LINDA SHAW
Something about Summer

Silhouette Special Edition
Published by Silhouette Books New York
America's Publisher of Contemporary Romance

SILHOUETTE BOOKS
300 East 42nd St., New York, N.Y. 10017

Copyright © 1986 by Linda Shaw Ltd.

ISBN: 0-373-09325-X

First Silhouette Books printing August 1986

America's Publisher of Contemporary Romance

Printed in the U.S.A.

Books by Linda Shaw

Silhouette Special Edition

December's Wine #19
All She Ever Wanted #43
After the Rain #67
Way of the Willow #97
A Thistle in the Spring #121
A Love Song and You #151
One Pale, Fawn Glove #224
Kisses Don't Count #276
Something about Summer #325

Silhouette Intimate Moments

The Sweet Rush of April #78

LINDA SHAW

is the mother of three children and enjoys her life in Keene, Texas, which she shares with her husband. When Linda isn't writing romantic novels, she's practicing or teaching the piano, violin or viola.

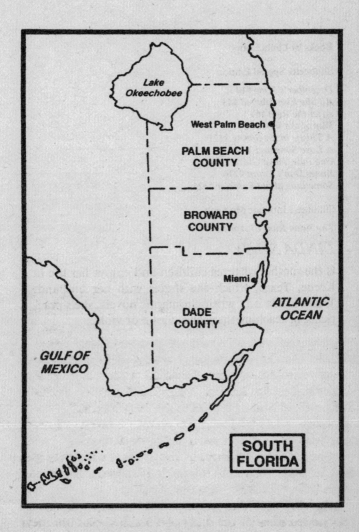

Chapter One

Lila Dean had the nose. When she began work on her infamous feature about the state prosecutor for the *Miami Herald*, she virtually smelled the story. The trouble was, the piece she ended up writing wasn't about Neil Jarvis at all.

"Ms. MacLean, definitely," several of the Metro-Dade detectives told Lila when she asked them who their first choice was over at Judicial. "You can depend on Summer. She puts in the hours it takes to get the job done."

"Hmm," Lila said with her notorious laugh. "I heard that Summer MacLean was a pretty tough cookie."

"She has to be," a sergeant said. "Do you have any idea how long we tried to put Reynoldo Martinez away on narcotics before she nailed him on fraud?"

Lila told herself that no one could be that good, and she interviewed some of the other one-hundred-plus attorneys who assisted the state prosecutor.

A number of them privately admitted, "Hey, yeah, I'd like Summer's job. She's a division chief. She'll undoubtedly move up when Neil does, though I don't know why she wants to. The state prosecutor's job doesn't pay worth a hoot. It does look good on the old résumé though, doesn't it?"

"Summer MacLean is a rags-to-riches story." Summer's neighbors in Coconut Grove knew the MacLean family from way back. "But she keeps her lawn as neat as any man. Gets the garbage out every Monday and Thursday."

Reynoldo Martinez's opinion was brief and to the point: "Bitch!"

When Lila took Summer MacLean to lunch at Versailles the last week of June, she expected to meet either a sterling-silver paragon or an ambitious shrew. She was surprised to find a petite, pretty woman in her mid-thirties whose toughness consisted of a pleasant smile and an unassuming manner and whose ambition consisted of only the desire to have a nice lunch.

"I do my job, Lila," Summer said with a charm that went well with her smile. "Like everyone else."

"Some say you do yours and the prosecutor's too," Lila pointed out. She privately hoped for at least one scrap of scandal to justify the time she'd invested in the story. "Some go so far as to say Neil Jarvis wouldn't have gotten a second term without you."

"It's true that Neil's duties are primarily in administration now," Summer said and was too clever to nibble at the bait. "Miami's carrying a heavy load. It's ridiculous to think that Neil can stay in the courtroom."

"Ridiculous?"

"If you're thinking what I think you're thinking, Lila, Neil Jarvis is one of the most conscientious, hard-working men I know."

"And the fact that he's good-looking and a bachelor doesn't hurt a bit, does it?"

"No more than the fact that you are good-looking and single," Summer said with a shrewd smile.

The one thing Lila was not was good-looking, and she knew it. "Do you want Neil's job?"

"Only if he's finished with it."

Laughing, Lila accepted her defeat gracefully. "I knew there wasn't any truth to that rumor that you're a tough lady."

"Of course there isn't." Summer's cinnamon-brown eyes twinkled with a dozen hints of candor as she swept up the lunch tab before Lila could signal the waiter. "And if you print that, I'll break your knuckles."

Lila was stymied. Paper-selling stories got into people's laundry, and she couldn't uncover even one grain of dirt on Summer MacLean: no penchant for wild parties—not much of anything since the tragedy involving her husband a year before—no off-duty sex with a man, no questionable relationship with a woman, no pills, no booze, no unsavory characters rattling around in her closet.

Her piece for the paper ended up being a comparison between the ten best and the ten worst of the Florida judicial system. At the top of the "best" was Summer MacLean. "MacLean is evidently a title of excellence in this state," she wrote. Midway down the "worst" list was the state prosecutor. Lila also accused Neil Jarvis of being "a master of evasive moves" and said that the only case he had gotten close to in the past year was "a five-hundred-dollar, endangered-species one." She concluded with, "If it weren't for assistants like MacLean, the state prosecutor might very well find himself an endangered species."

By Friday afternoon the feature was old news. Neil Jarvis was over his purple funk and his threats to sue the *Herald* for slander. Summer, no longer amused by Lila's alligator-style critique, was standing at the window of her office in the municipal building, listening to the bronchial wheeze of the air-conditioner.

She gazed moodily down at the traffic creeping along Thirteenth Street and unconsciously slipped a fingernail between her teeth and nibbled on it. Annoyed at herself, she jerked down her hand, walked to a desk drawer, petulantly ripped off a piece of tape and wrapped it around the nail to prevent future lapses into old habits. If anyone had asked her at this moment if she was tough, she would have shaken her head.

"Not today," she would have confessed. "It happened a year ago today."

The truth was, Summer had several titles that Lila Dean had hardly touched upon. The diplomas on her office wall were penned by hand: Jacqueline Summerfield, B.A., M.A. Her marriage certificate, in a box inside her closet with Martin's things to be sorted through one day, was officially typed: Jacqueline Summerfield MacLean. The sign on her desk had come with the office: Chief MacLean. Summer prosecuted cases of fraud for the state of Florida. To her son Tom, now twelve, she was simply, "Mom."

As far as physical aspects went, Summer had never been overly enamored with her body. It was healthy and functional, with breasts and hips and all the right equipment for having babies and sex. To her mind, when a woman was five-feet, three-inches tall and the world's glamour queens were nearer to six, there invariably came a day when she stood before the mirror stark naked, wished her nipples were noticeably turgid, held in her stomach and turned so that her thighs didn't look quite so mushy—though then she noticed that her fanny was beginning to droop—and she said, "What the heck? At thirty-four, a woman's nipples don't have to be buttons and the photographer for *Penthouse* isn't coming. Cover it all up."

She had a very nice face though. She liked her brown eyes with their long, spidery lashes and her mouth that was a little too wide and its lower lip fuller than it should be. Even her nose with its perky little tip had a tendency to tilt upward. Her teeth were pretty. Her fair complexion was more than nice, and her hair was outstanding. An ash-brown mane with a mind of its own, it tumbled over her shoulders and down her back when she let it down—a thing she rarely did, however, literally or figuratively.

Some people were of the opinion that Summer's small stature was what lent her her legal wallop. Sort of like a gun looking more frightening in the hands of a woman than a man. Summer denied that. In Miami, whose largest natural resource was a toss-up between seafood and crime, professionalism was the ticket. And whatever Summer did, whether it was giving an interview to a newspaper or sitting at lunch with one of the municipal mayors, meeting with an informant or addressing the courtroom before a jury, even intimidating the detectives next door, no one could question her professionalism.

Now Summer scrutinized the clock on her office wall for the dozenth time. The minute hand had to be paralyzed. It wasn't, of course; she was having an anxiety attack.

"To hell with this," she finally muttered.

She strode briskly to the door and down the hall that led to the half-glass, half-panel liaison booth where secretaries struggled, not always successfully, to keep the courts from becoming snarled. She poked half of herself around a door and broke her own rule.

"Angelica," she called out, "I'm taking off early. If anyone wants me, I've headed for West Palm."

One of the receptionists shot up like an exclamation point. She hung up her phone and screwed up a lovely Puerto Rican face.

"You can't," Angelica said and walked over. "That was Neil. I think Judge Starky just put his tail through a wringer. Among other things, Neil asked . . . Did I say asked? His voice was trembling. You know what happens when Neil's voice trembles."

"The earth moves," Summer replied dryly. "I'll wait."

Angelica rolled her eyes in gratitude toward heaven. "Thank you."

Summer and Angelica Santez had been friends since college. Though Angelica was a few years younger and saw everything in almost total reverse of Summer, there was something to be said for the old axiom of opposites attracting. Perpetually single, Angelica was always madly in love with someone. She shed her clothes as easily as she got into them and passed through one flaming affair after another with ease.

Summer secretly admired anyone who could do anything with ease, even if it was taking off their clothes. Angelica had been the only person she had trusted with the secret about her marriage.

"Martin's parents want Tom to come up for the summer," she explained to Angelica. "What they'd like is for Tom to live with them, period. They just don't have the nerve to come right out and say so." She frowned at her mutilated fingernail. "Things are a bit tedious these days. Tom needs a break from me, I think."

"Maybe it's time you took a break from Tom."

When Summer didn't respond, Angelica added gently, "It wouldn't be a sin, chief. Martin and Bobby have been gone a year now. You can be a regular person and get tired, you know. You could lose your temper. I would forgive you. You could even . . . don't get mad now, you could even go out with this really nice man I know."

Not in the mood for a pep talk and particularly disinclined to admit that getting propositioned was the furthest thing from her mind, Summer knew better than anyone how long it had been—that drive up to Martin's parents' with the twins, her hands controlling the wheel, the big semi gone wild and skidding straight for them, intensive care, the nightmare of those two caskets....

Leaning forward, Summer twisted her mouth into a grimace and said in a mock whisper, "Angelica?"

"What?"

"Love doesn't cure everything."

The girl giggled. "I was thinking more in the lines of good, casual sex."

With a doleful shake of her head, Summer started walking toward her office. "And that may leave *you* having to get cured."

Laughing, Angelica called out, "Are you driving up to West Palm?"

With a lift of her brows, that clearly stated, "You know I don't drive anymore," Summer retorted, "We're taking the train, and I'm not staying but one night. You can reach me at home tomorrow."

Intending to bury everything in tons of work—her weekend, her memories, her lonely bed—Summer removed an attaché case from the portable closet that served as a partition between her office and that of her two-person staff. She tossed it onto her desk and began cramming it full.

Workaholic, she called herself. *Why don't you go to a nice bar instead? Afraid no one will try to pick you up?*

She pulled on the unsculptured linen jacket to her suit and pushed up the sleeves. Sighing, she placed her handbag on the stack of take-home work and sleeked back a wisp of hair that had dared to escape from the severity of the bun at her nape.

As an afterthought, she plunked her dirty coffee cup on top of the case and, sighing again, folded her arms and tried to look hurried. At the last minute, she remembered the coffee pot. Whirling around, she yanked out the plug and straightened to collide with Neil Jarvis who was walking in, rapping upon the open door as he entered.

"John Brown, I wish you wouldn't do that!" she gasped with a half laugh. "You scared the life out of me."

"You're in a hurry," he said and took in everything at a glance. "Well, push the hold button. All hell's broken loose on the Pinnacle case."

Not even Lila Dean could say that Neil Jarvis was a mongrel. He was a vastly sexy man with his athletic club fitness and Bay Point tan and glitzy bachelor's wit. His dark curly hair was streaked with gray, and his custom-made shirts and Ralph Lauren ties were prime yuppie stock. His jewelless pinky ring cleverly made you wonder if a macho chain nestled beneath that Ralph Lauren tie, for Neil Jarvis was unquestionably a comer. His instinct for the high life was flawless.

Summer had known Neil long before Neil became the state prosecutor. Though she had no doubts that he hired her merely as a favor to her husband, that didn't really matter. After seven years of doing every unwanted drudge job in the legal business, she had no trouble taking anything Neil could dish out.

Except one. Six months after Martin's death, Neil, who'd been a pallbearer at the funeral, had crossed paths with Summer at a party up at Palm Beach. In an unfortunate moment of misguided sympathy, or perhaps just too much rum and Coke, he had kissed her.

Summer wasn't offended by the kiss. It was, on the whole, boringly sterile, sort of like being kissed by one's brother. Before she realized it, however, Neil had her trapped in the hallway and barred against the wall. He was very drunk. She expected to be mauled or pawed or something equally disgusting, but he didn't even try to reach up her dress. As he swayed against her and pressed his face into her hair, he uttered some of the most shocking vulgarities she'd ever heard.

Too flabbergasted to say a word, or even to push him away, Summer simply stood there, shivering.

She'd been lucky. Some faceless person had walked out into the corridor and brought everything to a ghastly and undignified halt. She fled from her friend's house as if demons were chasing her, and for the rest of the night she huddled bleary-eyed and furious in the center of her bed, raking her fingers through her hair and despising Neil for the position he'd put her in.

When Neil walked into her office the next day with his handsome, glitzy smile, it could have never happened. To Summer's amazement, he said sweetly, "You were at the party last night? Gee, Summer, why didn't I see you?"

That was when Summer realized that the state prosecutor had a slight problem holding his liquor. She was discreet; not by so much as a word did she even hint that she'd been insulted—her first hands-on lesson in "willful gullibility." Willful gullibility, she'd learned over the years, was a regular stock item of the lawyer's profession.

But today Neil was his usual dapper self. He braced a hip against the edge of her desk and flamboyantly sent a sheaf of papers sailing helter-skelter across its surface.

"There's your claim to fame, Summer, me darlin'," he announced in silvery tones as he pulled out a long, fashionable cigar and a gold lighter with his initials engraved on it. "When you're up at the governor's mansion, remember I gave you your big break."

As Neil lit his cigar and turned his face to one side to blow smoke at her ceiling, Summer picked up the papers and swiftly read the auditor's report that implicated Rex Jernigan, the president of Pinnacle State Bank, on a number of fraudulent charges. She read Pinnacle's declaration of bankruptcy. And a statement made by Jernigan. Also, a confession of graft signed by Jernigan.

"When does the bankruptcy go into effect?" she asked, surprised. Things were going down awfully quickly. Pinnacle was her case. Her people were working on it.

He said, "As of five o'clock this afternoon."

There was also a handful of felony warrants. Summer read the top one for Jernigan, then those for three Pinnacle vice-presidents named by Jernigan as his co-conspirators. "You went ahead and worked these up?"

Neil considered his ash with a fond smile. "Actually, Herschel Starky did most of the working up. I was more like a witness to the proceedings."

Laughing, Summer shook her head. "The good judge must have had an account at Pinnacle. Who's Harris Chandler?"

"Some hot-shot Miami developer who's been doing some work up at West Palm the last few years." Neil's shrug was an elegant gesture of disinterest. "You know that million-dollar loan the auditors found at two percent below the going interest rate?"

Her brows lifted in a reply.

Neil said, "It turns out that the note was made out to this Chandler character. They had a real nice operation going, he and Jernigan. Chandler would get Jernigan to loan him money at a low rate, see, then he'd buy a T-bill with it and hold it for a year."

Summer mused out loud, "And Jernigan is represented by Underhill, Case, and Hancock? Impressive." She laid down the papers. "How many other people has Mr. Jernigan made deals with?"

"Chandler's the only one the auditors have turned up so far, but he's enough. Once the little FDIC boys get in on this, heads will really roll. The city fathers want this dirt cleaned up before the Feds move in. Starky's put a red tag on it."

Since Castro's overthrow in 1959, crime had exploded in Miami, and the city was working desperately hard on its image. The Society of Arts and Sciences was making Miami into the national mecca for the arts. The city fathers were fighting to protect their greatest source of annual income: tourism. Every season brought its case of legislative nerves, and law enforcement got the lead out.

"Well," Summer dismissed her misgivings about the haste, "if Judge Starky thinks there's enough here to merit the arrests without a grand jury, I'm sure there is. I'll get my people on the paperwork immediately."

"Good girl."

Finding a pen in her drawer, Summer took a seat and scribbled her name across four of the warrants and sent them skimming, one by one, back to Neil. Holding her pen poised over the last warrant, she pondered it a moment longer.

Her mouth pursed into a pretty moue. "Starky wants to subpoena Chandler's business accounts and personal accounts?"

"That's what he says."

Summer flipped up the warrant to read some notes in pencil clipped to it. It seemed that Chandler was responsible for much of the unincorporated expansion west of West Palm Beach. She was about to say that Chandler had a good business head and that it would be strange if he were to do something so stupid as play bank games.

"This Chandler fellow—" she began.

"Has a criminal record," Neil cut in with unexpected vehemence. "He's served two sentences, for Christ's sake! What's the problem here, counselor?"

Nothing! Summer leaned back in her chair, her eyes wide and her lower jaw loose. Not a problem in the world until his protest sounded as if he'd been rehearsing it for days.

As if he realized that he'd come on too strong, Neil slouched theatrically. With his cigar held between his first two fingers, his hand came up to pinch the bridge of his nose, and he sighed dramatically. Summer had the disturbing sensation that she was involved in some kind of crazy chess game and had just made a ridiculously stupid move.

She stared at Chandler's name, then groped through half-buried facts in her memory. "I know this man," she said and waved her fingers. "At least, I know his name. Chandler, Chandler. Yes, something...I can't recall exactly. Didn't it have to do with a war protest?"

The corners of Neil's mouth turned cynically downward. "A year in the penitentiary for protesting Vietnam back in the late sixties."

"Yes." She snapped a finger and thumb. "Up north."

"Michigan. A few of the magazines picked it up, I believe. Sheer sensationalism." His look drilled deeply. "Who does the kook think he is? Margaret-Brenman-Gibson?"

Summer blandly ignored his rude reference to the activist professor from Harvard. "It's sort of an extenuating circumstance, wouldn't you say, Neil? This criminal record of Harris Chandler's?"

Neil's tone bordered on exasperation. "Why are you defending the man, Summer? What's with you today?"

She wasn't defending Chandler, damn it, and if anyone was behaving queerly, Neil was. She asked curtly, "Would it be so terrible if I were?"

He was too wrapped up in his own train of thought to notice her pique. "Demanding to go to jail instead of Vietnam may be extenuating in come circles," he leaned over her desk and stubbed his cigar, "but it's cowardice around here, baby. Preservation of democracy and the Bible Belt and apple pie and all that."

Quite a speech. Summer lifted her shoulders in a shrug. "Sorry I brought it up."

"And even if his first sentence did have overtones of civil disobedience, Chandler's second arrest was for out-and-out violence. Willful destruction of property. Starky has justification here for an arrest. Sign the warrant, Summer. I haven't got all day."

Finding her own temper entering the tropical zone, Summer waved him down. "Hey, cut me some slack, Neil. All I did was raise a question." She reached for her pen and chalked up the whole incident to early male menopause. She added offhandedly as she put pen to paper, "What would you have done if I didn't? Rip off my fingernails?"

Summer actually expected her facetiousness to clear the air. She thought Neil would make a face at her or laugh and say he'd have her black-balled by Lila Dean.

"It would save a lot of trouble all around, my dear," he said so calmly and quietly that a series of alarms went off in Summer's head, "if you simply did what you were told."

It was a deadly moment—his words like small stones dropped into a still pond: troubling, disturbing. She was much too practical to say "Take this job and shove it, Neil." Her most reliable instincts warned her to pull back and stay back. Which she did, with her face congealed into a stiff, opaque mask.

Neil studied her for a moment. "Hell, Summer." His laugh was nervous. "There's no need for this. You're causing a stir over a man who's guilty as sin." He walked to her window and peered down at a police motorcycle beside the sidewalk. "Have you ever met Chandler?"

"No." *And I don't want to hear your opinions, buster.*

"Well, spare yourself," Neil said. "No one likes him. He doesn't fit in. Some Lone Wolf McQuade or John Rambo type. The kind of man who'd walk into a luncheon with the governor wearing jungle fatigues. Come on, don't make such a big deal about it."

Summer envisioned a bare-chested man with fatigues bloused around combat boots, a headband buried in dark hair and Sly Stallone muscles rippling across his chest as he zig-zagged down Flagler Street packing an M16. She wondered if that weren't the real crux of Neil's antagonism—the fact that Harris Chandler was a loner and a rule-breaker. Neil tended to like everything in neat little rows. Judge Starky lined everything up in neat little rows behind himself. Perhaps the two of them were going to make an example of this Chandler.

Still chafing, she thought how easy it was to look at other people, men in the service, for example, and demand of them, "Didn't you even resist your orders? Did you just blindly carry them out? Are you a lemming just following along because it's easier than going against the current?"

She couldn't pretend that she wasn't thinking about the cost to herself. She was sitting on the razor's edge of a great career, for Neil's political eyes had strayed to the green pastures of the Dade County mayoralty. Everyone knew he would name her, Summer, as his replacement when he announced his candidacy. She would be a shoo-in for state prosecutor in the next election.

Sighing, she touched her pen to the warrant but peered up at the state prosecutor one more time.

"Your objection is duly noted," he said with a drab smile.

Summer glumly wrote her name across the form. Now the warrants would go down to the sheriff's department. Deputies would be assigned to serve them. Guns in hand, they would pick up Rex Jernigan and Harris Chandler, et al.

Hardly had her pen finished when Neil Jarvis scooped up the papers. Giving them a cursory glance, he said that he would drop them by the Metro-Dade building next door.

"It's on my way," he added with his usual sexy smile.

"Aren't you going to give me a towel?" she asked dryly as he reached the door.

Turning, Neil lifted his athlete's shoulders in bafflement.

"So Pontius Pilate can wash her hands," she said sarcastically.

Leaning against the door frame, he gave her his most generous absolution. "You're making too much of it."

"I'm sure."

"There was nothing you could do. It came from the top." He toyed with a smile, then grinned broadly. "You know, Summer, you're going to make a great prosecutor. You've got compassion. And, the most important thing, you've got great legs."

He stopped her accusing look with a palm. "Joking aside, that's what it takes to be great, and that's why I take my orders. I don't always like them, but I know someone could have this job who doesn't give a big rip about the people. And I do care, Summer. We all do the best we can."

Summer's angry smile felt as if it would crack her face. It had corrupted her, hadn't it? Her hope for her career? The sweet smell of power?

"That's b.s., Neil." Rising, she turned her back on him and walked to the window.

He roared with laughter. "Exactly! It makes the world go 'round."

Spinning on his heel, he breezed through her door in an aura of happy success. Summer could hear him chatting and joking with everyone as he made his way to the elevator.

In disgust—more at herself that at him—Summer dumped his ashes into the wastebasket and made a face of distaste. Returning to the window, she watched two black women with badges strolling along beneath her. What did they do to get up the career ladder? she wondered. Would someone say about them that they were tough?

Except that she wasn't so tough. Martin had been the one who'd taught her how to fight. From the first moment when she'd sat in Prentice Hall at the university and listened to him make law come alive, she'd known he could teach her everything.

Their relationship had been destined from the beginning, she supposed: one loser to another. But the wonderful thing about losers was that you could sometimes put two of them together in a dice cup and throw out a winner—she, the determined, penniless girl working at McDonald's to put herself through Florida State; he, the handsome, published professor who had never been allowed to give personally of himself to a woman.

No one knew Martin was impotent, not even his parents. He'd been to countless specialists. No one could help. At first Summer had backed away from the arrangement Martin had suggested to her. Then she'd talked things over with Angelica.

It had been Angelica who had convinced Summer it could work. Summer agreed to marry Martin and give him children by one of the modern medical choices open to couples. Then, if she wanted to, Martin promised her, she could leave or do anything that struck her fancy. He would take care of her for the rest of her life.

Though it seemed cold-blooded at the time, she'd gone home with Martin. Everyone in his elite circle of friends had been flabbergasted when he'd married her, a woman twelve years his junior who'd just waltzed in one day, looking like exiled royalty searching for a new home. Martin crammed her down the throats of Miami's fashionable, upper-crust matrons who decided, since they were stuck with Summer, that they would make her over into someone as chic as they were.

She'd disappointed them, naturally, along with Martin's parents. Except for the twin boys. Never were two babies

loved so much, by parents and grandparents alike. Summer
and Martin crazily felt as if they were children themselves,
with a spanking new toy, and they loved sharing every minute of it. Neither of them counted on how much they would
grow to care about each other.

Summer grew to respect Martin, to love him for his
goodness and his kindness, his devotion to her children and
his desire to see them flourish. It was Martin who put her
through more and more school and exposed her to all the
right people. It was Martin who picked her up when she
wanted to quit and who drove her on and on and gave her
the courage to want it all.

The sexual problem of their marriage was worked out
with patience and honest affection. Martin was an incredibly caring man, and if Summer ever missed making love the
conventional way, she was never tempted to be unfaithful.
She'd had the best part of a man. Why wish for seconds?

In those first hours after she learned about Martin's
death, Summer didn't know how she would go on. She had
lost her best friend in all the world. When she returned to
work at the municipal building and moved among the doz-
ens of people she knew, loneliness was like a fever that refused to break. But she had a son left alive, and it had been
Martin's boundless love for her that gave her the courage to
pick up and go on.

She still missed Martin. Terribly. And her eyes had hurt
all day from having to force back the tears. She guessed that
Martin would have been disappointed in her for not pin-
ning Neil against the wall about Harris Chandler.

As some form of self-inflicted penance, Summer placed
her fingernail between her teeth and cruelly peeled it off.
Tossing the tiny piece into the wastebasket then gazing in
satisfaction at the ugliness of her otherwise neat manicure,
she snatched up her case and strode through the door.

But ruining a fingernail did not a hand-washing make. "I should have refused to sign that warrant on Chandler," she muttered irritably to herself. "I should have called Neil's hand. I should never have let him get by with railroading me like that."

Summer took the escalators because the elevators were too slow. Even the escalators didn't take her out of the building quickly enough. She rushed down the moving steps and almost raced for the front doors. She didn't look back as she pushed through the glass door and hurried along the sidewalk feeling doomed, as if a gray goose had just walked over her grave.

The moment Deputy Hank Delaney stepped out of the passenger side of the air-conditioned police unit and stood in the wedge of car and door, one booted foot in and one foot out, he started to sweat. Patting his pockets for a fresh pack of chewing gum, he opened it and pulled out a piece, unwrapped it and wadded the wrapping into a tiny ball.

"Whew!" he said, gazing out at Palm Beach County as he tossed the wrapping into the car. "Ten o'clock in the morning and it's already ninety degrees."

Pete Cavassas eyed the Dade County insignia on his old friend's uniform. He and Hank Delaney had been football heroes at high school in Haverhill. They had gone through officer training together and vowed to be best buddies forever. Then Hank had up and taken a job in Dade County.

"It's cooler up here than down at Miami," Pete said reproachfully.

"It may be cooler," Hank retorted, "but it don't look it. This place is the end of nowhere, man. I don't see how you stand it."

Removing his Stetson, Hank fished out his handkerchief. After meticulously blotting the headband, he carefully arranged his thinning thatch of fiery red hair and resettled his hat and stroked his hand over his neatly trimmed beard.

"Miami's where it's at, man," Hank said and rolled the chewing gum around in his mouth.

Cavassas snorted. "You wouldn't catch me down there with all those junkies."

Hank chuckled. That was why Pete would still be a deputy sheriff when he was fifty while he, Hank Delaney, would be at the top. Not only was he now the youngest deputy in Dade County's employ, he was today's lawman—in possession of a degree, a man who knew the game and how to play, who knew how to dress and act the part. He could handle any man and any situation.

He felt the .38 lying with familiar weight against his thigh and closed the car door.

As far as he could see, building plots were in the process of development and had been laid out like pieces of a patchwork quilt. The water system was going in now, and three backhoes were stitching gray threads through the cloudless sky with the needles of their diesel smokestacks. A shirtless crew was laying forms for street curbs. They operated out of a motley collection of battered vans and trucks.

In the middle of it all, sticking up out of the flatlands like a hitchhiker's thumb, was a metal building. Inside, hopefully, was the man Hank had given up a Saturday fishing trip to pick up: Harris Chandler.

"This won't take long," Hank told Pete and kept his eye on the drooping power lines that carried electricity to the building. Two humming air-conditioners projected from each end, and three mud-spattered pickups were parked out front.

Pete called out, "You want me to come with you?"

"Just to deliver a warrant? Nah, no problem."

All this was costing Harris Chandler lots of overtime on a Saturday morning, Hank guessed as he leisurely strolled nearer, his boots kicking up small gysers of dust. He watched as a buff-colored clump clawed its way out from under one of the trucks and scrambled to its feet—a fully grown hound that could only be described, pedigreewise, as a junkyard dog.

Hank came to an instant and a prudent halt.

The hound twitched one floppy ear. With the hair on his neck bristling and a growl rumbling from deep in his throat, his approach was in a wide circle and with a lumbering, cockeyed lope that made the hair on the back of Hank's own neck do funny things.

"Hey, Cavassas?" Hank yelled over his shoulder, not removing his eyes from the dog for a single second.

"No problem," Cavassas laughingly taunted his friend. "Don't let him smell fear, Delaney. You'll be okay."

Hank shifted the chewing gum to his other jaw and sincerely hoped the dog knew how he was supposed to behave.

"Good dog," he called out in a polite greeting as he extended a hand. "Easy now. Don't get spooky on me. I'm not going anywhere. Good dog, good boy."

Not finding the words particularly persuasive, the dog came to a stop and curled his lips back over a set of well-honed teeth. The hoarse barking he set up virtually shook the walls of the metal building.

Inside, three men were leaning over a table. The tallest of them was in the process of drawing the tip of a long, callused finger over a blueprint. At the sound of barking, all of them lifted their heads and looked at each other.

The man who'd been pointing straightened to an impressive height, and the blueprint rolled up with a snap. Closing his eyes, the man pressed the lids wearily with his fingertips. His lashes were long and almost femininely beautiful, but the stubble of beard on his chin only partially concealed the rugged lines that forty years had placed on his face.

"Hold what you've got," he said with quiet authority. "I'll be right back."

By now the barking outside was reaching a feverish pitch. On the way to the door, the man snatched up a thermos cup of cold black coffee and tossed it down, and, grabbing the burned down cigarette in a nearby ashtray, took the last drag, which tasted almost as vile as the coffee. Stubbing it, he grasped the flimsy metal door and sent it crashing back on its hinges.

"Shag!" he yelled over the furor of machinery as sixty-eight-degree air rushed out to blend with the ninety. "Hush up!"

Hank Delaney's relief was heartfelt as he watched Shag's ears perk up and his huge feet turn around. As docile as a kitten, he loped back up to have his ears scratched. Hank placed the heels of his hands on his gun belt and pushed it farther down upon his hips, managing a small swagger.

"Mr. Chandler?" he called out.

The weathered, tightly wound man who stood in the doorway didn't appear to be a particularly menacing man, Hank thought. He was a tall man and possessed the kind of muscular lankiness that invariably retained its trimness of buttock and slenderness of waist as the years went by.

Harris Chandler, if this was indeed the man he'd come to find, obviously spent most of his time outdoors. His dark, russet-brown hair was heavily streaked by the sun and his skin was deeply bronzed. His black sleeveless T-shirt, stretched over a chest of solidly knit muscles, was tucked into the elastic waist of putter pants that looked as if they'd been slept in for a week. Blobs of spattered cement had dried on their hems. On his feet were deck shoes.

Hank intuitively guessed as he drew close enough to see the man's hawkish blue eyes that his suspect possessed more than ordinary strength—not only a physical strength but one of the will. He had obviously dispensed with the frills of life and laid down a set of ground rules: his own, and anyone who set foot into that self-declared territory had better respect them.

"Who wants to know?" he called out. He detached himself from the doorway of the building to take the makeshift steps with an hypnotic economy of motion, then waited, slouching and scratching the hound's ears.

Behind him, Hank saw movement. Two more men—one, a tawny-skinned and muscular youth with hostile eyes like bullets, and an older man with a salt-and-pepper beard and glasses whose thick lenses were set in small, round frames.

Reaching inside his jacket, Hank carefully withdrew a bronze shield and proffered it. "Hank Delaney," he said officially as he stepped forward. "Dade County. I'm looking for Mr. Chandler."

In silence Hank watched as his insignia was studied, as if every detail were being committed to memory. Then the man eyed him up and down with a cool dispassion that made Hank shift his weight. As he returned the badge, he drawled, "I'm afraid that Dade badge don't hack a great deal up here, deputy."

Hank sighed. This wasn't going to be as one-two-three as he'd hoped. "Are you Harris Chandler, sir?"

For a brief moment, icy blue eyes glittered at him, but they softened with self-mocking amusement. "That depends." His face cracked into a winning grin. "You're not a jealous husband, are you?"

Not for a hundred dollars would Hank have smiled back. "Failure to identify yourself, sir, could get you in a lot of trouble."

"Oh? I'm under arrest? You're going to take me in?"

"Could I see some ID, sir? A driver's license?"

The identification was promptly produced, and Hank read it aloud as he compared the man with the ludicrously bad picture on the Michigan driver's license. "Harris Joseph Chandler."

"The dirty rat," Chandler replied with a flash of strong, white teeth. "In the flesh."

Hank avoided looking straight at the man but focused instead on the crow's-feet at one of his temples. "You know that you're supposed to have that license changed, sir, if you're going to be in the state for any length of time."

"I just spent six months in Michigan with my dad. I do that ever so often."

Anxious to get the warrant served, Hank dutifully removed a card from his jacket pocket along with the folded warrant signed by Summer MacLean. He began droning out the words. "Mr. Chandler, it is my duty to inform you that you have the right to remain silent. You—"

The bulletlike Hispanic eyes behind Chandler fired two rounds: *bang, bang, you're dead*. Hank glanced back at the waiting patrol car and wondered how long Pete Cavassas would take to get here if there was trouble.

"For not gettin' my driver's license changed?" Harris Chandler said with a light scoff. "Hey, you Dade County guys really are tryin' to clean up the old place, aren't you?"

Chagrin stung the curves of Hank's freckled cheeks. "You have the right to an attorney, Mr. Chandler. If you cannot afford one—"

"What's the charge?"

There was suddenly no mockery about the man now. The tightly wound tension that could be cocky and amusing could also be vicious—not a mean, bullying nastiness, but a cold and controlled toughness that could give back in kind of what it received.

Hank had the alarming sensation of having just lit the fuse to a keg of dynamite.

"Grand larceny, sir," he said as he swallowed down a rush of fear. "If you cannot afford an attorney, one will be provided."

Chapter Two

Blame was a word that was never spoken out loud. Never once since the accident had Arthur and Pat MacLean confronted Summer with that fish-lipped pucker of reproof. Nor did they ever intimate by so much as the lift of a brow that their son would be alive if she hadn't been driving the car that tragic night.

But to Summer, the silence of Martin's parents called attention to her blame the way a detour sign warns of a washed-out bridge.

"Now, Tom, dear," they would say, "we wouldn't want to stop playing football, would we?" Or, "Keep on the tennis team, dear. You need your old friends now, more than ever." Or, "I never see you with any boys, Thomas, darling. Why don't you bring some of them up and we'll go skiing out on Lake Mangonia?" And when they thought she wasn't listening, "Has your mother been dating anyone lately, sweetheart?"

The awful part was that the MacLean's possessiveness was well-meant and unconscious on their part. How could Summer say to them, "Back off, people. I'm not going to turn your grandson into a warped sissy. Tom needs time to heal. He'll find his own stride."

One night at the MacLean's affluent West Palm Beach estate was all Summer's maternal insecurity could stand. She was the one who suggested that she leave early to catch the next train back to Miami.

"I have an idea," Pat interrupted with an announcement from her grandmaternal throne behind the silver coffee service at ten o'clock in the morning.

Tom was slumped on his spine on Pat's plush damask sofa, browsing through the Saturday newspaper, and Summer thought he looked marvelously out of place in his chaotic mixture of jeans, tank top, baseball cap, iridescent tennis shoes, iridescent punk socks and bulky, waterproof, shockproof, date/calendar/alarm/compass wristwatch. They rather complemented her own off-work attire of Jag khaki jeans and mesh top and jellysandals.

"What's your sign, Mom?" he asked as he peeped over the top of the paper with a pair of impish brown eyes.

Summer's smile adored him. "My child genius. It's Sagittarius, and what are you reading?"

Pat MacLean was oblivious to any trains of thought other than her own. "Why don't I get out the Seville and drive us to the station myself?" she suggested.

Tom continued to search through the horoscopes until he found November. Fixing his mother with a lopsided consideration, he grinned. "You'd better be careful, Mom. Today you're going to take a trip."

"Of course I'm going to take a trip, silly." Summer laughed. "I'm going back home."

"'Travel is broadening,'" Tom continued to read. "'Delay your normal routine and take a journey to allow the real you to emerge.'"

"Who wants to know the real me?" Summer groaned.

Tom affected the part of a conspirator and stage whispered, "You're also going to face a challenge and meet a stranger."

"I don't think there's any need to bother the chauffeur," Pat was saying to herself as she serenely poured two cups. She lifted her flawlessly coiffed head and looked up. "Thomas, you can come, darling, and we can stop by the ice cream shop on the way. Well, what do you think?"

"The last thing I need is broadening," Summer said to her son with a slap to her derriere as she kept part of her attention on Pat MacLean and part on her wristwatch. "Now, the stranger part I'm interested in. Tell me, is he tall, dark, and handsome?"

"It doesn't even say he's a man," Tom replied gravely and squinted at the print. "But it does say that you...let's see...you 'could venture off the beaten path with far-reaching con...conse...consequences.'" He crinkled his nose at his grandmother and added, with a gagging moan, "Ice cream in the morning, Gran'Pat?"

Accepting the cup that Pat leaned forward to extend, Summer nodded her thanks and said to Tom, "See? It proves that horoscopes are a waste of good ink and paper. I never wander off the beaten path, and nothing I do has far-reaching consequences."

Pat bestowed her grandson's thin hand a pat. "Ice cream is fattening, smartie pants, and we're going to have to fatten you up."

Sipping, Summer said by way of a gentle hint to her mother-in-law, "Tom's afraid of cellulite, Gran'Pat."

The older woman missed the point entirely. "No bag o' bones allowed in this house. You listen to me, Thomas MacLean, and you'll be filling out those jeans in no time."

The twins' resemblance to her had always been a source of reassurance to Summer, but when Pat MacLean drew her glasses down on her expensive nose and surveyed her grandson from his scalp to his feet as she was doing now, Summer's heart invariably missed a beat. Arthur and Pat must never know that Tom wasn't Martin's natural son— not that they would think the worst of her, which they would—but Tom was all they had. To lose him would destroy them both.

"My horoscope says I'll meet an old friend." Tom privately wished his grandmother would stop nagging him about his weight. "What's your sign, Gran'Pat?"

Summer brought everything to an abrupt halt by glancing at her wristwatch and giving a terrible performance of surprise. "Mercy, would you look at the time! I'll miss my train."

Bounding to his feet, Tom scurried across the room to where his mother's tote bag waited beside the door. He swung it over his thin shoulder. "Well, I'm ready. I've got the luggage."

"I'm just no good without my second cup of coffee," Pat was complaining. "Oh, dear, no matter, I suppose. Well, you two get in the car. I'm coming."

As Tom heaved open the heavy glass door from the MacLean's breakfast room to the four-car garage and tore through it, Pat brought up the rear and made a final inspection of herself in the mirror.

"Thomas is looking so frail, dear," she said to Summer as she meticulously scrutinized the arch of her brows. "I declare, I think someday he'll just up and blow away. Does he take vitamins every day?"

Not for a moment did Summer allow herself the luxury of turning around and withering the woman with a look. Through a congealed smile, she added another lie to the million she had already told the MacLeans. "Of course he takes vitamins. He's just like his father. You remember how thin Martin was as a boy."

Harris Chandler didn't take the Miranda warning lightly. On the contrary, as Hank Delaney read it, his freckled hand resting casually upon the butt of his gun, Harris was remembering his youth and wishing for the millionth time that he'd done things differently.

Even in the beginning, he'd known his fatal flaw—that stubborn, bullheaded pride that refused to let him bend the knee—and as he listened to the now-familiar words and stared sightlessly into the living color of his memory where a nineteen-year-old kid took everything much too seriously, he knew he'd never overcome that flaw.

But then, things had been very serious in the early seventies. He'd been a naive and free-spirited young anarchist—all that oath-swearing along with several dozen other naive and free-spirited young anarchists and their glowingly righteous vow to resist Vietnam to the final breath.

No shortage of idealism in those days. He'd thought he was Mr. Supercool when he'd packed a suitcase and parked upon the steps of the Ingham County Courthouse in Lansing, Michigan. He didn't believe in killing, he declared passionately to the authorities. He didn't believe in war in general, nor Vietnam in particular, and there was no way he was going to Southeast Asia.

He'd made headlines. "That's Chandler," he said cockily to one reporter, so eager to be a martyr that he'd leaned over the man's pad to watch him write it down. "C-h-a-n-d-l-e-r."

"A true desperado," a newspaper called him. "A modern-day Don Quixote from the timberlands of upper Michigan."

He received fan mail calling him a hero. Women sent him their pictures, along with generous propositions. One school teacher offered to adopt him. But not one of his pledged cohorts followed suit after he'd made his big announcement to the world. His first crusade had cost him a year in the federal penitentiary.

So much for free-spirited anarchy. When the amnesty issue came up, Harris was released, but he still hadn't learned that The System, like The House, never loses. Then he righteously announced that to accept amnesty was to admit that he'd done something wrong. He had only acted according to his conscience, he told reporters, and he was ready to fight it clear to the Supreme Court.

That was when he'd been deposited outside the gates of the prison with the same tacky suitcase he'd walked in with.

No sooner did he return home than he found himself engaged in yet another battle, with somewhat less fervor this time, however, and a good deal less brashness. This time he locked horns with a private contractor who had been hired by the state highway commission to cut an interstate highway straight through the middle of his father's school for delinquent boys.

Bud Chandler was himself an ex-con. While spending three years in the state prison for manslaughter, he fell in love with a surgeon. After he was cut up in a cell riot, Bethel Raines put sixty stitches in Bud's back and then married him.

Unfortunately, Bethel died in her early thirties of cancer, but she left her husband and small son a magnificent legacy: four thousand acres of prime Michigan timberland. For fifteen years, Bud worked hard to establish the school, which was no small accomplishment in the fifties; such institutions hadn't gained the recognition they were to receive in the eighties. But Bud's three appeals to the state against the highway commission availed nothing.

By the time Harris returned from his draft caper, heavy equipment was already at work on Bud's property. Noble trees lay with their great roots naked and dying. Whole hillsides were in the process of being cruelly gutted and ripped away. Wholesale butchery. It made him sick to his stomach.

Later Harris said that he regretted the way he'd handled the situation. But at twenty, after considering the problem and having already learned that a person didn't get anywhere reasoning with the powers that be—and after discovering that the highway could just as easily be shifted twenty miles to the west—Harris came to a solution that seemed quite tidy at the time. He placed a crate of dynamite beneath several million dollars' worth of heavy John Deere equipment and calmly lit the fuse.

That last protest had cost him another year in prison.

As he neared forty, Harris's past was scarred by hassle after hassle with the law. Now he couldn't remember how many times he'd been accused of things he didn't do. He was forced into championing countless unpopular causes by default. His name was linked to situations that he'd never heard of.

Heartsick, bleakly disillusioned, bearing the financial burden of keeping the school operating—Bud's school was the one thing that escaped Harris's razored cynicism—Harris went south to Miami where money was quick and a bank was on every street. He worked hard and became one of the best at what he did. He gambled huge fortunes because he had nothing to lose, and he turned impossible Florida land into towns for the exploding population.

In some circles he possessed an enviable reputation. He could'nt have cared less. He had no friends and didn't want any. His women were faceless creatures, coming out of the night and fading back into the same night. It ceased to matter. He had his regrets to keep him company, and the money kept flowing back to Michigan.

At least his mother would have been proud of him. As she was dying she had called him to her side. "Whatever happens, my darling," she said, "don't ever become a yesman." Little did Bethel Chandler know how completely her wish would be granted, Harris thought grimly as Deputy Delaney finished with his Miranda ritual. Far and above her wildest dreams.

"Very good, deputy," he said in a flat, arid tone. "There's only one thing wrong. I haven't committed grand larceny, see? I haven't committed anything except to stay in this godforsaken state too long. Now, why don't you do us all a mega-favor and take your little popgun back down to Dade County where it belongs?"

Hank flushed as red as the hair on his head. "Look, Mr. Chandler, don't give me a hard time, okay? I don't make out these warrants, I just deliver 'em. Now, you could be as innocent as a new-born babe, and I'd still have to take you back to Miami."

Harris didn't believe any of it was for real. It was all a bad joke. He was on *Candid Camera*, right? Wrong, convict-breath.

He turned the deputy's words over in his mind the way a beggar turns a coin. "You don't mind if I take a look at that warrant, do you?"

Proffering the warrant, Hank stood with one cautious eye upon the dog and one upon Harris.

Harris stared incredulously at the words typed above S. MacLean's signature: grand larceny. "Perhaps you've got the wrong Chandler."

"I don't think so, sir."

"Who's S. MacLean?"

The more nervous Hank became, the faster he chewed his gum. "The assistant prosecuting attorney, sir. Assistant to the state prosecutor."

"This Mr. MacLean—"

"Ms. MacLean."

A woman? Harris conjured up the image of a sadistic prison matron with great pendulous breasts and bulging calves and pornographic books hidden beneath her mattress. He hated her bitterly. "This *Miz* MacLean thinks I committed grand larceny against the State of Florida?"

"Pinnacle State Bank had declared bankruptcy, Mr. Chandler." Hank rolled the chewing gum around in his mouth. "As of five o'clock yesterday afternoon."

It took more control than Harris had exerted in a long time to keep from slamming Hank Delaney back against the building and running as fast as he could. His thoughts veered crazily.

"That has nothing to do with me," he said.

"Auditors have turned up a number of fraudulent situations, Mr. Chandler," Delaney was saying. "The officers of the bank have all resigned. Other people are being arrested besides yourself. It promises to be . . ." He popped his gum nervously. "Does Watergate ring any bells?"

At Harris's flammable glare, Hank instantly wiped the smile off his face and cleared his throat. But Harris was aware of the sunlight burning into the top of his head like a laser. He said, "I'm supposed to have done what?"

"There were several notes issued to you by Mr. Jernigan."

"Of course there were. I've done business with Rex Jernigan for years."

Hank grimaced. "I'm afraid you'll just have to come with me to Miami, sir. All the charges against you will be explained."

"Miami?"

Hank had wearied of the gum, and sweat was streaming down his sides. Turning his back to the sun, he spat out the gum with a *thwoot* and said with exaggerated patience as he wiped over his mouth, "It's your legal residence, sir."

Harris raked his fingers through his hair. Not one of his projects with Rex Jernigan had lost money. How was it possible that his notes weren't legal? Of course they were legal. Then the truth dawned. They weren't talking about real notes. Rex has other notes with his, Harris's, signature on them, notes the he hadn't signed at all. He was being set up!

Feeling reality hurtling away from him, Harris indicated the patrol car parked a distance away. "We're going to Miami in that?"

"Only to the train depot, Mr. Chandler. Would you give me back the warrant, please?"

Harris watched his own shaking hands crumple the warrant signed by S. MacLean—*Miz* S. MacLean, he thought nastily—and he thrust it hard into the deputy's chest. "Here, make that into a pizza box."

Ignoring the .38 glinting in the sunlight, Harris spun around to where the two men, Riley and Sib, were visibly puzzled, their expressions demanding the answers to some obvious questions. He motioned them out of the way and swiftly climbed the steps back into the building.

He heard the deputy following, and he pretended to gather up scattered blueprints. He could see the man scanning the ratty chairs huddled around the air-conditioners, and the half-dozen empty beer cans on a table beside a plate of wilted lettuce and tomato and cold cuts and the empty sack of whole-wheat bread, the two empty cartons of milk.

Deputy Delaney was smoothing out the crumpled warrant and replacing it in his pocket. The unsnapping of the holster and the removal of the .38 made a sound that Harris supposed he would recognize in his sleep. *Easy does it, Chandler!*

"Mr. Chandler," the young man was saying, "I'm going to have to ask you to step over to the wall, if you would, please." He took a nervous breath. "Face it and place your palms flat upon it. Spread your feet."

A cold, murderous rage swelled inside Harris, but he moved with a strict deliberation and grace and, keeping his head high and his back as straight as a timber, continued to arrange the papers upon his desk—plans and forms bearing releases from the county. He gave no indication when he felt the barrel of the gun jab into the center of his back.

"Please remain exactly where you are, Mr. Chandler," Delaney said in a shrill voice.

Turning, lifting his brows at the young Hispanic who stood blinking sooty black eyes, Harris reached for a pad on his desk. As he did so, Hank Delaney lunged forward, and the gun barrel did a terrible number upon Harris's right kidney.

In pain, but hiding it with a stone-cold mask that dropped instantly over his face, Harris stood perfectly still. He said icily, "If you don't mind, deputy, I'm going to write out a few instructions. I assure you that this pen is exactly what it appears to be. No James Bond tricks. It doesn't shoot bullets or spray knockout solutions. You, sir, are safe from me."

With admirable control, Harris wrote several of the crew members' names on a pad and, still hurting, ripped off the top sheet and handed it to Sib. The part-time accountant squinted.

"See that the backhoe operators get paid," Harris told him with an ugly smile, and added, "Use cash. I don't think I trust checks anymore."

"Sure, Mr. Chandler."

"Riley, shoot the grade on the sewer lines one more time before they cover them up."

The Hispanic's handsome young face came alive. "I'll take care of everything, Mr. Chandler. And I'll take care of Shag, too."

"Will you step to the wall, please, Mr. Chandler?" Deputy Delaney was insisting.

I will turn off my mind now and block out everything that will happen, Harris thought. *I won't dream about making anyone pay for this. That's a lie. I want revenge. I want to get my hands on someone's throat. I want to beat someone senseless. Ms. S. MacLean, the high-flown witch. I want to drive her against the wall and hit her and hit her....*

"Have you selected a wall?" Harris snarled.

Hank Delaney's youth finally got the best of him. "Any wall!" he shouted.

The feel of the smooth young hands frisking him was the ultimate humiliation to Harris. Even so, far back in his mind, he maintained enough presence to know that he was a twice-convicted man. Anything he did from this point would be used against him. He must be careful, very careful.

He thought of trying to reach Rex Jernigan. He thought of his record books in a safe inside the model home where he'd been staying weekdays. If someone was setting him up, it was conceivable that they could alter his accounts, too.

Damn it! Harris tolerated the slaps up and down his legs, his trunk, down his groin and over his hips, his thighs. But when he heard the handcuffs rattling, some superficial control in him snapped.

"Wait a minute!" he yelled. Spinning around with the blood pounding in his heart and his blue eyes slitted with rage, Harris swore a terrible oath.

The young deputy paled and held the gun extended shakily with both hands.

Bitterly, quietly, Harris said, "You don't need the cuffs."

Delaney licked his lips nervously, his words almost a plea. "Please don't make this any harder than it has to be, Mr. Chandler. Come along peacefully, now."

Letting his shoulders slump, Harris grimly turned and placed his hands crossed, behind his back. He had sworn to himself a lifetime's worth that he would die before he'd go through this again. He winced as the steel bracelets snapped shut.

Not knowing how to retrieve his lost composure, Hank tried for lightness. Chuckling, he gave the prisoner a slap on the shoulder to turn him around. "Try to think of it as a little side trip, Mr. Chandler. Travel is broadening. You know."

Harris's flashing eyes would have cut through steel. "I don't need broadening," he said with deadly intensity. "I need a lawyer." He turned to his men. "Riley? Sib?"

"We'll take care of everything, sir," Riley promised.

Hesitating, thinking again of the safe, Harris said, "Sib, in my front pocket on my key ring is the key to the model home on Broken Wing. I've got some account books there—"

"Sir," interrupted Hank. "I suggest that you don't touch anything or allow anyone else to. It is my understanding that Judge Starky will subpoena your accounts."

Harris's facade faltered, and he was once again that naive and hotly idealistic nineteen-year-old kid. "The hell, you say."

"I'm sure your attorney will advise you, sir. Now, if you don't mind, we have a train to catch."

Harris strode swiftly toward the door of the building and hardly felt his feet absorbing the thud as he dropped outside to the ground. His whole head pounded. The draining of his rage left him exhausted.

Hank Delaney didn't even have time to prod his prisoner forward; Harris was heading across the dusty expanse with long strides. Hank sighed. For a reason he couldn't quite pinpoint, he wanted to let Harris Chandler know that he sympathized. Maybe it was Chandler's eyes. They didn't look away enough. Did thieves take the time to pay off their help as they were being hauled away to the cooler?

One thing for sure, Chandler's lawyer would have his work cut out for him. Judge Starky meant to have these arrests.

When Summer and Tom walked the length of the chain-link fence that enclosed the railroad terminal, she guessed that nobody could look at them and tell that they'd survived a tragedy—Tom in his funky garb and herself carrying a trendy tote bag slung over her shoulder, crammed with enough feminine paraphernalia to keep her going for at least a week. She didn't even look like a lawyer with her bun exchanged for a loose, Andie MacDowell-ish topknot.

She worked at maintaining a pleasant expression on her face. Brushing back undisciplined wisps of hair, she licked her ice-cream cone. "What do you and your grandfather have planned for this weekend?"

"Trolling." Tom's tongue circumvented walnut ripple and a tiny cream mustache appeared on his upper lip. "That's what he usually wants to do."

"Wear a life jacket." She teasingly swiped off his mustache.

No sooner were the words out than Summer could have bitten her tongue. There she went again, trying too hard, treating him like an infant.

"Mo-om," he chided in a singsong way.

Summer smiled, but still she saw him as the boy in her memory. She saw both of them, flopped on their backs with their feet propped on the walls and their heads stuck into the stereo speakers. She could see the two of them running and riding their bicycles, could hear their fond insults as they waged battle at a computer terminal.

A pain nearly ripped her in two. *Need me,* she wanted to say to him. *Don't see me as your mother. I have terrible holes in me.*

She pretended to consider her ice cream. "You don't want to go trolling? Don't you enjoy spending time with your grandfather?"

Tom's only response was one of his vague shrugs. "He thinks I want to."

"But you don't?"

"It's okay, Mom." He stared for a moment in preoccupied silence, then said without facing her, "If Grandpa didn't have me, he'd stop doing anything."

What a responsibility for such young shoulders! Summer wanted to hold him, but Tom was walking ahead, skirting the corner that flanked the parking lot. He stopped dead in his tracks.

"Tom?" She was instantly attuned to him.

He walked back, all the color having drained out of his face. Bewildered, Summer lowered her cone. "What is it, honey?"

"Nothing." Heeling sharply, he took off in the opposite direction in order to reach his grandparents' Seville the long way around. "I thought I recognized someone. It's nothing."

Summer took several backward steps so that she could lean back and see around the corner. A local police car was parked there. Men were in it; three of them, two in the front seat, one in the back. No one out of the ordinary, nothing familiar.

"The man in the back seat was handcuffed," Tom explained when she caught up with him.

She tossed her uneaten ice cream into the trash can and shifted her tote bag higher onto her shoulder. "Did he remind you of Bobby?"

"Dad." Tom brushed a fallen lock of hair back from his eyes.

She should have taken him to a counselor, Summer thought with a stab of regret, right from the beginning instead of trying to heal him herself.

"I do it, too, sweetheart," she said and slipped her arm around his slender, boyish waist. "All the time. I see a man from a distance and—"

When, to her surprise, Tom tightened his thin arms around her like a vise, stuffing his sweet face into her neck, Summer clutched him desperately to her breast. His heart was racing against hers, and over his head she stared blindly into space, overwhelmed by the ruthless vortex of the past and the present.

She whispered tenderly into his hair. "Please be safe and happy, my darling. Please have a good life and grow up to be a fine, strong man."

In the distance the daily passenger train to Miami announced its approach with poignant melancholy. To ward off the tears that pressed blindingly behind her eyes, Summer blinked at Pat who waited in the distance. She telegraphed the older woman that she should come and take Tom now.

But before Pat reached them, Summer cupped her son's face urgently in her hands and caressed him with her eyes. "Tom, listen to me. You don't have to be brave, sweetie. You don't have to take care of anyone. Not your grandfather, not me, not anyone. Just you."

Tom grimaced, but when he hugged her goodbye Summer knew that he was as aware of her needs as she was of his. She watched him shuffle toward the shiny white Seville, his head bent low and his hightops scuffing the cement, and she wanted to run after him and say she hadn't meant it, that she couldn't bear to be away from him, not even for a week.

But she couldn't go on seeing a tragedy in every parting. People did leave one another and come back, after all. *Watch over him,* she prayed, dying the death of those who love.

"Chief?"

The Seville was dipping its elegantly grilled nose into traffic and disappearing when the masculine voice behind Summer sent her whirling around to come face to face with a beaming Hank Delaney.

"Hank!"

Summer thought that if she could do tricks with her mouth and eyes the young deputy sheriff wouldn't guess she'd been crying. Laughing, she ducked her head and blinked furiously. "Where did you come from?"

Hank jerked a thumb over his shoulder to indicate the parking lot where Tom had seen the police car. "They can really get to you, can't they? Kids?"

He'd seen the tears. Summer gratefully dispensed with the false bravado. "Do you know what the worst thing is, Hank? The fairy tale they tell you, that once they're out of diapers the hard part is over. The bigger they get, the harder it is, believe me."

"It's only been a year. You ought to expect a few hard places, chief."

A few? Summer unzipped her tote and poked around for a tissue. Finding one, she vigorously blew her nose. "Well, so much for the perils of motherhood. You're a bit out of your territory, aren't you?"

"I live up here, remember? Come home on the weekends?" Hank gave her a crooked, conspiratorial grimace as he muttered, "Now, I don't live around the lake with your in-laws, understand. 'Way back in the boonies I got me a double-wide and a boat and a little gal who can love the socks right off my feet. What more could a guy want?''

Every so often a lawman came along whom Summer truly liked—one who took pride in what he did and kept straight, a man who really cared about what was happening to the world but had no illusion about his place in it. Hank was young enough to be ambitious and still dedicated.

"Now I remember," Summer said laughingly with a wave of a finger. "You have a ficus tree in your backyard. But you're surely not going back to Miami on a Saturday. You can catch a lot of fish and love a lot of woman before Monday, Hank."

He winked at her. "It's all your fault."

With a bewildered smile, she urged him to explain.

"The warrants you sent down? Inspector Clouseau got right on 'em, said he'd had some pressure from the higher-ups. The truth is, he gives your warrants priority. He's a little taken with ya, chief."

Summer chidingly shook her head. "Hank . . ."

"Anyway, since Chandler was alleged to be in the area, guess who got stuck with the warrant?"

So it had been Harris Chandler whom Tom had seen! Something vague moved inside Summer, something alive that she hadn't known was there. She shook off the feeling of foreboding. "I'm sorry, Hank."

"Aw, I don't mind. One of the deputies from Palm Beach County and I are old friends. We drove out on highway Seven-ten where Chandler was working."

"You're not taking Chandler back to Miami on the train?"

"Easier than carryin' him piggyback." Hank shrugged. "I don't have a car up here with a cage."

As if by command, Summer followed Hank's line of vision. In the distance a man was unfolding himself from the back seat of a Palm Beach County police unit. From where she stood, she could only see Chandler's back.

Caucasian male, she assessed from habit: six feet and one or two inches, one hundred and eighty-five pounds that he carried with a graceful but definite masculine independence. His clothes were a fright, and his dark, chestnut hair covered the tops of his ears and furled a bit too long at his nape.

Her heart kicked with an unexpected thrill. Tom had been right; there really was a vague resemblance to his father—the color of Chandler's hair, perhaps, or the trim taper of his waist. But Martin had never possessed such reckless defiance in his shoulders, nor such arrogance in the spread of his legs. Chandler's thighs were straining against the tautly stretched pants, and his buttocks were neatly and provocatively delineated.

Show-off, she thought. *You're forty, if you're a day, and you flaunt yourself as if you were thirty.* Yes, definitely rough-cut, and Harris Chandler wanted to make sure the world knew he didn't give a damn. No wonder Neil didn't like the man.

Summer turned swiftly away, past getting excited over a man's behind, and certainly not an ex-con's. "Frankly," she said, "I've never known of a warrant for fraud to go through so quickly."

Hank patted his pockets for his chewing gum, found it, and unwrapped a piece. He fit it into his jaw like a wad of tobacco. "You know, Chief, there's something about this bust. I don't know, a lawman gets a feeling sometimes..."

Summer waited, but he didn't finish his thought.

"Well," he said, sighing and crushing his gum wrapper into a tiny ball and winding up like a baseball pitcher to throw it at the tracks, "I guess I'd better be getting back. See you on board, chief. Take care."

Summer didn't want to see the deputy handcuff himself to Harris Chandler, and she didn't try to analyze why because that would start her to thinking about Martin. Nor did she want to think about the disagreement she'd had with Neil over Chandler.

Moving quickly to the tracks where the monstrous hissing machine would screech to a stop and stand rumbling while passengers boarded, she hugged her tote bag and smiled wanely at the porter when he placed the step in place.

"Watch your step, ma'am," he said.

Purposely, Summer selected the last seat in the coach. From here she could lean her head against the glass and not have to worry about anyone watching her. From here she wouldn't have to think about anything. Or, if she wished, she could try to remember more innocent days when both boys were alive. If she wanted to, she could really be ridiculous and map out her future.

The one thing she would not do, she promised herself devoutly as she placed her bag in the rack overhead and looked away as the other passengers began to fill the coach, was to take a guilt trip because of a perfectly legitimate warrant she'd signed on a cocky, two-time loser who had gotten himself accused—rightly or wrongly—of fraud.

If he was innocent, Chandler could prove it in court. That was the law. For better or worse, it was all there was. Right?

She sighed. She wasn't sure she knew what was right anymore.

Chapter Three

Ladies love outlaws—a fact well-known enough for Waylon Jennings to write a song and for Harris Chandler to be wary.

When he'd been younger and his blood was hot, Harris had used the lady-outlaw phenomenon to his advantage, but age, alas, had its way of tarnishing even the most golden of substitutions for love.

Upon stepping out of the police car, Harris had found himself the object of every stare and speculation possible. He should've been used to it—awed children openly gaping at his wrist and tugging wonderingly on the arms of their parents, grown men hurling him a condemning, serves-you-right look and twisting away in masculine disgust.

But the women's glances? They were always different, bless their hearts. They looked at him with shy longing, wanting to mother him and make everything all right. The lady, for instance, who came face to face with him as Deputy Delaney was selecting the first seat up front in the coach.

"Lady" perhaps stretched the imagination a bit; she had a young body but an old face, and her bleached-blond hair sprang out from her scalp in a stiff helmet. But as her gaze fell to his wrist, she tilted her head as if to say, "What you need, honey, is a good woman." Her smile was a combination of curiosity and invitation.

Giving a mental shrug of "what the heck," Harris made the bold sweep of her that she wanted. Her reaction was predictable; pleasure pinkened her cheeks, and her tongue flicked flirtatiously across her lips as she flaunted her hips and walked past.

Having paused to watch the same pair of hips, Hank noisily cleared his throat and even stopped chewing his fresh stick of gum. He took his seat and carefully adjusted his handcuffed wrist upon the armrest.

A wry smile threatened to curve Harris's mouth, but he slumped on his spine to peer out the window at the ugly backs of buildings that flanked the railroad tracks where women, heavy-armed and unsmiling, leaned on the windowsills and pigeons flew in a sudden sweep and caused the children playing in the alley to pause and look upward.

Harris said to the deputy, "Put a lid on it, Matt Dillon. You'll die young."

Hank's reply was smothered in a cough. "Uh, I was just wondering if you, ah, if you wanted anything, sir."

If Hank thought he was going to nibble at that one, Harris decided, he was younger than he looked. He thrust up a shoulder between them. "What I want is a stiff drink and a good lawyer. Not in that order."

"Aw, you'll be out on bail by tomorrow, Mr. Chandler."

"I don't want bail, I want justice."

Hank couldn't promise that, and the wheels of the train began to creak and to inch the monstrous weight forward—

whining, rumbling as the big diesel engine gathered its strength to propel them toward Miami.

Harris leaned back against the headrest. With very little effort he could put himself into a near trance, a trick he'd taught himself in prison. By disciplining his brain mercilessly, he could actually visualize each detail on the blueprints, every angle, every slant, every joist.

He opened one bloodshot blue eye. "You ever do any construction work, Delaney?"

"No, sir," Hank replied meekly.

"What about timbering? You ever been a lumberjack?"

Hank compared the older man's big, roughly capable hands to his soft ones. "No sir, I don't guess I have." Presently he said, "I am married, though. Does that count?" He fingered the sideburns his wife had neatly trimmed only this morning. "Are you? Married, I mean?"

"I was."

Both men fell silent again until Hank said sympathetically, "That's too bad. You seemed to have survived it though."

"Divorce is a mother." Harris sighed, then grudgingly added, thinking as he did that Hank might not be such a bad guy if he'd change his line of work, "One of us had to put the other out of his misery. We were just kids."

The deputy chuckled, having more and more difficulty picturing his prisoner as a criminal. "Well, cheer up, Mr. Chandler. There're a few good ones left. If you look hard."

Harris said, "You got one of 'em, I suppose."

"You bet."

Another lapse of silence was filled with the *clack, clack, clack* of the wheels gaining speed.

Since Harris was sitting in the first seat, he had to look over his shoulder at the array of other passengers: the men in their walking shorts and Izod shirts who were taking their families to Miami's entertainment parks for the day; the students returning to the University of Miami for the summer term. A pair of lovers cuddled in a seat midway back. A few older women alone held empty shopping bags tucked in their laps that would be filled with goodies from Macy's and Bloomingdales on the return trip.

Domesticity, he thought with a familiar twinge of loneliness. Nice, pleasant, routine domesticity.

With the possible exception of the woman in the farthest rear seat. She had a double all to herself and had turned sideways in it, tucked her legs beneath her. She was reading. There was nothing routine about her. When had he last seen such a regal, unattainable woman? The kind of woman who always made him feel dressed wrong?

Harris unexpectedly wished he could see more of her—her face—but her head was tipped at a downward angle and a filmy lock of hair had slipped free of the twist at her crown to form a charming but troublesome veil. As the breeze from the air-conditioner stirred it, the lock fluttered silkily over her cheek.

Frowning, she brushed at it, and Harris found the gesture so innocently erotic that he sat stupefied and spellbound. She had to be in the indeterminate thirties, though with skin like hers it was difficult to tell. Margo had had expensive skin like that.

Funny, he hadn't thought of his ex-wife in years; Margo, with her sleek pantherish walk and her small, boyish breasts that she let everyone else touch but him.

The oversized top this woman was wearing was a meshed, flowing affair. He could even perceive the curves of her breasts and, unless he was miscalculating, a tiny waist that flared out into trim but well-curved hips. Her thighs were long to be as petite as she was, and her calves were very nice, slender and coltish.

He pictured her in a sleek Grecian gown of white silk slashed daringly low, only hinting at petal-pink nipples and a belly as white as porcelain. Then he pictured her without the gown. But that was masochism in its most hardcore form—imagining the negligent hollow of that spine and the milky whiteness of those hips, the forbidden crevices.

He wet his lips, for they were suddenly dry. As if she somehow sensed a danger in the air, she threaded her fingers through the lock of hair and drew it back from her face.

There was no way she could see the handcuffs that bound him to the deputy, yet Harris found himself self-consciously covering them with his hand.

He straightened himself slightly and, before he thought, wished he'd had a shave and haircut. He started once to turn away, but it was too late. She looked straight into his eyes.

Caught! Harris didn't know anything to do except to smile. He waited for her to smile back, the way a man uncomfortably waits for the wind on a hot summer day.

She didn't. Her pink lips parted, and her eyes widened until they seemed to fill her whole face. She wrenched her head harshly around, as if he had flicked some offensive sign at her.

Her expression had been something Harris couldn't identify: horror? contempt? shock? He felt like a fool, and a physical burn crept up the sides of his neck. Damn it, what was the matter with her?

Before he could puzzle over it, she leaned back against her seat and let her face turn around again—a weary, beaten lolling, her stare at first glazed, then blurry with quicksilver tears that rolled, glistening, over the beautiful slopes of her cheekbones. She spread a hand upon her breasts, whether to protect them from sight or because they ached from grief, he did not know. Yet she didn't turn away from him again. She stared and stared and stared.

"Yep," Hank's voice was drifting in from outer space, "I've got the prettiest, feistiest, lovin'est woman in the world."

Harris twisted around, feeling vacant, transparent and outside himself. *Get a hold of yourself, Chandler. Get real. Don't look at her again. She's a crazy woman.*

"Well, Hank," he said, and listened to himself talk with disinterest, "you don't have to sell me. I'm not soured on all women. Only one in particular."

The deputy made a sound through his teeth. "Your ex-wife?"

"The bitch who put me here."

Harris was fighting a losing battle. He would not turn back to the woman, he promised himself. If there was anything he didn't need, it was that kind of intimidation. Yet even as he reasoned with himself, he flicked another stolen glance over his shoulder and mumbled distractedly to Hank, "I wish I had my hands around her neck right now."

Astonished, Harris didn't think the woman had moved. Perhaps she hadn't even breathed. She was a frozen portrait of shock. Against his better judgment—what did he know about judgment the last five minutes?—he risked communication with her: an inclination of his head, a casual, inquiring nod.

More tears welled in her eyes, and Harris felt a sting of failure. *It's all right,* he told her with a helpless, embarrassed expression. *You're a special lady. I didn't mean anything.*

But the deputy was tugging on his wrist, dragging him back to the unwelcome present. "Speak of the devil."

"What?" Harris swung sharply around.

"The neck you'd like to get your hands around," Hank said with a gradual dwindling of his voice. "It's sitting in the last . . . seat . . . behind us."

If he'd thought things through, Hank guessed he wouldn't have told Harris who Summer MacLean was. But once the words were out he couldn't take them back. Besides, Chandler would know sooner or later.

"What d'you mean, deputy?" Harris's imagination, being light-years faster than his words, was in a state of vertiginous despair.

"Ms. MacLean." Hank belatedly wished he hadn't said anything. "On the last seat back there. She's the reason you're wearing these." He rattled the handcuffs in question.

She was S. MacLean? That lovely, feminine creature he'd been watching was the sadistic prison matron with the great breasts and the bulging calves and kinky books under her mattress?

When Harris looked at Summer this time, not as a lovely woman but as the assistant prosecuting attorney of Dade County, he not only despised her sparkling tears, he despised her for making him care she was shedding them.

"She was bringing her son up to stay with his grandparents for a few days," Hank volunteered the information.

Which solved that problem, Harris thought with strangling fury. The bitch was married and had a son!

Harris felt an irrational betrayal like that when he'd found Margo in bed with another man. Then he'd gone outside and looked up at the massive Michigan timber and, giving a horrendous howl of fury, he grabbed an ax and started tempestuously bringing down a two-hundred-year-old tree. He'd broken his anger before he'd broken the tree.

But now he could only twist around and face the front of the coach and slump down onto his spine like some sullen, hand-slapped boy. Past his window he could see the blur of West Palm Beach's industrial buildings. He despised them. He despised being in Florida and on this train. He wished he'd never come to the south. He wished he'd never fought the army, and he wished he'd never blown up the highway equipment. He wished....

Damn it, he wished that he didn't have a notion in hell of who S. MacLean was!

It had been, Summer thought, like an excruciating form of shock therapy.

She guessed her eyes had actually seen Harris Chandler before her brain had, her pupils like a camera—snap, snap, snap. Then the hurry into the darkroom only to realize that something was in the picture she hadn't known was there— Martin's face, superimposed upon the stranger's startling face, rising up out of the murky solution to assault her with memories.

No wonder Tom had been disturbed at the train depot. Harris Chandler could have been his father's double!

Except for the eyes, she thought. Where Martin's had been light, almost a colorless blue, Chandler's were a strong, Viking azure with the translucent quality of pure crystal. And they looked at her with a brutal, clothes-stripping rudeness that Martin's would never have been guilty of.

She scrubbed the outsides of her arms. Numbness was creeping all over her. She felt as if she were being sucked down into some watery grave, and the waves were closing over her head. How many times in the past had she pridefully brushed sympathy aside? How many times had she said the words, "I'm fine."

Everyone had thought she was so courageous. They had bragged on her maturity and balance. She had even thought it herself, congratulating herself with the thought, *How many people could suffer what I've suffered and still go on?*

Oh yes, she had grieved. She had mourned. Deep unfathomable holes had formed inside her. But sometimes it didn't seem as if Martin and Bobby were really gone. Somewhere there was a door that still wasn't closed, a haunting door that invariably eluded her. Angelica had often given her that best-friend's look and said, "It just hasn't hit you yet, sweetie. But when it does...."

Then she'd looked at Harris Chandler and had seen Martin's mouth smiling back at her. She had seen Martin's fair skin darkly tanned and stretched over rugged, sharply boned features. But where Martin had lived easily, this man had lived hard. His white teeth flashed at her and his lashes lowered until his eyes were friendly blue slits, and she'd fallen headlong into that smile without thinking.

Then, *then* it hit her: a thousand, million watts of voltage knocking her down! This man, this stranger whom Tom had warned her about in a silly horoscope, this stranger with whom she had, for an instant, communicated on a level so basic that she couldn't even articulate it—man to woman, body to body, sex to sex—this man was alive! He wasn't Martin! Martin was dead! And Bobby was dead!

Summer thought if she didn't reach the lounge, she would vomit where she sat. Swallowing, gagging, moaning, she pulled to her feet. She didn't care who watched her or what they saw, she wanted only to be alone, like an animal craving seclusion for its suffering.

Reeling between the seats toward the front of the coach, Summer didn't look at Harris Chandler. She didn't want to see the handcuffs she had caused to be there. It was like having betrayed her lover. Dear God, help her make it!

As she pushed through the door of the lounge and found it blessedly empty, she ran, stumbling, the last few steps. It must surely be like coming alive after having been frozen for a year, for she draped herself over the lavatory where the clattering of steel upon steel deafened her to anything outside the tiny cubicle. Closing her eyes, she lost everything.

Summer didn't know how long she wept. She vaguely remembered rinsing her mouth and staggering out into the tiny anteroom and leaning against the wall so that she could look out at the city going past. She felt as if the tears had washed scales off her eyes. Emptied, it was as if she could now look at her life and see it through the eyes of a scowling, handcuffed stranger for the very first time.

The truth was, she didn't even know what she was doing on this train. Or what was she doing, period. Who was she? Where had she come from? She was no one, from nowhere. She had pulled herself up by her own bootstraps and had lucked out by marrying well. She was the assistant to the state prosecutor.

So what? That had come about because of Martin's friendship with Neil. What had she really done, all by herself, except to conceive and bear two sons? Her marriage had been good because Martin was innately good. She was a good mother because Martin made it easy for her to be so. She had gotten through law school because Martin made it possible. But all she had managed to do with her own two hands was kill Martin. And one of her sons.

Oh, this was no good! She was letting a ghost rattle her into thinking like a crazy person. The simple fact was, she had looked into Harris Chandler's face and seen something that made her want to reach out and feel things again— feel.... She didn't know.

When a tap came at the door of the lounge, Summer looked with disbelief into the mirror. Her eyes were swollen and red-rimmed. Patches of discoloration splotched her throat and her cheeks. Her lips were puffy and colorless. A year's worth of grief had taken its toll all at once.

Again the rapping.

"Just a minute!" she wailed and frantically fished foundation from her bag and dabbed it on the red spots and brushed blusher on the pale spots.

Why had this happened to her? Why had she lost so much that she loved? People always blamed God for trouble. *God, why are you punishing me? Why are you doing this to me?* God didn't kill people. Evil killed people.

She inspected her face in the mirror. Terrible. But she had to return to her seat and rejoin the world of living things. One step at a time. One step. She could take one step, couldn't she? Yes. She just wouldn't make the mistake of looking at Harris Chandler again.

Sweeping up her makeup, she flung it all, clattering, into her bag. She took a deep breath and prepared herself to walk out. She told herself to be careful as she balanced against the swaying and jostling of the train. The last thing she wanted to do was trip over Hank Delaney's foot that was poking out into the aisle a few inches away.

Milliseconds later, as the engine derailed and plunged its nose into the ground, and as the coaches screamed and whipped and bucked then flipped over onto their backs, Summer did more than trip over Hank's foot. Somewhere during the unholy cataclysm of metal ripping and rivets being stripped from their moorings, she screamed.

She heard her own voice over the pandemonium of glass shattering and dust, debris, paper, food, bottles, and luggage raining down like an avalanche. For the second time in her life, she looked eternity baldly in the face.

To Summer, the weightlessness of being turned upside down was incredible. Through the roar that brought pain to her ears, she realized with perfect clarity that she was conscious and not dreaming. She was clutching the shoulders of Harris Chandler with all her strength, and he was gazing back at her, not in wonder of the hellish violence around them but in some terrifying pleasure that they were enduring it together, as if she had this coming for what she'd done to him.

But then time returned to normal. A second was a second again and not an eternity.

Summer spat dust from her mouth and raked dirt from her eyes. She was lying sprawled upon the two handcuffed men, and what had been the floor was now the ceiling. Where there had been a fiendish and unearthly roar, there was now silence, except for the delayed sounds of isolated glass tinkling and metal slowly shifting to its final resting place.

The sounds of people began immediately, each one seeking survival in his own way. As Summer ventured to lift her face—it was buried into the hard span of Harris Chandler's belly—she saw Harris's T-shirt where it had pulled free of his pants and twisted up beneath his arms. His bare chest, strong and sculpted, branched out into perfectly torqued arms. His breast was cleanly articulated and as deeply bronzed as the roped muscles of his arms. Dust was sprinkled over the sparse design of curls on his chest.

She braced her weight on one hand. Harris Chandler's eyes, which had plunged so callously into the depths of her own, were closed now, as heart-tuggingly peaceful as Tom's when he slept. Robbed of harshness, his mouth was oddly tender, and a fine sensuality was evident in its curve.

"Mr. Chandler!" she gasped and scrambled backward off him, feeling her heart throb painfully in her throat. She steadied herself and waited for him to wake up. Cautiously, like a night prowler, she ventured to whisper, "Mr. Chandler?"

No response.

Horrified—that same recurring nightmare since the accident—she clapped her hand over her mouth. Oh, no, oh, no!

Be calm. Giving herself a mental shake, Summer forced herself to take a deep, steadying breath. *Be logical. See if he's breathing. Easy now, you're in control.*

Overtimorously, as if she might receive a shock if she touched him, she bent over Harris Chandler until her face almost grazed his. He smelled faintly of tobacco and coffee and sweat and fabric softener and soap. She held her breath and drew her tongue across her lips. When she felt his breath stirring gently against her moistened mouth, she wanted to laugh—giddily, ridiculously.

Just to make sure, she tentatively laid two fingertips against the vein in his neck. Yes, his heart was beating. Quite strongly, as a matter of fact. She timidly touched his shoulder and was amazed at how hard and solid it was, how capable of leverage. It had seen a lot of physical labor, that shoulder.

"Mr. Chandler?" When he didn't move, she closed her hand upon his bristly jaws and worked his head back and forth.

"Oh, Mr. Chandler," she said sadly. Her search over his body for injuries was hasty and superficial: ribs, sides, waist, thighs, legs. Shakily—what would she do if he suddenly came to?—Summer slipped her fingers into his thick hair and felt the well-formed contours of his scalp. No damage that she could tell. No blood, except at his wrist where the band of steel had taken its toll during the wreck.

And then she saw the blood of Hank Delaney.

"Ms. MacLean?"

Hank's voice sounded like that of a child a long way off. Coming around, Summer took one look at the young deputy and knew he must be kept still at all costs.

"Don't move, Hank." She swiftly searched for something to place beneath his head. Someone's corduroy jacket lay in a dusty twist nearby and she clutched it, rolled it into a pillow and eased it beneath Hank's head.

"You're going to be all right, Hank. Just keep still."

Hank flicked an inquiry toward his prisoner whom he could not see. "What about him?"

"He's okay," Summer lied.

People were beginning to stagger to their feet amid the rubbish now, trying not to step on one another. Parents were searching for children, making sure they were all right, and the children were oddly adult about the whole thing. From what Summer could tell in that first hazy glance, the personal damage was miraculously slight—mostly bruises, and a few cuts that she surmised were being bound up.

Through the shatterproof windows, which were shattered, Summer could see pandemonium on the streets—cars were pulling up to the curbs, and horns were blaring, people were shouting, running to help. Not ten feet away, two women were trying to collect their belongings.

Summer called to them. "Over here! This man is hurt."

But Hank was tugging at her wrist to shush her, and Summer, twisting back to explain that this was not time for heroics, watched in mute astonishment as he slipped the handcuff from his own wrist and snapped it shut around her own.

She sat gaping at him. "Wha—"

He lifted his free arm and tossed something far over her head. Too late, Summer realized that he had just thrown the key away.

"Hank!" she yelled in disbelief and grabbed at his hand, but his eyes were slowly closing. "Hank!"

So great was Summer's panic, so stark and complete and horrible, for some seconds all she could do was sit with her hand pressed to her mouth. But then, when she moved and felt the dead weight of Harris's arm connected to her own, she stupidly began battling the handcuff.

"No, no," she wailed, and clawed at the shiny metal steel bands.

The more she struggled with the steel, the more frantic she grew until small, strangled sounds were bubbling up out of her throat. Desperate, she searched about for something she didn't know: someone to help, some instrument, some *thing* to sever the devastating connection between Chandler and herself.

But everyone had too many problems of their own. They were crawling out windows. Someone had gotten one of the doors at the end of the coach pried open. Others were haltingly picking their way toward it.

Oh, God! Slumping into a huddle, heaving to catch her breath, Summer tried to think what to do. She spied a bottle of spilled shaving lotion and reached out with her foot to kick it over. She ridiculously began banging at the lock with it. What had possessed Hank to do such a thing? she wanted to babble to anyone who would listen. Did he think he was going to die?

She looked wretchedly at the unconscious deputy and, clutching a handful of his jacket, started going through his pockets. Perhaps he had a spare key. Perhaps she would find some miracle to set her free.

She found nothing. Opening her mouth, knowing nothing to say and whimpering her helplessness, she finally clutched the front of Hank's jacket and shook it with an utter frenzy. "Hank? *Hank!*"

Hank didn't open his eyes when she screamed, Harris Chandler did.

After the Korean War, long before it was the fashion for a woman to do so, Summer's mother became a success. Estelle Summerfield bought her own insurance company in a respectable, nation-wide franchise. She and the Gainsville Savings and Loan managed to swing a modest cottage on the outskirts of the city, and she drove a moderately priced '57 Chevrolet with a few trimmings. She topped her tweedy suits with expensive frilly blouses and a genuine ivory cameo brooch.

In all of her commendable successes, Estelle made only one fatal mistake; she married a sweet-talking man. The trouble with Barney, so Estelle always claimed to Summer, was that he sweet-talked every woman he knew. When Summer was three, he left town with one twice his age.

For years Barney wandered in and out of Estelle's life, and a good deal of Estelle's money wandered in and out of Barney's pockets. After a long struggle, Estelle found her own way into a bottle of Smirnoff's vodka.

Estelle died shortly before Summer and Martin were married, a broken woman without a penny. Summer swore, literally over her mother's grave, that she would never, never trust a man who called every woman "darling."

As she knelt beside Harris Chandler and watched him return to consciousness, Summer figured she could relax with this man. By the way Harris's chest filled suddenly with air and he jerked irately up to sit, the way his brows flew fiercely together and his nostrils flared when he comprehended that he was no longer handcuffed to Hank Delaney but to her, it was obvious that he didn't care a great deal for women. She doubted that he'd ever uttered the word "darling."

With his free hand he gripped the steel bracelets that imprisoned them and said, "I'll be damned."

Summer stared, wide-eyed, for several speechless seconds, not at his hand but at the unavoidable reality of his chest where his T-shirt was still bunched up beneath his arms. She saw what she had not noticed before—a long, thinly drawn scar maring the curve of his left breast, frightfully wicked, like that of a blade.

Prison? she wondered with a tingling shiver and snatched up her head in the same second that his rib cage expanded and seemed about to pierce the lean surface of his flesh.

His drawl was nasty and insulting. "A neat trick," he said and shook the handcuffs. "Someday you must tell me how you did it."

Feeling like a silly girl caught with mischief on her mind, Summer shook her head. "But this isn't . . . I didn't—"

"Save it."

"But—"

Swiveling, he crawled over to Hank Delaney, and his movement nearly jerked her arm out of its pocket.

"Wait a minute!" she cried and pulled back on her wrist, which was an even more painful protest. "Just...ohhh, you— *Wait!*"

Forced to scramble after him, whimpering and cursing him with a barrage of names that she couldn't even articulate, Summer crawled over her bag and other people's spilled luggage and tried at all costs to protect the flesh about her wrist that now felt as if it were the nerve center of her entire body.

He ignored her outburst completely. His only interest seemed to be inspecting the deputy for wounds.

Having found that she must coordinate her moves with him or suffer the most excruciating agony, Summer bent with Harris as he discovered the tiny trickle of blood at Hank's ear and forced open his eyes to see the dilated pupils. She leaned over as he shook Hank's shoulder and called his name.

Harris searched for a pulse and, satisfying himself that there was one, bent low to listen to Hank's heart. Then he felt along the deputy's back. When he straightened, Hank's revolver lay in the palm of his hand.

Summer recoiled in horror.

"He's alive," he said as if to himself and jerked Summer's hand unceremoniously into his crotch as he fit the gun beneath the waistband of his pants. He pulled the T-shirt down over it and pushed a crumpled cigarette pack back down into the pocket.

"I could have told you that," she snapped, hating him now and bracing herself away by shoving hard against his thigh.

"Okay." He blew a stream of air up into his lashes to dislodge the clinging dust. "Now that we've got that business out of the way, hand it over and let's get on with it. No hard feelings, you understand. We'll just chalk it up to experience. Live and let live. That's the way the cookie crumbles. Take a nurse to lunch. Whatever."

Summer clamped her mouth shut and mutinously narrowed her eyes. "Give you what?"

"The key, lady! The key!"

He was suddenly ablaze with fury, and his look swept with stripping cruelty over her. Martin's sweet blue eyes, Summer thought in a disoriented daze, turning her most precious memories to dust.

"The key?" She had utterly lost her train of thought. "The key! Are you insane? I don't have any key."

"Oh? I'm to assume that you performed some great feat of magic to get these bracelets off Hank's wrist and onto yours? Hmm, Houdini?"

"Oh, great." Her shoulders dropped into a dismal curve. "If you'd give me a minute to explain, you'd see that this is all a perfectly innocent—"

"You will make this brief, won't you?" He showed a lot of perfect, white teeth in a malicious smile. "As you can see, I'm a bit pressed for time."

How dare he use that disgusting tone with her? She was the only one who'd raised even so much as a question about his innocence to Neil. Who did he think he was?

"Look!" she cried distraughtly. "In case you don't know who I am, Mr. High-and-Mighty—"

"I know who you are *Miz* MacLean." He slashed across her explanation with an insensitive lack of regard. "*Miz S.* MacLean."

Feeling like ten kinds of an idiot, Summer slumped again. "Take time off from your regular routine," her horoscope had said. "Let the 'real you' emerge." She should venture off the beaten path? Wasn't that what Tom had read? What a laugh, what a ludicrous, heartbreaking laugh!

She swallowed hard, refusing the tears that threatened.

"Our nice mutual friend told me," Harris was aridly explaining before she could ask. "Now, you and Hank may be the best of buddies, Miz MacLean, but this is taking things a little too far, don't you think? So, if you'll just give me the key..."

When it was all said and done, Summer seriously doubted that she could have stopped Harris Chandler from doing anything he had his mind set upon, yet when he shoved her arm aside and grasped her bag, she lunged forward and tried weakly to fight him for it.

He held the bag out of her reach as easily as a teenage boy tormenting a sibling.

"You monster!" she said through her teeth. "You son-of-a—"

"Uh, uh, uh."

One flick of his piercing blue eyes, and Summer slumped back onto her heels. She clamped her mouth furiously shut as he rifled rudely through her things and finally flung the bag aside in exasperated futility.

Grabbing the tote and clutching it to her bosom, Summer regained some shreds of her composure. She was a mature woman, a professional woman, for crying out loud. She didn't have to take this kind of browbeating from a rude, boorish *ex-convict*!

She spoke with the insulting deliberance of explaining something complicated to a slow-witted child. "I know that you are upset, Mr. Chandler." She exaggerated every syllable. "I am upset, too. But the fact is that we have a very injured man on our hands here. Half the people on this train are injured, and as you can see, many of them are climbing out the windows. I suggest that we do the same."

Summer didn't think, as she paused for his reply, that Harris heard a word she'd said. He was staring baldly at her breasts. No, worse. He was looking lower, to where her knees splayed out in a position Estelle would have blushingly called "highly unbecoming to a lady."

She looked down at the explicit V and felt the heat of embarrassment slide up from her waist to her scalp. Yet she would have sat before Harris Chandler stark naked before she would've given him the satisfaction of adjusting her legs one inch.

With her dignity completely wrecked, she compressed her lips, then said with the nastiest, most hateful tone she possessed, "Do you think you could find something better to do than that worn-out chauvinist gambit, Mr. *H*. Chandler?"

He came very near to laughing, but he caught the corner of his mouth between his teeth and chewed on it as if he were envisioning her deliciously skewered on a stake.

"You should know, dear," he murmured with saccharine sweetness.

"What are you talking about?" She threw back her head in a blaze of righteousness.

"Isn't that how you get your kicks? Hmm?" He leaned irately forward until the end of his nose was practically assaulting hers.

Flinching, Summer clamped hard on her jaw.

"You couldn't take your eyes off me before," he drawled mockingly. "What's the matter, Miz Prosecuting Attorney? Turning shy on me? Well, I'll tell you what, you take your kinky head trip on someone else." Here, an intolerable leer. "Because if you don't, I'm going to strip every stitch off that kinky little bod of yours and find that key for myself." His smile vanished, and icy bitterness took its place. "Now, give it here, damn it!"

There was nothing, Summer supposed, like a fist in the stomach to get the adrenaline truly flowing. She hardly knew what she did first, strike him across the face with her open palm or scream at him, *"You're disgusting!"*

With the impact of her blow ringing in his head, Harris sank back onto his heels and dropped his hands slackly to his knees. In amazement he cocked his head to one side and stared dumbly at the diamond sparkle of her tears. No woman had ever struck him before. He wasn't sure if he should laugh or hit her back.

He didn't do either, for all through the stricken coach people were collecting their belongings and throwing them over and across and going through broken windows. After having found out that they were all in one piece, parents were now snapping at children, and children were whining at parents. Passengers who knew each other were calling out. From the outside, strangers were rushing up, waving their arms wildly and trying to help.

"My glasses," an older woman was wailing. "I can't find my glasses."

"Come along, Mother," her husband consoled as he wobbly picked his way through the debris. "Be thankful you can still see."

Several people were calling back to companions. "Over here, over here."

"My mother said that I shouldn't travel today," a woman's voice complained. "She had this dream..."

"Gerald," a father barked, "hold your brother's hand."

"Someone's going to pay for that vase I was returning to Bloomingdales," another declared.

"Hail Mary, full of grace..."

"First thing, I'm calling my lawyer."

Outside, things were nearly as chaotic. Far in the distance sirens were beginning to wail, and on Interstate 95, traffic was backing up. People from the residential districts, having heard the noise, were driving up and parking their cars, hungry for the sight of blood.

Harris stared with unseeing eyes beyond the railroad tracks where West Palm Beach stretched for miles. In his mind he went swiftly beyond that, to the edge of the county across miles of sand and waist-high saw grass, savage palmetto and anemic thickets of scrub pine trees.

What was to stop him, he wondered, from going through one of those windows himself? With any luck, he could walk across the city and out Beeline Highway. He could reach his house before the authorities could untangle this mess enough to know who he was and that he was missing. His chances of getting his records and at least letting a lawyer see them before they were subpoenaed were very, very good.

Escaping, however, would place him in violation of the law for real: evading justice. And he wasn't absolutely positive that having his original records would help, in any case. Why should they? If Rex Jernigan had had his signature forged to a handful of bank notes, who would believe the word of a twice-convicted man?

But it was the best chance he had. At this point, it was the *only* chance he had.

He wiped a hand over his mouth and tasted the bitter regret of his youth. Then he looked at the woman who had changed his future with the flick of a pen. He almost regretted what he was about to do to her.

Grabbing both her wrists, he hauled her roughly to her feet. "Come on, pretty lady," he said and began picking his way through the ankle-deep clutter of the coach before she could protest.

Astounded, Summer grasped one of the stalactitic coach seats and clung desperately to it. "What are you doing?" she demanded on a shrill note of panic.

Harris turned to consider her soft expensive skin that he'd coveted only moments earlier. And her luxuriant mind-blowing hair and lovely, irresistible breasts, all feminine assets that could drive a man to murder but which were no help where he was planning to take her.

"Up until this second," he admitted with a more honest and less fierce sigh, "I hadn't really made up my mind. But I'm going over to that broken window, Miz S. MacLean. I'm going to climb through it, which means that you must climb through it, too. I am, as I believe you legal people put it, going to leave the scene."

Summer felt her color drain away. Along with the final shreds of her courage. She tried to speak, to come up with a sane and logical suggestion, but she dipped her head at a disbelieving angle and threw a helpless gesture over her shoulder. "But Hank..."

"I'm sorry about Hank, and I mean that sincerely. But there's nothing I can do. You can't do anything, either. The paramedics will be here in a matter of minutes, and our staying or leaving won't matter a whit."

Harris knew there was no way he could justify his actions to her, and to waste time trying to do so was more stupid than some of the other things he had done in his life. He began dragging her to the window again.

Summer's composure spiraled out of reach, like a charred cinder disintegrating in the wind. "If you do this, Mr. Chandler," she cried, wrestling him futilely for her wrist, "I swear, I—"

"You'll what, Miz MacLean?" His challenge was a final stripping glare that hacked straight to Summer's bone marrow. "Make a citizen's arrest?"

Chapter Four

Neither heaven nor hell could stop Harris Chandler from leaving the wreck. Summer saw that now. It was as if Martin were doing and saying everything, and she had always trusted Martin. She'd let him map out her career, even her life, if the truth were told. She had always taken Martin's advice. But now....

She waved helplessly at the bulge at Martin's—no, Harris Chandler's—waist. "If you must go, for God's sake please don't take that thing with you."

Harris glanced down at the outline of the gun beneath his T-shirt, then at the unconscious deputy, at the handcuffs which imprisoned the woman and himself. If things had been different, he guessed he would've taken her face in his hands and told her not to be afraid. He wondered, too, if they had both been born fifty years earlier, when life was a more simple matter of treating people decently and being treated decently in return, if she would have seen something in him to admire. He would oddly have given much to see her smile.

"Oh, hell," he muttered and, puzzling at her strange attraction for him, slipped the weapon from beneath his shirt. He dropped it into the debris beside Hank Delaney.

With her shoulders drooping in relief, Summer followed as he led the way through the clutter to the window. Lifting his foot, he karate-kicked the worst slivers of glass to the ground outside, and then, while both of them bent into contortions that they would have found enormously funny under different circumstances, he crawled through.

When only their cuffed hands spanned the breach over the glass, he gave her a surprisingly endearing grimace. "Please do be careful, counselor. All I need is a bleeding albatross around my wrist."

Summer flung the tote bag through the opening to land beside his deck shoes. Humor? At a time like this?

Once she was out, he thrust her bag into her arms and drew her against the side of his hip in a way that would have been quite suitable had they been lovers. Now it was presumptuous and infuriating. She elbowed him sharply in the ribs.

He flicked her a sidelong look of mockery. "Try and think of this as a marriage of convenience, Miz MacLean," he drawled. "You stay on your side of the bed, and I'll stay on mine. We'll get along just fine."

"You can take your marriage of convenience," Summer flung her tart retort at his familiar profile, "and go straight..."

He was narrowing his eyes at her again. She finished lamely, "Go straight to hell...with...it."

In the face of what had just happened, hell didn't pose too much of a threat. Not breaking his stride, Harris threw back his head in silent, chest-deep laughter.

Summer was of a mind to say something exceedingly waspish, but before she could do anything a police car screamed to a stop not fifty feet from where they were. She and Harris came to a startled halt as four uniformed officers spilled out of it and ran toward them.

Behind that car, another swerved into the curb. And another and another. And an ambulance with its radio blaring and paramedics hitting the ground at a hard run.

"Damnation," Harris said, his face rigid as he heeled hard to his left and turned Summer into the hollow of his side so the handcuffs wouldn't show so badly. "Where is a cop when you don't need him?"

Even as the climactic seconds ticked past, Summer knew she would reconstruct the moment over and over again in an attempt to understand what happened between Harris and herself to topple that first domino in a long, long chain. For one thing, the outlandish circumstances of the past hour already had her senses spinning. Then, Harris Chandler so uncannily resembled Martin. Perhaps it was her stringent chastity over the past year that threw her logic out of kilter.

Whatever it was, she didn't remember being so acutely aware of a man before. Every nerve in Harris was so visibly stretched that her own nerves trembled in empathy. His thighs were tense and poised for flight, as a sprinter's would be, and she could feel the bones moving powerfully beneath his skin. He was a strong, determined man, but he was on the edge of breaking. And his eyes, glittering with recklessness and despair, swept over her, plunging past the externals as if they didn't exist and stripping her to the bare essence. He entered her, mind, body and soul, in the most profound act of coupling she had dreamed possible.

A gap appeared in Summer's stomach. As if the ground had just dropped ten feet.

Radios were squawking from all directions now. Some of the uniformed men were climbing into the capsized coaches and helping people out. Others were locating railroad officials and commencing upon plans to evacuate people from the area and to control traffic. Summer guessed that if she were to call out for help, the worst Harris could do would be to break her arm. She could walk away from this nightmare unscathed. It could be over. Just like that.

Do it! she demanded of herself. *This man isn't Martin. He's a fugitive from the law. The law you have sworn to uphold. Don't be a fool!*

"Hey!"

Coming from behind, the policeman's yell went through Summer like the blast of a shotgun.

She jerked around to view the concerned face beneath the uniform cap, then twisted back to the dark and volatile face hovering inches above her own. Open-mouthed, speechless, she watched the stain of fear creeping above the ribbed neck of Harris's shirt.

"In case you're cherishing heroic ideas," he said, his voice distorted and pulled by fear, "let me remind you that I'm a desperate criminal. I know terrible things to do to a woman."

Which was nonsense. What he was really saying was, *For God's sake, could you possibly extend yourself to stand in my shoes for one minute? Could you bring yourself to trust me? Please?*

Summer couldn't believe what she was contemplating.

"Are you two all right?" the officer demanded as he strode toward them.

"Yes, thank you," Summer shockingly heard her most professional voice saying. She felt transparent and detached from her body. Not for a second did she break the riveting connection between Harris and herself. "We... We're not hurt."

Relief went through Harris like a shudder, and the strength seeped out of Summer's legs, leaving her like a crumbling puppet. Harris Chandler had to have felt the overwhelming magnetism. There was no way he could have been alive and not have felt it.

Sealing her guilt even more, Summer smiled feebly over her shoulder at the officer and inclined her head. "We're okay. Thank you."

The man started to ask something but the radio clipped to his belt spit static at him.

"Just checking, ma'am," he said as he lifted it to his mouth and said offhandedly to Harris, along with a motion of his arm to step back, "If you would, sir, please stay clear of the rails until we get some evacuation vehicles here." This, into the transmitter, "Two-niner-four, requesting air backup at the intersection of Industrial and Seventh Avenue North."

Summer stared dumbly at the ground. Had she finally snapped? Had she survived that other horrendous tragedy, coming out of it alive while those she loved had died, only to be destroyed by this one?

She pulled her head up to see what Harris would do now and found Martin again, studying her with open bewilderment. Or was it the stranger with Martin's face? Upon the screen of her imagination she saw Harris with Martin's face, or Martin with Harris's face, waiting for her. The image was breathtakingly vivid: she was running to him, and when they met, they embraced as if they had known each other forever. There was a breathless flurry and the sigh of clothes being removed. They kissed ravenously and, without breaking the embrace, they sank to the ground, and when she looked up into his burning face, she found nothing of Martin MacLean at all. Only this man—this dark, compelling, and unlawful man.

No! she shouted at the fantasy as it ate into her senses with the lethal burn of acid. *This is not what I bargained for.*

She lurched as far back from Harris as possible, as if his fingers upon her arm were the corrosive acid.

Yet, putting distance between them didn't erase the image of seeking mouths and hot, chafing flesh. He was looking at her as if he had seen the same image in even greater detail, and Summer wanted to blurt that she had been momentarily hallucinating. But her statement to the police—had that been a hallucination?

"I want this thing off my wrist!" she cried with a sudden clawing hysteria, unable to free herself of him quickly enough.

Harris blinked down at her hand torturing the steel clasp and said nothing, for he was consumed with his own blinding recriminations. Some of them were old enemies: his fear, his horror of being locked up again, the sick knowledge that he had structured his own life to be the way it was, and his fresh determination to get away from people and stay only on the fringes of the thing they called life.

Why had this woman saved him just now? He had seen things on her face, puzzling things, but not disgust or repulsion. And it had been that, he supposed, which had triggered it all: her look—not the professional toughness he expected, but a pale, frightened vulnerability that could break a man's heart. Her helplessness had awakened the other sensation, the hard, driving one from the center of himself that he recognized only too well but which was as beyond his ability to touch as his bitterness and the past.

Desire wasn't a thing he felt indiscriminately anymore, yet sweat was running down his back, under his arms and down into his crotch; and he wanted to reach into his brain and rip out the sudden passion that hung there, taunting him with its throbbing, primal blood.

But it overpowered even his desperation to escape this place, and the funny thing of it was, he could have scorned the danger and closed the space between himself and her right then. He could have thrown his freedom away and taken the smell of her into his lungs and kissed her and driven her to her knees until there was no mystery existing between either of them.

"If I have t' chew 'em off with my teeth, S. MacLean," he said, hardly recognizing his own slurred, passion-drunk voice, "you'll be free before nightfall."

Then Harris told himself that he was a fool. Lacing his fingers with hers, trying erratically to clear his head of the images that drugged him, he walked her swiftly toward Tenth Avenue.

At least twenty miles lay between the site of the train wreck and the locked safe in the model home where Harris lived. Alone, he knew he could walk it easily. But handcuffed to a woman, he had no idea, and his responsibility toward Summer, once they left the site, weighed more than he reckoned on.

His strategy was to keep to the crowded sidewalks—two faces hidden among hundreds. It didn't take long to discover that by unfastening the strap of Summer's tote and relooping it, he could carry the bag upon his own shoulder. They could rest their hands upon it, not only camouflaging the steel bracelets but also keeping a little more skin on their wrists.

The assistant prosecutor had an admirable resilience, he discovered with short, guarded glances. She was hot and tired and hungry, and at times she hobbled as if her shoes were wearing blisters on her feet, yet she nonetheless gamely, or perhaps bullheadedly, swallowed her complaints.

They skirted warehouses and restaurants and fast-food places and shopping malls. They hurried across blistering, clamoring intersections and bustling shopping plazas. They tunneled through crowds of oddly dressed, weary-eyed people waiting at bus stops and dodged streams of boys in tight pants that showed off their behinds and young girls who wore short skirts and spike heels and cheap blouses that showed the shadows of their nipples.

Most of it they walked without talking, but they moved as if they had walked in tandem for years. With each step, Harris's instincts of self-preservation warred with a growing fascination with Summer. While he kept sharply on the alert for the danger of a uniform stepping out from behind a parked car or from a doorway, he was privately wishing he dared pick up that fragile thread from before, when she had looked at him with such naked and poignant longing in her eyes.

Perhaps he was watching out for the wrong danger, he thought wryly, and abruptly mistrusted himself. This... whatever it was—curiosity? interest? infatuation?—was happening much too quickly.

"I need to use the telephone," she said presently as they waited, out of breath, at the intersection on Lake Worth Drive.

Lest some of his interest show, Harris dropped a wooden mask over his face. "To call your son?"

Her reply when she swung around was laced with defensiveness. "What d'you think, that I'll tell on you? Do you think I would have lied to the police if I were going to do that?"

Her misconception irked him immensely. No, it hurt, damn it! Harris touched his forehead as if summoning great patience.

She took a step back and asked lamely of the traffic light, "How did you know about my son?"

Harris hesitated, then brushed off his pique. "Hank told me."

"I see."

She smiled without really smiling, and Harris saw the sun glint off a white tooth. Her hair was pulling loose, its knot drooping low upon her nape. With the erotic grace typical of women who rarely worried about their sex appeal, she ignored it, and Harris pictured her standing in a room of dusky shadows, her naked back visible with one smooth hip thrown higher than the other and her hair floating down her nape.

His impulse of desire returned, much stronger this time. "You really are quite beautiful," he murmured without the slightest intention of doing so. "Did you know that, Miz S. MacLean?"

At first Harris thought he'd offended her. She caught a sharp little breath, coughed into a loose fist, and dipped her head until all he could see was the finely boned slope of her cheek.

"I'm short, Mr. Chandler," she presently said, and straightened to look at him with an amazing lack of coyness. "Short women aren't beautiful. They're cute, or they're cuddly, or they're piquant. They're pleasant. Attractive. Nice. Even delightful. But never beautiful."

Harris couldn't remember the last time he'd thrown back his head and let the laughter just roll out of himself as he did now. It poured straight from his gut, wonderful, cleansing, restoring.

People glanced aside at them and smiled, and Harris found their amusement satisfying. They thought she belonged to him. He found that even more satisfying.

When he could speak again he said, "I didn't realize that height was so complex a matter."

"It's the first thoracic vertebra."

"Is that so?"

She pressed a smile out of her mouth in a most charming way. "You've obviously never gotten a crick in your neck by kissing a tall man."

"Can't say that I have. Nope, can't say that."

The traffic light finally changed, and Harris stepped off the curb, wondering, with a sudden rush of excitement, if she would get a crick in her neck by kissing him.

Still chuckling and finding her lightness infinitely appealing, he leaned over as if sharing a well-kept secret, "I hate to say this, ma'am," he murmured, "but I'm afraid the only people I allow to call me Mr. Chandler are those who're impressed with me."

"Oh, I'm very impressed with you, Mr. Chandler." Her brown eyes twinkled. She tipped her head aside, as if she knew wonderful things no one else would ever know. "Extremely impressed."

"I should've said that I let people call me Mr. Chandler who are impressed in a *positive* way. You know, the old pedestal. Laud and adoration. Next president of the United States, etcetera."

"Well then, *Harris* . . ."

At last, her laughter, and its melody was worth waiting for. Harris was enthralled with the lines crinkling beside her eyes and the way her merriment showed all her teeth and wrinkled her nose.

"I have a question for you, Harris," she said after a moment as her amusement dwindled down to a wistful and melting sigh.

But Harris was thinking how no one woman should be so perfect. She was smart and able and professional, yet could be shy and elusive. An irresistible combination. He would always be two steps behind a woman like her. Always? Why in hell had he thought that? Was he about to get himself in trouble here?

"Shoot," he said, abruptly on guard.

"How much did Hank Delaney tell you about me?"

Harris reached for his cigarettes from habit. Placing one in his mouth and pausing to cup his hands around it, finding it difficult to light in the wind and hampered by the handcuffs, he glanced down to see a smile tilting the sides of her mouth.

"Is this conversation giving you a nicotine fit?" she asked.

He twisted his mouth out of shape. "You're giving me a nicotine fit, Miz MacLean."

Her eyes widened in mock surprise. "Me? I don't mean to. What can I do to help?"

"Stop wearing that face, for one thing."

She shrugged off the compliment.

"And stop being so...wonderful," he added and tried to replace the bent cigarette into its pack. It crumbled in his hand. Tossing it away, he grimaced at her, laughed, then resumed walking.

"Hank didn't tell me much more than that," he answered her question. "He said that your son's grandparents live in West Palm. That you had taken him up for a visit."

"How did the subject come about?"

"I was saying that I'd like to get my hands around the throat of the bitch..." The look he shot her was one of comic guilt, and when she merely lifted her brows in amusement, he continued, chuckling. "I was saying that I'd like to get my hands around the throat of the woman who put these on me."

She laughed again. Harris was under a spell so sweet he had no desire ever to wake up. He collided with a man and took the force of his weight hard upon his shoulder. Hobbling around on one foot for a few seconds, he glared at the man and grimacingly drew Summer out of the stream of traffic.

After a superficial scan of the street and a thrust of his shoulder to protect them from it, his caution evaporated. He let his look take baldly improper liberties with her face and the quick rise and fall of her breasts.

Returning to her mouth, he asked the question that had been bothering him for blocks. "Hank didn't tell me if there was a Mr. S. MacLean."

She didn't blink or turn away. She did, however, lower her eyes to the vicinity of his Adam's apple. "I'm not wearing a wedding ring, am I?"

"Not all women do."

"Mr. MacLean is dead."

She grew withdrawn with the statement and looked out into the distance. The mood was shattered, and Harris was sorry he'd asked. She walked a few more steps, brushed back a troublesome strand of hair, but her topknot, having withstood the wind's tugging as long as it could, finally freed itself and spilled haphazardly to her shoulders.

Instantly the wind snagged it, whipped it free and threw it out like a sail. Strands of hair floated out to graze the rough stubble on Harris's jaw, and he had to steel himself to keep from telling her that he was sorry about her husband and that he was sorry...for what? He wasn't sorry she was free.

Then he knew; he was sorry they had met as they had. He was sorry they weren't people who bump into each other on buses and in grocery stores and who say nice things that go somewhere and open up the future. He was sorry—God help him for being such an utter fool, for he knew there was no chance for him with a woman like her—he was sorry that she and he had no chance for a future.

She began burrowing about in her hair in a search for pins and jerked him back to reality when she pointed to the bag between them. "In there I have some pins," she said with a hoarse, brittle edge to her voice. "My hair..."

"Leave it down."

Harris's mouth was dry. When she stopped walking and faced him, he said foolishly, "It makes you look like a girl."

"I'm not a girl, Mr. Chandler."

No, she wasn't. Now Harris saw a white circle running around her mouth and nostrils. The lines around her eyes were tight, in a different way. And her eyes.... He could see her grief, a terrible, aging sadness of which the physical evidence was only the tip of the iceberg. He felt himself being drawn into the vortex of her ruined eyes. In the name of sweet sanity, what had happened to this woman?

"I was driving," she explained and didn't resist when he reached for her fingers and laced them reassuringly with his. "There was an accident. My husband and one of my sons were killed."

Jesus! Harris felt the breath knocked out of him. He shook his head. Jesus! "I'm sorry."

A muscle pulled at the side of her mouth. "There're still nights when I dream . . . when it happens all over again."

Harris forced himself to calmly follow the mountains and peaks of her knuckles with a fingertip when he wanted to fold her into his arms and make promises that made no sense. He asked, "How long has it been?"

"A year now. A year yesterday, as a matter of fact."

"You were married a long time?"

"Thirteen years."

A fractured moment of time passed. She simply stared at his hands communicating with hers. As if she realized, then, that the intimacy was preempting normal conventions, she shrugged and pulled away.

"That's all in the past." Looking up, she seemed a wistful distance. " 'The past is like a funeral gone by.' "

Before Harris thought, he finished the Gosse verse, " 'The future comes like an unwelcome guest.' "

Her distance disintegrated, and she measured him until he flushed sheepishly.

"Right?"

For an answer, she commenced a distracted search through the bag. After a bit of difficulty, she drew out a pair of sunglasses and stabbingly fit them on her face. She plucked jerkily at the strands of hair lodged between the earpiece and her temple.

Unable to bear not touching her in some way—man's eternal fumbling to comfort—Harris dared to fish out the wisps of her hair from beneath the glasses. She didn't move away, but he thought he saw her flinch, like some skittish, trembling mare unused to being handled.

"I know it's trite to say that I understand," he said.

"Everyone says they understand. They don't understand."

"Sometimes I think there has to be a certain ratio of good and bad in this world. The strong ones get the bad because they're the only ones who can bear it."

"But it isn't fair."

The loveliness of her cheekbone as she stared out into space miraculously seemed the apex of Harris's whole existence, and she gave a quick, convulsive shiver and hugged herself, as if the sun had suddenly gone under and the cold had pierced to her bones.

"No," he said thickly. "It isn't fair."

Then, because he had lived forty years with a brain inside his head, and he knew that if this had ever happened to him before he would remember it, Harris stepped into her legs and drew her close so that she could feel his intense longing to make things better. He wet his lips and tried to take a deep breath but couldn't.

"Something is happening here," he muttered uncertainly. "Something . . . I don't know."

She seemed to swim up from the place where she had momentarily drifted. The lines at her eyes tightened and answered his. She was on top of it again, recovered, restrained, aloof. She shook her head. "No."

Harris followed her for the step she had taken. "You know there is."

Mutely, she denied it.

His courage faltered, and Harris loathed the handcuffs that prevented him from walking away, from leaving her standing there with her regal distance. "Don't play this game."

"It's not—"

The vehemence of his posture cut off Summer's protest. He was right, she was playing games, but not teasing ones. The truth was, she could no longer bear such intimacy from a stranger, particularly not a man as destined for trouble as he was.

And Harris Chandler was headed for trouble, there was no doubt about that. His world of clear-cut blacks and whites was on a collision course with her world—a larger, more powerful planet of grays. His defeat was inevitable. With the same inevitability, she didn't think she could bear to witness his defeat.

She twisted her face away because it was easier than watching the confused anger she knew would appear on his, and as she wove the hem of her top in and out between her fingers, she said, "You know you can't beat this charge of grand larceny the way you're going at it, don't you?"

The breath he took was abrupt. He stood chewing the inside of his jaw for a moment in a hard challenge of silences. Then, "You have a better suggestion?"

"Yes, I do, Mr. Desperado. Come down from your fences and trust a little bit."

Harris remembered the last time someone had called him a desperado. "Trust!" he snorted scornfully and threw his hair back from his forehead, rubbed at a furrow. "What a word, trust."

"You're hardly in a position to flaunt yourself at the system, Harris. You need the system. It's all you've got."

"Hey, babe, you're talking to the wrong guy. I trust the system and men like Starky like I trust—"

All of Summer's nerves abruptly turned into stinging nettles. She jerked up her head. "What do you know about Judge Starky?"

Summer wasn't sure why she asked the question. She was, unexpectedly, Harris's lawyer, though she neither meant to be nor wanted to be. She wasn't even sure if she believed he was innocent.

He lifted a shoulder. "Not a thing in this world. Except that Starky's leaning on me. I have to ask myself why a judge, a respected man of the bench, would do that. Why would he even waste time on an untried felon? Who told Starky to subpoena my business records? Who planted the lie that I made deals with Pinnacle? Rex Jernigan?"

Summer shrugged, her attorney's mind in a dozen places at once. "It's possible."

"But what would Jernigan have to gain by lying about me? The guy needs all the friends he can get, and that makes me wonder if maybe Judge Starky didn't make the illegal notes with Pinnacle Bank himself."

Summer laughed incredulously before she knew she was going to; Herschel Starky wasn't her favorite judge in all the world, true, but what Harris was saying was very far out.

Anger was a crimson stain along the sides of Harris's neck, and Summer swiftly sobered, moistened her lips and shook her head.

"I'm not saying a judge can't be corrupt, Harris. Judge Starky may be for all I know. But when you talk about the law like that, you hit where I live. Even though it has faults, I believe in the system. You can't fault me for that."

A muscle twitched at the side of his mouth. This time he did get his cigarette lit, and Summer watched him inhale. He held the cigarette as a European would do, hollowed in his palm, and he blew a stream of smoke at the street.

"You live in your world, Miz Prosecutor," he said flatly, and made his profile a statement of his determination, "and I'll live in mine."

He made her want to slam her foot to the ground. Hadn't he learned anything yet? "At least mine's outside the bars, Mr. Chandler!"

When Harris swung to confront her, his lips were curled thinly back over his teeth. "Let's get one thing very straight, okay? I was in prison by choice. I knew exactly what would happen when I chose to ignore the law, and I took the consequences. That's what's wrong with your system, Miz S. MacLean. There's no provision made for someone whose conscience tells him to do things differently. Everybody doesn't have to be stamped from the same mold, you know. Everybody doesn't have to think the same thing at the same time. But the only place someone can go to be different is outside the law. Well, I refuse to pay those kinds of dues, see? And nothing you can say will change that."

Summer had to make fists out of her hands while he delivered the speech that he had obviously thought about long and often. She found herself comparing him with the hundreds of brash, cocky defendants whom she'd looked at and thought, "I'm going to bring you down, Mr. Smart Guy."

And she wanted to do that to Harris Chandler. Oh, how she wanted to make him admit that he was wrong! But deep in her deepest private self, she knew she could never bring Harris down.

And that was the reason she was becoming so embroiled with him, wasn't it? Because from the very beginning she had sensed a strength that couldn't be broken. Not by her, and definitely not by the military. Oh, they might take his freedom and lock his body up in a cell, but nothing could really break Harris Chandler. And she envied him that strength.

"What d'you mean, dues?" she demanded, though the fire had gone out of her argument.

He didn't flinch at her question. He watched his toe crushing out the cigarette. "Those things you pay, counselor, every time you do as you're told when you don't want to. Every time your conscience tells you that you shouldn't, and you do it anyway." He lifted his head. "Ring any bells, MacLean? D'you know what I'm talking about? Did you ever cop out? Hmm?"

Summer wished that she could scream no at him, but his words struck at the very core of her guilt. "Doesn't everyone cop out?" she asked him quietly, turning away in surrender. "At sometime or another?"

Knowing how ruthlessly he had pushed her against the wall of her own morality, Harris guiltily let his eyes reap the spoils of war, sweeping them over her, touching all of her as he chose—her proud, slender back and determined posture, her shoulders that kept him at bay when he would race ahead and defy the limits of convention.

How many times had he promised to never again let himself invest in the future? No woman would ever charm him, he'd vowed. None would steal away his loneliness and make him hope. Yet now he gazed down at the top of this woman's bent head, and he saw the open spaces of his own life and how unbearably empty it all was, and he didn't know how it had come upon him so stealthily. Did he dare put a name to what he was feeling?

"About little things maybe," he said softly, fearing to want something as much as he wanted her in his life, "but never big ones. Never about principle. Never when it counts."

Summer had been blindly studying a crack in the sidewalk. Her first mistake was in looking up without warning so that she glimpsed the hunger on Harris's face before he could disguise it. Her second mistake was in being so enthralled by that hunger that she lifted her hand up to his jaw.

Time froze, trapped in a frame. Somewhere a horn honked. A door slammed.

Summer couldn't see her gesture through, nor could she call it back. She couldn't turn it into a flirtatious pat on Harris's cheek, so she simply stood with her hand suspended while both of them stared at it, then ricocheted looks and speculations as they imagined where all this would lead if they were somewhere else, in some other time.

Stinging, Summer jerked her hand down to her side. It was much too late, of course; Harris's recklessness had already got the best of him, and he caught the offending hand and turned up its palm. As she battled him for it, he raped the soft slopes and hollows with a thumb.

She stumbled as dizziness swirled up from the sidewalk. As he let her hand go, she clumsily steadied herself and brought the backs of her fingers to press her mouth, as if to wipe away kisses he had yet to take.

"We have to be sensible," she mumbled, even as she felt him calculating what lay beneath her surface. "We have to..."

The one thing Harris knew, in all of its vast shapes and forms, was rejection. If Summer didn't understand the rivers of bruised pride that flowed through him, she certainly saw the results. One of the coldest smiles she'd ever seen in her life slowly formed upon his lips.

"Yeah," he said, slashing her to ribbons with the cutting edge of his voice. "Such a sensible answer from a sensible lady with a sensible life and a sensible career in the sensible system. Tell me, Miz—what's your name? I'm tired of calling you by a damn initial. What does the *S* stand for?"

"Sensible!" Summer snapped, suddenly wanting to make him feel the confusion and embarrassment she was feeling.

People were having to swirl around them in eddies now, for the sidewalk had grown more crowded. The handcuffs were in plain view.

"Oh, hell," he mumbled and, yielding, drew them into the crowd once more.

Chapter Five

Summer and Harris were like lovers who had quarreled. As they trudged along the crowded streets of West Palm Beach—two sullen adults, too self-defined and independent to make peace and too suspicious of life to trust anything that felt right—their conversation was little more than monosyllables. The sounds were the street noises: honking horns, loud radios, the squealing of brakes and roar of buses, sirens, yells of workmen, the collective hurry of strangers.

Summer alternately hated Harris, then worried about him, then hated herself for worrying. Harris Chandler wasn't her concern, she told herself. He was a grown man. He'd been taking care of himself for a long time.

The one time she tried to apologize she sounded like a maligned and misunderstood child. "I shouldn't have been so rude before." He didn't even look at her when he answered.

"I forgive you," he said unenthusiastically. "You're so obviously broken up about it."

"Well, you know what they say." Now Summer regretted the shred of sympathy she'd felt for him.

"What do they say?"

"That I'm a tough lady."

"It figures, doesn't it?" He smirked. "Of all the people in the world, I get handcuffed to the tough lady."

Summer wished she knew a terrible enough word for the occasion. Harris, wondering if any man alive could swallow being outranked by a woman he'd like to make a good impression on, resented being in Summer's debt. He resented needing what she had, what she was. He wanted to do or say something that would shake her down to her roots.

They walked so long without speaking that the next thing Summer realized was the sound of Harris saying, "We'll take some of the cornflowers, I think. And a bit of baby's breath. Yes, that's nice. Now, give us some snap dragons. Perhaps a few of the asters. No, those over there."

Astonished, Summer blinked at the flower stall edging the shopping center.

Harris? Buying flowers? An apology? How unexpected. How...Martinish? No. No man could be so different from Martin MacLean as Harris was. Now she couldn't imagine why she'd ever thought they resembled each other.

She smiled up at him, her own wane apology in the hesitant nibble of her lower lip. "Venture off the beaten path with far-reaching consequences," she presently murmured.

"What?" Turning, his blue eyes moved quizzically over her.

Summer shook her head and remembered Tom's laughter and his hug. "Nothing."

The proprietor, with his defeated shoulders and meager, scuffed shoes, was much more interested in the twenty-dollar bill Harris casually laid upon the counter than the handcuffs that bound them. He stuttered when he thanked them and, with a greedy rustle of tissue, told a couple of bad jokes, took the money, accepted his handsome tip with a counterfeit surprise and extended the armful of blossoms.

"You're just trying to make me feel bad," she told Harris with a smile pulling at the sides of her mouth.

Like the errant prince he was, Harris grinned crookedly and unzipped the bag. He poked the flowers inside as if it were a vase.

"Pretty flowers for a pretty lady," he said and clicked the heels of his deck shoes. "Hate yourself while I enjoy my humility."

"Humility, my foot." Laughing at his zany and endearing unpredictability, Summer poked her nose into the flowers and sneezed.

"Oh, no." He arranged a disappointed face. "You're allergic to baby's breath."

"The Case of the Killer Baby's Breath." She crinkled her nose and sniffed, went through the process of, "Ah...ah, ah—"

They waited, but the sneeze didn't happen. She sniffed again, then said, "No, I think I'm allergic to you, Diamond Jim. What are we going to do with this hothouse you've bought?"

"We'll live recklessly." He studied her lingeringly, carefully, then huskily said, "How about a date?"

Summer found her quick rush of pleasure frightening. She took a breath. "You've spent all your money."

"True." He gave a wounded sigh.

"But then, I'm a cheap date."

When she lowered her head, her sensitive skin fiery with sunburn and her upper lip glistening with droplets of sweat, her slender hands betraying her nervousness, Harris felt like the flawed hero in the last scene of a tragedy. Only this time the flaw wasn't his pride. It was a shameless lack of it. He wanted this woman, any time, any way he could get her.

"Ah, dear Mrs. MacLean," he murmured quietly, "there's nothing cheap about you that I can see."

A fine trembling spread over Summer's limbs, and her customary eloquence deserted her. She spoke distractedly to the sky. "Then you haven't seen all of me."

Her words hung on the noisy afternoon, and they both laughed when they realized her unintentional double entendre.

Summer lowered her head to her fingertips and flushed. "So much for the old sophisticated-worldly-woman ploy. Forget I said that, all right?"

"Not on your life." He chuckled. How was it that even her worst moments made him want to throw himself at her feet as a human sacrifice? "I'm not that crazy, counselor."

Then presently, when he saw that he might not have a more opportune moment, Harris asked, because it was what he truly wanted, "Why haven't you offered to be my attorney? All this time I've thought you would at least make the gesture. What will it take? If I get down on my knees and beg, will you?"

Summer stopped walking and distractedly fondled a spire of the baby's breath. He'd taken her by surprise. She thought he would have taken any hack lawyer over her. "I did offer you my advice," she reminded. "You didn't take it."

"Aw." He stroked the roughness above his lip. "I've hurt your feelings, haven't I? Okay, tell me what to do, counselor, and I'll do it."

She confronted him squarely with it. "Turn yourself in."

His big shoulders dropped, and his gaze flicked skyward with a what-did-I-tell-you twist of his mouth. "Forget that, Miz MacLean."

"See?" Summer stabbed with a finger. "That's why."

His voice had an edge to it now. "Why won't you believe someone is framing me, damn it? What do I have to do?"

Partly because she was weary of fighting her hair, and she was also desperate for a way to avoid his hawkish scrutinies, Summer began ploughing through the tote bag for pins. Beneath the flowers she found three, and two tortoise shell combs. The pins she placed between her teeth, and with the combs she tried to make some order of the flyaway mass.

Around the pins, she explained, "I don't *not* believe you, Harris, I just don't see any motive for a frame. People have motives for what they do."

"Well, try thinking more in terms of convenience."

"How so?"

Harris watched her anchor the combs into the charmingly wanton disarray. He said, "You have to realize that a developer is always neck deep in hock at the bank. I happened to have two notes with Rex Jernigan for real, in case you're interested."

"Of course I'm interested. Go on."

"Okay, let's say that Rex Jernigan sticks his neck out for someone—really far out, by loaning him money at a low interest rate, maybe."

"All right."

"The bank gets in trouble, say. Maybe Rex is even tempted to take a risk or two on real estate or the stock market, just to put things a little more into the black. But things don't work out. The auditors come in, and our Mr. Someone is caught with his pants down. He comes down on Jernigan and demands to be covered. Are you following me?"

Summer shook the cuffs between them and almost smiled. "Whither thou goest, I will go."

"That isn't funny."

Now she did smile. "Sorry."

Fascinated with the range of expressions playing over Summer's face, Harris had to think to remember where he was. "Oh, yes. So, maybe now Jernigan is scared enough to perjure his soul to hell. Maybe he types up a few bad notes to cover the liabilities of our ficticious someone. Then he forges a signature or two. A crude but efficient technique, wouldn't you say?"

"Do you have any ideas about who this Mr. Someone is?"

He blinked at her. He hadn't an idea in the world. He said with a brisk spit of his tongue against his teeth, "Maybe it's Starky."

Laughter bubbled out of her. "That kind of talk will really get you locked up, Harris."

"Any kind of talk will get me locked up. Who wants to risk believing an ex-con?"

Seeing his point, Summer sighed and caught the center of her upper lip in her teeth. "A handwriting analyst could be brought in."

"And if the forgery is bad, I'm in luck. But what if it's good? It would be like a polygraph test damning a truthful man."

She stood a moment, thinking. She reached up for a stray wisp of hair and twirled it around and around a finger. "Harris?"

But Harris was distracted by the way her bra played hide-and-seek with the mesh of her top, and a whole series of subliminal scenes of her naked flashed through his mind. Strange things happened to his pulse rate.

He jerked up his head. "What?"

"Do you know Neil Jarvis?"

"The state prosecutor? Who doesn't?"

"Personally, I mean."

Harris wasn't keen on being intimidated by Summer's relationship with her boss. "Should I?"

"He says he knows you."

He was instantly sober. "When was this?"

"The day I signed your warrant. I got the definite impression that Neil had known you from before, and you two hadn't gotten along."

"I don't know the man." But tiny alarms were going off in Harris's head. He tried to be generous, but it was all too easy for him to imagine the state prosecutor neck-deep in scandal.

He patted his pocket for a cigarette, found it, placed it in his mouth, removed it and squinted at her. "Do you think the state prosecutor is having me framed?"

"Neil?" Laughing, Summer shook her head. "Don't get the wrong impression about Neil. He may have his faults, but he wouldn't do something like that. My goodness, Harris, if I don't go to jail for what I've done, Neil will probably ask for my resignation. To him, the law and the Ten Commandments are synonymous."

She had hardly gotten through speaking before he demanded, "What faults?"

"Faults? Well, all I meant was that he's just a human being like the rest of us. He has...weaknesses, habits. Human habits."

"Habits? Coke?"

"Cocaine? Goodness, no."

"Pot? Pills?"

She waved away his guesses. "Actually, he doesn't hold his liquor very well. And that's stretching things grossly. I don't think that he even drinks very much. Look, Harris, you're going off on a futile tangent here."

"Wait a minute, wait a minute." Tossing the cigarette away, Harris pressed a fingertip to Summer's mouth to hush her. "You're not serious about being in trouble, are you? Because of me?"

Trouble? Where did she begin the list? *Oh, by the way, Harris, if I defend you I can kiss any political endorsement by Neil goodbye. I've only worked seven years for this.*

"Would you really be in trouble?" Harris repeated, more fiercely this time.

Heat singed the lobes of Summer's ears. "Yes!" she wanted to cry. She was already in trouble, and not because of Neil Jarvis!

She flicked Harris a nervous smile that was all wrong and averted her face. She didn't want Harris to go down if she could do anything to prevent it, and it wasn't right for her to have to choose between the two.

"I don't know," she replied drearily.

"Bottom line, Ms. MacLean," he said sharply. "And if you try to hide something, I'll know."

Yes, Summer thought with a jolt as she felt the impetus of his strength that she not only admired but was now growing warily to respect. Harris Chandler was the kind of man who would always go for the bottom line, even with her.

She wet her lips and in a guarded, lawyerish voice said, "In the eyes of the law, Harris, either you will have kidnapped me, or I will have aided and abetted you."

Harris jammed his free hand into his pocket and scuffed at something on the sidewalk with the toe of his deck shoe. He stared out at people moving along with folded newspapers beneath their arms and started to speak, then stopped.

"I guess I knew that," he said after a moment. "You'll have to say that I kidnapped you, of course. As soon as we can, I'll get these handcuffs off, and you can call the police to come pick you up. I don't think you'll have trouble getting someone to believe that I threatened your life to get you off the train."

She should protest such words. Summer knew they were all wrong. But then she would have to explain what she was feeling, and she didn't understand what that was.

"You're not becoming discouraged, are you?" she asked in a hollow, evasive move.

He huffed his bitter laughter. "Why should I be discouraged? I've only been accused of grand larceny. The one chance I've got to protect myself is in a set of books twenty miles away. I'm evading justice. I've left the scene of an accident. And now I'm kidnapping. I'm supposed to feel good about that?"

"I would expect you to go on fighting."

"Look where fighting has gotten me."

Summer knew, before she even spoke, that she had stepped up to a line that was unexpectedly drawn across her life. It was a clear, distinct line. There was time enough to stop herself from stepping over. If she truly wanted to, she could turn around and tell Harris the matter was closed.

He was standing very tall, his raw vitality masked as he ventured to some private place that no one could see but himself. Summer wasn't sure she wanted to see it. Once a line was stepped over....

She hesitated. Words clung to her tongue like taffy. Whispering—for if he didn't hear, he would not answer—she asked, "Where has it gotten you, Harris?"

He didn't say anything. When he finally did speak, it was with a sad and princely dignity, a kind of unshakable, courtly resignation one sometimes sees in aging victims of war.

"It's gotten me lost from my youth," he said, then hesitated. "It's left me standing in the middle of life with a handful of worn-out dreams. It's gotten me empty. Alone, with nowhere to go."

The ticking seconds went nowhere. Summer stood in awe of the solitary man who had fought battles no one cared about. He had no medals, and he had no badges to prove that he had fought, only his own scars and a vast capacity to see the world for what it really was.

His terrible unhappiness touched some elusive part of herself that Summer had never quite been able to conceptualize before. In a panorama, she saw her own life from beginning to end, especially her life with Martin—good years, yes, very good years that she had really done nothing to deserve.

But Martin had never experienced the kind of need that Harris Chandler was expressing. Martin had loved her, he had taken care of her, he had made tough decisions that she could not have made for herself. But that was the point, really. Martin had done it. Martin had made the decisions. And he had never had an awful, gaping wound inside him that desperately needed healing.

Without warning, Summer was washed over with compassion for Harris Chandler. However unwise and illogical it was, she wished she could heal his unbound wounds. And, perhaps even more unwisely and illogically, she wanted to open herself up and reveal to him her own.

More afraid than she had been in a long time, she began walking. *This is silly,* her logic said. *You don't know this man.* I know enough. *Look at yourself, you're shaking.* It's no disgrace to shake. *This is nothing more than a mothering instinct. You would feel the same way if you'd stumbled upon an injured animal.* Shut up. For once in my life, I want to do something good and decent. I want to help this man. *Help? Don't kid yourself, sis. You're hung up because he wants you.* No! I'm not a sex-starved widow needing a party. *Sez who?*

Harris's footsteps were unerring beside her shorter ones. Summer watched them for some moments. Without looking up, she said, "I don't know what to tell you, Harris."

His smile, when he caught her by the wrist and swung her around, surprised her. And the boyish wistfulness that wreathed his strong, tanned face.

"Your name," he said and played his eyes over her brows and her hair and her mouth. "How can I fall in love with you, if I don't know your name?"

It was a joke, and it almost took Summer's breath away. She laughed nervously. But he didn't laugh. Sobering, she leaned back and shook her head. "You're a bewildering man, Harris Chandler. Do you know that?"

They were passing Christine's Boutique, a tiny but lavish establishment whose fancy display windows were in the shape of a *W* and which were seen every day by a person in Miami who read the header of the *Herald*'s classified advertising.

Without warning, Harris cornered Summer between two of those famous wedged panels and pushed her back into the crevice. He braced his free hand and pinned her in, kept her there with a pressing knee.

The protest fell automatically from Summer's stunned lips. "Just a minute. What're you—"

"Will you hush?" he murmured, not teasing her now. "For just one minute, will you quit being the professional and go with your heart?"

He was pressing closely into her side so that the handcuffs were hidden to everyone except a chiffon-draped manikin grinning at them from inside the shop. Summer felt longing rise in him like a fever, hot and throbbing and pulsing between them.

She pushed feebly at his chest. "Harris..."

Harris made a quick reconnoiter of the street, wondering if he were losing his mind. This time tomorrow he could be sitting in a cell. But if he was going to be in that cell, he wanted the luxury of telling this woman things—things such as how he'd like to start his life over and do everything differently, how he'd like to start over with her. How he'd stopped believing he would ever meet a woman like her, and that it had been good to know her for even this short time. He wanted to say that he needed badly to kiss her and to hold her and to dream for just a few sun-splashed moments of what might have been.

But he forced himself to lighten up, and he lazily poked a questioning finger through one of the tiny meshes of her top. "Tell me your name, Miz S. MacLean."

Hypnotized, Summer watched the tip of Harris's finger as it insinuated itself deeper between the woof and warp that lay over her bosom. With electrifying flicks of his nail, he blazed a trail toward one swelling curve. She crazily wanted to take his hand and press it hard upon that awakening part of herself.

She gasped for breath and whispered stupid words. "You don't need to know my name."

He grazed the side of her breast, so lightly that it was more a matter of the imagination than anything else. Goose bumps exploded upon the surface of Summer's skin, and she felt her nipples tingle and grow taut. Outside, everything felt sharp, but inside, all the moving parts of her seemed to blur.

"You can't begin to dream of what I need," Harris muttered hoarsely, for as he watched her he didn't understand what was happening either. He was seeing in his mind, not cutely erotic images of them entwined in some fairy tale place, but solemn scenes of the two of them together with her son, and with their own sons, and their sons' sons. He saw them in church. He saw them at play. He saw them at work. He saw them sick and well and laughing and crying.

Good God! What was he fantasizing? Desire was one thing, but paternal longevity? Legacies? No, no. Not now. Not after all these years.

He told himself to do something to shatter the spell, he laid one hand on the back of her neck and the other the side of her hips. "Do you believe me?" he whisper with terrible concentration, for it was now imperative th she did.

Summer couldn't bear to watch the pain drifting acro Harris's features. She let her head slump forward to curve of his neck and she struggled to regain her equil rium. "I—I know you need a good lawyer, Harris. I'll h you find one. I'll stand by you."

His fingers buried into her hair. "I want a friend. I w someone to believe in me."

"But you have friends."

The sudden search of Harris's lips for hers was its o kind of denial, Summer thought as she intuitively dodg the kiss as she had dodged Neil's.

"No I don't," he said and trapped her face between hands, "and neither do you."

Summer wanted to protest. She wanted to say some bla cynical remark about how he wasn't right and that she did need this and she didn't need him. But he was needing h She was insanely needing him. How often in this world w people truly needed?

The pride of her neck slowly yielded to the kisses he gan strewing along its length. As she lay wonderingly ba in the curve of his arm, she took that first, age-old step trust in allowing her breasts to be vulnerable.

"I'm afraid to be your friend," she gasped as he press his lips to the pulse in her throat.

"Then we're almost even. I'm just afraid."

Summer thought, as Harris's mouth slowly covered own, that neither of them would ever find the courage speak after this. Her lips remained closed beneath his, y even so, she felt his need to know, and when his tongue ressed the edge of her lip and moved to her eyelids and to ears, she closed her hands tightly into his shirt. She clung to him as a starving waif would scoop up fallen crumbs and hide them away to be cherished later.

"I want to say terrible things," he recklessly confessed against her cheek. "I want to make you . . ." He swallowed. "I want to make you promise me things."

She leaned back from him. "What things?"

His shackled hand was nearly touching her breast. As he lowered his gaze to it, it spread wide and slipped slowly, but definitely, beneath the curve to shape its fullness.

Summer moistened her lips as she watched, and when he closed his hand, she took a ragged, jerking breath. He met her eyes and saw heat stinging her cheeks. His hand tightened, and in that one gesture he closed the distance between them intellectually, spiritually, physically.

"Promise that whatever happens, this won't change," he said gruffly. "Promise . . . that we can find it again."

"Things will happen, you know."

He leaned against her with the whole of his weight. "Then it is real?"

From the center of the hazy, golden spell, Summer tried to remember when something had ever been so real. The birth of her sons? Was that it? Had she lived thirty-four years and could only name one thing as real as her bizarre, exploding need for this man?

And what if she told Harris the truth, that it was real? What would they do? What would they say? What would they call it? Love at first sight? No.

Love might possibly grow out of it, but it wasn't love. It was an instinct, an awakening of the mind to something that might someday be: the vision of a monument as yet unbuilt, the sure certainty that drives men beyond their borders, the need placed in mankind from the beginning to seek out the other half of the whole.

But at what cost? Summer couldn't hide from reality. To link herself to Harris Chandler was to invite a deluge of trouble and criticism. Everything that she and Martin had worked for could be shattered by a single bad decision. Her political career could be wrecked, and no one was guaranteed a second chance.

Feeling her ordered life breaking up so easily, Summer dragged her head around. At first she was too dazed to really see what she looked at. She was drugged. She was paralyzed. Then the shock of what she saw cleared her head like ice water in her face.

From the boutique, a tall, stout woman was staring straight at them, her shocked eyes fixed upon the handcuffs. A telephone receiver was held at her ear, and she was speaking into it.

Without moving a muscle, Summer gasped, "Harris, turn around quickly and look."

His reflex was instantaneous, and Summer knew when his hand clutched her waist that she had not been mistaken. "Damn!" he blurted explosively. "We've been made. Let's get out of here!"

"What?"

"Come on!"

In less than five seconds they were racing down the sidewalk, hands tightly clasped. It could have been some delirious chase scene from a Gene Hackman movie, except that the stitch torturing Summer's side was real. And her gasping was real, and so were their feet hitting the cement in harsh, painful slams.

Summer didn't dare look back at the colorful stream of snap dragons and asters and cornflowers and baby's breath they strewed as they flew across the boulevard. Harris darted and dodged on-coming cars with the agility of a dancer. He ignored their blaring horns and waving fists and yelled insults. With his elbow under hers so that he bore part of her weight, he sprinted at top speed.

"Oh!" She stumbled and lost a shoe, barking her wrist in the process.

As if in perfect sync with her, Harris stopped when she did and scooped her shoe up, shoved it on her foot.

"Do you think that woman called the police?" she gasped and stared in astonishment at her own hand gripping the hard, tanned thrust of his shoulder.

"You can lay odds on it, babe."

The muscles working beneath her fingertips were powerful, and they moved as truly on course as Harris did himself. Harris Chandler: the hot-headed Yankee who had left his territory to come down here and fall into her life and break it in pieces.

His head lifted to reveal an infinitely raw fear for himself and an upward-spiraling anguish for her. Summer knew then, with an instinct that rarely failed her, that Harris hadn't stolen anything. If anything, the man gave too much away. She knew, too, that she would risk whatever it took to see that he remained a free man.

She met his fear with her own wide, frightened eyes and fumbled for his fingers and clutched them.

"My name is Summer," she declared with urgency. "And, oh, I hope I don't regret this. Heaven help me, I'll take the case!"

Chapter Six

If Lila Dean had been chronicling the bizarre flight of Harris Chandler and Summer MacLean from West Palm Beach, she probably would have made note of the following statistics: the two principals ran due north for approximately ten minutes after they were reported to the police; the temperature was now a record-breaking one hundred degrees.

The pair of fugitives wasn't spotted, though a number of patrol cars in the area did respond to the call from Christine's Boutique, their sirens screaming. At a Gulf service station off Tamarind Avenue, they bought two Cokes and four Snickers candy bars from the vending machines outside. This was paid for by the assistant prosecutor's loose change because all Harris Chandler had on him were a few twenties and a checkbook of questionable worth.

An interesting side note might have been this: the Palm Beach County sheriff received an odd phone call from a young man named Riley. It seems that Riley had in his possession a hound belonging to Harris Chandler. His question was, if Chandler had disappeared, what was he supposed to do with the dog?

The sheriff's reply was not only unprintable, it was physically impossible.

The fact is, Lila had been seriously considering a follow-up story on the assistant prosecutor anyway. After learning that Summer MacLean had disappeared from the site of the train derailment—or had been kidnapped—she was inspired to telephone Neil Jarvis. When she learned that Summer had actually signed the warrant for Chandler's arrest herself, her nerve endings went on red alert.

"This is Ms. MacLean's case, not mine, Miss Dean," the state prosecutor hotly insisted.

"I see," Lila said demurely and rolled her eyes as she hung up the phone.

Rushing into her editor's office and slamming the door, Lila leaned back upon it. She told him that she would do just about anything for this one.

Although her editor, not a Puritan by any means, declined the offer, he generously gave Lila the go-ahead on the story. The first person Lila went to see was Christine Whittier at the boutique.

"Well, my dear!" Christine exclaimed when, after introductions, Lila asked if Summer MacLean had appeared frightened or distraught. "I hardly know what to tell you. It's not my place to criticize. And you know I'm no prude, but really, it's all over the television news."

"Of course not, Christine, dear," Lila purred. "I mean, of course I know that you're no prude."

Christine lifted her cultured eyebrows a fraction. "Decorous behavior is a thing of the past. You know that Elliot and I attend First Christian, and even there we feel the effects of laxity. I fight it with all my being, of course, but I must say, it just wears me out. Yet we all have to do our part to raise standards, don't we? There is no rest for the weary. I'm on the board of regents for the symphony, if you recall, and I can't tell you how much money I've put into the Humanities Research Center.''

Lila smiled her goody smile that she saved for occasions such as this one. ''Oh, you have the seal of approval from me, Christine.''

It never occurred to Christine that she was being put on. She lowered her voice so that her salespeople wouldn't hear her stoop to gossip. ''Well, the truth is, and I swear this on my mother's grave, Lila, the man mauled her. It was a disgrace. Right on the street in broad daylight. And she let him! I think she actually enjoyed it. Why, it embarrassed me to look at it.''

It promised to be a better story than she'd counted on. With a hand held up for Christine to pause, Lila extracted a tape recorder and pressed a button. Her smile was the signal to go ahead.

Christine continued. ''He pushed right up against her with his . . . well, you know. A blind person could have seen how . . . what word do I want? Libidinous? You could see how libidinous he was.''

''It's as good as any,'' Lila blandly intoned then brought her brows together in a bored frown. ''Mauled, did you say, Christine?''

''Well, it wasn't a peck on the cheek. Right on the mouth. All those tongues and everything. I was terrified to death that my daughter would see. She was here, you know, trying on dresses in the back. Permissiveness, Lila. I tell you, it's running rampant. It all started with Marlon Brando and Eva Marie Saint in that hideous waterfront picture. And the song lyrics today! Did I tell you I belong to the National Music Review Council and the National P.T.A.? Frankly, I think they had it planned from the very beginning.''

Lila sighed. So much for a story. "Had what planned, Christine?"

The sides of Christine's mouth curled. "Everything, darling. The getaway, everything. This MacLean woman is his moll. It was as clear as the nose on your face."

Not too fond of remarks about her nose, no matter how clichéd, Lila dispensed of the tape recorder with one stabbing finger. "Uh, Christine...I don't think they knew each other before today. It was my understanding from the state prosecutor that Mrs. MacLean didn't know the man at all. And as far as mauling goes—"

The matriarch of society reared back, her bosom the prow of a Viking ship. Her neck turned an extremely unbecoming lavender hue.

"Are you questioning my word, Lila Dean?" she screeched. "*My word?* Why, I'll have you know, there are people in this town who think *my word* is as sacred as holy Writ. My reputation is without blemish, I'll have you know. Why, I've never been so insulted in my life. I've half a mind to call Joshua Stern and cancel my ad in your *damn newspaper*!"

The first helicopter flew over during the lazy, midafternoon lull—that period between the time when women shoppers have gone wearily home to pick up their children at the pool and the men have not yet started to brave the rush-hour traffic.

Neither Harris nor Summer noticed the chopper at first. They were recovering from their scare, and Harris was telling Summer about his disastrous marriage to Margo, recounting the details with far less pain than he'd anticipated, for he couldn't remember when he'd talked about it last, much less laughed about it.

After he lead them off the main thoroughfares and guided them through a dizzying maze of West Palm's better alleys and along residential streets where the worst danger was being run down by boys on bicycles or having their heels nipped by overzealous dogs, he recounted his time in prison. He even told Summer about his mother, about her last words to him, and with tenderness, he told her about Bud.

"Despite what you think," he said, "Bud's a shy, quiet man. Most people, when they learn he's an ex-con, picture Karl Malden with a gun on each hip. But Bud's practical. He likes to have the feel of the land beneath his feet."

"What happened to him, Harris?"

Harris grimaced. "He also used to like the feel of a bottle in his hand. One day he and the bottle drove his car into a house."

"A house!"

"A twelve-year-old boy was killed. Dad's been doing penance for it ever since. The school's sort of a repentance and redemption thing, I guess."

"Harris, would it bother you to tell me how much money you put into the school in a year? Don't answer that if you don't want to. I know it's none—"

Harris had never told anyone. Without hesitation, he said, "About a hundred and fifty."

Summer blinked. "A hundred and fifty dollars? You're kidding me."

"Thousand."

"A hundred and fifty *thousand*?"

Before Summer thought to disguise her utter shock, she laughed. "Harris, no one gives away a hundred and fifty thousand dollars every year."

Her remark embarrassed him. His shrug was in his distance. "I've been pretty occupied with my own repentance and redemption lately."

Immediately he changed the subject. He described what it was like, growing up around a school for delinquent boys. With infectious, rippling arpeggios of male laughter, he added, "Man, I didn't take anything off those kids. Every time a new one came in, I'd have to go through this 'daddy's boy' routine. You see this nose? It's been broken four times. But I think the point got across." He chuckled to himself. "Though to this day I'm not quite sure whose point it was that got across, theirs or mine."

Still staggered by the enormity of his generosity, Summer thought she could fall in love with Harris's laugh. She was half in love with it already. "I think you were their king," she said, smiling.

"More like an erring prince." His sigh was slightly melancholy. "Some would have said I was the court jester." He raked his fingers through his mussed hair and added bleakly, with a heavier sigh and a more realistic shake of his head, "Or maybe I was just the fool."

Leaning upon his arm, Summer attempted to bring back his happy mood. "Why don't you just admit you were the black knight, Harris, and get it over with?"

Harris appraised her up and down and, with a sly pucker of his lips, took her shackled hand in his. She teasingly battled him for it. He won, not as easily as he expected to, however, and he matched his long calloused fingers to her short, slender ones.

"Gee, lady, when they said you were tough," he kissed her with a look, deeply, lingeringly and, Summer thought with shocking breathlessness, with a much more catastrophic effect, "they didn't say the half of it."

Summer tried to smile and couldn't. "You're a devil," she said low and huskily.

"Because I know what I want?"

She didn't have the nerve to ask him what he wanted; she guessed she knew. She said, as she took great care to match a step to his, "Because you move so quickly, Mr. Chandler."

"A man tends to do that when a price is on his head, Mrs. MacLean."

He didn't release her hand, and as they strolled, Summer thought, *We really could be friends. We could be lovers. We could be normal people, walking in the sunshine and enjoying each other's company.*

She wanted to find out a lot more about him. She wanted to ask Harris if he'd gotten the scar on his chest in prison, but he was reluctant to talk any more about himself. She told him about Estelle instead. When she explained her relationship with Martin, she chose her words carefully.

As they talked, however, she began having second thoughts about taking his case. Harris had his own life, and it was the way he wanted it. He would do well without her.

Harris told her about his developments, about his tiny house in Miami.

You're making a career decision, Summer, Martin would have said. *Reconsider. Make sure.* After all, Summer reminded herself, those years working up to the promotion as Neil's chief assistant had been hard ones.

Summer told him about Martin's huge house that gobbled up half her salary but made the MacLeans' blood pressure escalate alarmingly every time she mentioned selling it.

It's hard for a woman alone, Estelle would have said. *You have to be careful.*

Harris liked old Mickey Spillane books and Phil Collins's songs and prime rib.

Martin would have been so disappointed, Pat would have said.

Summer liked David Halberstam and Itzhak Perlman and broiled trout.

It isn't logical, Spock would have said.

Vaguely, then, Summer heard the helicopter. If she thought at all, it was to surmise that it was a traffic patrol from one of the local radio stations. But when the second one flew in a wide arc from east to west, Harris stopped dead in his tracks and reached across one lonely cornflower to take her by the shoulder.

Summer followed the direction of his troubled squint.

"I don't like the looks of that," he muttered as the lines beside his eyes tensed.

"They can't be hunting for us."

"I wouldn't count on it."

"Harris, are you sure mine is the only warrant out on you?"

He didn't find her humor remotely amusing. When the second helicopter made another sweep, he took hold of her arm. "Enough of this," he snarled.

Hurling himself against the light into the line of traffic on Okeechobee Boulevard, he began dragging her across the lanes to a huge, sprawling supermarket lot. At first Summer thought he intended to hide in the crowd of shoppers, but when he headed straight for the parking area and veered between Chevys, Fords and Plymouths, she had a premonition of unspeakable proportions.

"What are you doing?" she shrilled at him, pulling against the handcuffs as hard as she could.

"I'm going to get those cuffs off you and get you out of this mess," he yelled back. "That's what I'm gonna do!"

Summer knew his intentions like a farmer knows when rain is in the air. She dug her fingers into his arm. "Listen to me, Harris, you can't even think it."

As he spun around to tower over her, the blaze of his determination hacking through words that had yet to be spoken between them, Summer didn't flinch at his touch. She had lost count of the times he had touched her.

"It's no good wandering around out here in the open," he insisted and gave her a shake. "It's only a matter of time until they see us."

"You'll only make things worse."

"Things couldn't be worse!"

No, she guessed they couldn't. Summer winced when Harris whirled suddenly and kicked the tire of the nearest car, causing the pain to go through him in waves. What violence lay beneath his surface? she wondered with a darting alarm. What terrible destruction was he capable of?

He turned back to her, desperate. "I've been out of my mind. I don't know what I've been thinking."

"Harris—"

"Look, I'm taking one of these cars long enough to go somewhere and break these cuffs. Then I'll put you out and I'll leave the car. Tell the police whatever you want to. Tell them I kidnapped you. Tell 'em where the car is. This thing... it's... out of control."

Clutching the front of his T-shirt in her fists, Summer compelled him to look at her. "You said you wanted my advice, Harris. Well, they'll hang you. You said it yourself. You've got two convictions already. I don't care if you drive a car three blocks, you'll wind up in Joliet."

"But you haven't done anything. You don't deserve this, for Christ's sake!"

"Forget me, damn it!"

The helicopter was now sweeping up and down the boulevard. It made a wide circle several blocks away and retraced its path. High over the supermarket lot, it orbited.

Harris dragged her down between a Chrysler and a dual-cab truck, pressed her against a fender with his side. Forget her? She was all he could think about. "Next thing, they'll have the bloodhounds," he mumbled.

As the chopper made its third sweep, a dilapidated quarter-ton pickup rumbled and sputtered its way onto the lot and veered into a parking space several slots away, a lamentable excuse for a vehicle with smoke boiling out its tailpipe and the engine sounding as if one of the rods would crash through the housing at any moment.

A frayed young Chicano—fourteen or fifteen, tawny-skinned and muscular with heavy, long hair and thick black lashes all but hiding his burning eyes—opened the door and swung down without locking it. He wore a football jersey and stained jeans, bottomed out with heavy-toed sneakers. A cigarette dangled from one side of his sultrily beautiful mouth.

Pausing to glance in first one direction, then the other, he took a final drag on the cigarette and threw it down with a cold, reconciled stare at where it fell. He slammed the truck door shut.

From the corner of his mouth, Harris whispered, "Miami license plates and no inspection sticker? The driver underage? Ten to one this truck is stolen already."

Summer pictured Harris in a cell, and felt sick to her stomach. "Stop this foolishness, Harris. Please."

As if reconsidering, the youth returned to open the door and reach across to the glove compartment and remove a packet. Opening it, he shook out some pills into his palm and, after picking them over, put several in his mouth.

Throwing back his head, he swallowed. Smiling faintly to himself, he flicked a glance to the helicopter, then rolled the packet into a tiny wad and stuffed it into his front pants pocket. Shrugging at the chopper, he began trotting toward the boulevard traffic light, heading for an open-air arcade some blocks away.

"Well," Harris mumbled as he pulled Summer to her feet, "he's out of the picture for a while."

Summer thought of a half-dozen things to say to Harris, but none of them would've been what ought to be said: *I care about you now. What hurts you will hurt me.*

She strained back against the fender of the car, and when he began striding toward the old pickup truck, she grabbed the passing handle of a door and battled him in a ludicrous tug-of-war. He pried her fingers loose by force.

"Oh, Harris," she wailed. "How can you do this stupid, self-destructive thing?"

As Harris opened the pickup door, glanced over his shoulder and climbed in, he hauled her up with him. "Like this, sweetheart."

He reached across her to pull the door shut and, without explaining, doubled himself into as small a knot as possible, spun around on the seat and dropped his head back beneath the dash.

In disbelief, Summer gazed down at the long legs stretching across her lap. She felt as if she were pressed between the pages of a book. First he jerked on something, then another something. She bit her lips to keep from crying out. Two wires dangled from beneath the dash, and Harris finally extricated himself from the tiny space.

Sweat was streaming off him in sheets. Wiping it out of his eyes with the back of his hand, he leaned down and grasped the two wires and touched them together. The engine kicked over. Straightening, he gripped the wheel and revved the engine of the old truck.

"I might have known you'd be able to do that," she said acidly.

"Baby, I was taught by experts."

His profile was fiercely set. Like a sullen boy, Summer thought, determined to have his own damned way!

In the split second before she moved she asked herself if she had ever physically taken destiny into her own hands. Once, her memory brutally reminded her, when she'd tried with superhuman effort to swerve the car out of the path of that truck. Now she didn't ask herself if she could be electrocuted, she simply flung herself around Harris's side, grasped one of the wires, and jerked.

The engine died instantly. Harris's blistering oath filled the silence. "What the bloody hell . . . Are you crazy?"

Twisting around, he pushed her back by her shoulders so that her head snapped on its slender axis and swirls of her hair swept over his face.

Maybe I am crazy! she wanted to shriek. *You're breaking my heart!*

"What're you going to do now?" she cried out a challenge. "Hit me?"

He looked as if the thought had occurred to him already. Mumbling something unintelligible, he jerked around and bent forward to savagely connect the wires again. Summer clawed her way up and went with him, grabbed his muscular, sweat-slick arms. Burying her nails into the straining biceps, she flattened her breasts against his back and clung with all her strength.

Defeated by the fearful racing of her heart against his back, Harris slumped over the steering wheel. "I'm doing the best I can do," he declared bitterly, his knuckles crested with white. "What d'you want from me, for God's sake?"

They were both cowards, Summer thought as she collapsed against him, her breath coming in hard, heaving gasps. He feared prison and she feared her own feelings.

"Nothing, Harris," she said dejectedly and moved away. The man was a virus, and he was in her blood already. Oh, he was there, enflaming her with fever, infecting her with his sweet laughter and dreamy-eyed reflections and outrageous generosities. "I don't want a blessed thing from you."

Swiveling, he pushed her backward. Theirs was a silent, bitter struggle of minds and flashing, sparring eyes, but somehow, in the warring, the reason for it changed and the harshness of Harris's features softened. His hands, no longer ready to wreak destruction, released her shoulders and slipped upward to cradle her face as tenderly as if she were made of thistledown and would float away on a summer breeze.

"Ah, Summer," he sighed her name as she raised her hands to tremblingly circle his wrists. "I swear on everything I know, this has never happened to me before. I don't know... I don't know what to do with you."

He pressed her down beneath him on the rickety old seat and, with a shift of his weight, fit so easily between her legs that Summer wriggled for a moment—a wasted, useless, feminine writhing that served only to fan the bizarre flames that circumstance had lit between them.

If fate had given them time, perhaps she could have told him that for the past year the only thing that had sustained her was the tenacious hold she had upon the structure of her life. There had been no romance, no dreams.

But he didn't ask, and his mouth was suddenly dipping to hers. Yet it stopped before he kissed her, and Summer's breath was trapped in her throat as he hovered, a tiny frown creasing his brow. He started to say something, then didn't. Her eyes flared, and she started to push him away, and didn't. The touch of his lips to hers, when it happened, was a startled reflex, a questioning blink.

Then nothing.

No kiss, no breaths, no thoughts.

Then everything as Harris's mouth suddenly claimed hers with a hunger as immeasurable as their lives were empty. Summer was staggered and dizzied and hurled out into a strange, time-stopped place. His hands seemed everywhere upon her, and she couldn't outrun the flames that chased her: part of the spell was the danger of where they were, part of it was the contradictions of who he was.

Harris was arousing her, despite her clothes, and rescuing her from sterility in a way that Martin had never been able to do. The romance she'd been denied all her married life was unexpectedly, incredibly there: the lure of the great outlaw.

"Harris!" she gasped and fought her way up because she was way out of her depth and she knew it, "I have to talk to you."

Never had she seen a man less inclined to talk. The passion on his face thrilled her. It terrified her. He was moving his hands over her, watching them touch and inquire.

"I want to talk to you, too," he mumbled and found the hem of her top and slipped beneath it to fan his hands wide upon the span of her ribs. "But not now. Not now."

His hands on her bare skin were electrifying. Voices sounded from outside, and Harris was suddenly wired and alert. His gaze shot upward, dangerous and calculating.

Summer gasped as the words grew louder, then softer and faded altogether. "Now," she demanded.

"We've both known from the very beginning what this would come to."

Yes, perhaps she had known. She whispered, "You're a good man, Harris, but I—"

His eyes were slits of deadly, unreadable blue. "The one thing I'm not is good. We're not children, Summer, who can't stop this. You say the word, and I won't touch you again. But by heaven, you'd better mean it."

Words tangled in her throat. Her inhibitions would have embarrassed a teenager. "I want...what I want... Oh, God, Harris, I'm not ready for someone like you in my life. I don't even know you!"

A small smile flitted over his face. He eased himself down upon her and kissed her with such delicate persuasion that Summer wanted to cry. He traced every feature of her face slowly, then made an adjustment to his crotch. Summer felt desire trapped between them, throbbing to the rhythm of their racing hearts and saying more than words ever could.

"You know me," he said thickly, and moved his mouth to her ear. "You may not know what to do with me, but you know me."

When she turned her face away, Harris was glad she did. He wasn't sure he wanted her to know how deeply he was involved with her. She would always outdistance him. He would always need her more than she would ever need him. What kind of fool would set himself up for that?

He was suddenly seized with a raging desire to bring her down and to make her want him as he was wanting her. His fantasy was flashing and brutal. He saw himself tearing off her clothes and mounting her roughly and violently. Then, literally, his fingers searched beneath her jeans, found her, touched her.

Her eyes flared wide and disbelieving as she grabbed at his hands. He thought she was prepared to fight, but she grasped his hand that was already bound to her own with steel, and it was she who controlled the moment—holding him fiercely pinned against her and moving quickly, drawing in her breath with a tiny sound, then whimpering as she lay back, her eyes closed and her lip bitten between her teeth.

He bent to kiss her, but she turned her head away. Ignoring her, he dragged her again into a hurricane with no calm eye at its center. And again. Then, when she was dazed and depleted and the perfume of her hair had him drunk, Harris felt his own flesh—hot, unbearably hard. His mouth found her ear, and he touched himself to the innocence of her hand lying curled between them.

Her reaction jackknifed through Harris's body with ten times the speed of light, long before the comprehension reached his brain.

Harris didn't really know how many forms of fear he had witnessed in his lifetime. Enough. There was no describing Summer's, and there was no mistaking it, either. He felt as if he'd been dealt a blow to his groin. Desire drained from him as if it had never existed. Then Summer, to his horror, turned her face away and began to cry.

Hers was like no weeping Harris had ever seen. She slid down until she was lower on the seat than he, and her body knotted into slow, twisting rails of pain. Her grief had no sound, only a terrible, gut-wrenching anguish for which he had no understanding and no comfort.

Humiliated and feeling the most abysmal despair, Harris wanted to get down on his knees and beg her to forgive him. But he lay there holding her in his confusion, crooning to her, stroking her, pushing back the rebellious disarray of her hair.

"I'm sorry," he said when he finally felt her tears subsiding, though he was privately asking himself what he'd done that was so bad. Summer was a wife of thirteen years and a mother. It wasn't that she didn't know what happened between a man and a woman, for pity's sake.

Her voice was a hundred miles away. "It's not your fault."

"Of course it's my fault. What d'you think I am, Summer? I don't force women."

Summer was too drained to explain, too crusted over by life—a kettle that had rusted. She pressed her cheek with the back of her hand. "I take full blame—"

"Blame!" The word exploded with his utterance. "Summer, hardly an hour ago, you blamed me because I didn't trust. Do you? Do you trust anything? Anyone? If not me, then yourself?"

They were the kinds of questions she should be asking, Summer thought distractedly. Damning questions in cross-examination. The trouble was, the relationship she had shared with Martin had left her sexual education sadly lacking. Oh, she read, she talked, she heard talk. But talk was theory, and theory wasn't knowledge. Harris Chandler was a man of knowledge. She wanted to tell him about Martin, but it seemed like a betrayal.

He released her. He sat up and stared out the window without seeing anything.

"I wanted you on that train," he said, as if searching himself for an answer. "The way you sat, the way you moved, the way you touched your hair—everything made me want you. I closed my eyes, and I made love to you right there. I don't know what I saw when I looked at your face...your heart was there, Summer, in your eyes. It's true. Nothing you can ever do or say will make me believe that in that one moment, you didn't want me, too. It was as if a lifetime had passed between us."

To have deceived him, Summer thought, would have been the ultimate cruelty. But how did she tell this man the truth, this strange, brooding man who was now in her blood like a virus? What man could bear knowing that he reminded a woman of her dead husband?

"What are you thinking?" Harris demanded. He looked over at her swollen nose and the pink tear stains that marred her complexion.

She flinched at his bark like an anemone tightening upon itself. Her disheveled hair covered all her face except the slope of one glistening cheek. She sounded as if she had a terrible head cold. "It's nothing."

"What is it you're keeping from me? I want to know. I have the right to know."

In the end, it took a courage Summer wasn't sure she possessed. She didn't resist when Harris found a tissue in the bag and blotted her eyes, but when he tried to tip her face so that she must confront him, she closed her eyes.

"I wasn't trying to come on to you or anything," she said with excruciating effort. "I know how it looked. I knew the conclusion you were coming to. But you have to understand that I couldn't help being drawn to you, Harris. Yet that has nothing to do with this. I'm not some part of the sexual revolution trying to make a learning experience out of you. What I just felt, and what you just felt—I mean, there's a reason, but it's not... What I'm trying to say is that you could be...you are..."

She couldn't get the words out, and she gazed up at Harris with such unfeigned misery that Harris thought his heart would break. "Say it, Summer," he said through the walls of his frustration. "Will you just say it?"

Summer heard some strange-voiced woman coolly saying, "You are an uncanny image of Martin, Harris. An eerie...double. Even Tom saw it, at the station. He saw you, and..."

A beat of time passed between them—one so long and so frozen with exchanged exceptions and misconceptions, that Summer finally lowered her eyes to her lap. She'd made a mistake. She shouldn't have told him such a thing.

The sound of her flicking fingernails made her focus on the nail she had peeled off in such a frenzy. Harris Chandler had brought her to a crisis point before she'd even laid eyes on him. Did her attraction have all that much to do with Martin, after all? Was it, as Harris had said, meant to be?

With a low growl, Harris kicked open the door of the truck and sent it crashing back and dragged her along with him as he slid out. Grasping her wrist, he pulled her out. When the door slammed shut, he lifted her painfully by the shoulders until her feet left the ground.

Summer's outcry was silenced with a quick, ruthless kiss whose point had more to do with revenge than romance. He released her just as abruptly and took several harsh strides around the truck.

"I ain't a dead man, babe," he growled as she stumbled along behind him. "Don't bury me yet."

She became dead weight at the end of the handcuffs, her attraction passing over the frail line to fury. "You belong in the dark ages, Harris Chandler! Crash, bang. Grab a woman by the hair of her head."

"Yeah? Well, you're not the first one to tell me something like that."

As the boy returned from the market to his truck, Summer supposed that she and Harris saw him at the same time. If they could have gotten past their own thundering conflict and had waited five seconds longer before reacting, they would have realized that the boy was so stoned that he probably would have climbed into the truck and sat for some moments before he even noticed the ignition wires dangling beneath the dash. Even then he probably wouldn't have had the presence of mind to look through his front windows in time to see them.

But neither Harris nor Summer was thinking clearly, and Harris wasn't willing to take the chance that the kid would report them. Before Summer knew what was happening, he swiveled hard on his heel and took two swift steps so that they came up behind the boy before he could get the truck door open.

With several well-timed moves that made Summer's eyes widen incredulously large and her lower jaw drop, Harris slammed the youth hard against the door. He forced his head through the open window and held it down so that he was sprawled half-in, half-out of the truck.

"Hey," the boy bellowed his dazed protest. "God-damn!"

"Watch your mouth, scrub, and spread 'em." Harris proceeded to kick his legs apart and said in a surly voice, "If you stand perfectly still, I won't have to smear you all over the asphalt here."

...be tempted!

**See inside for special
4 FREE BOOKS offer**

Silhouette Special Edition®

Discover deliciously different Romance with 4 Free Novels from

Silhouette Special Edition®

...be enchanted!

As a Silhouette home subscriber, the enchantment begins with Lisa Jackson's DEVIL'S GAMBIT, the smoky passion in his cold gray eyes drew her like a magnet—despite his reputation and mysterious behavior...Natalie Bishop's STRING OF PEARLS, when two former lovers meet again, passions are sparked anew—but so are the lingering doubts...Patti Beckman's DATELINE: WASHINGTON, his rugged good looks challenged every move she made and every promise she made to keep their relationship strictly business...and Linda Lael Miller's STATE SECRETS, the story of a man and a woman who discover that too much curiosity can lead anywhere—even to love.

...be our guest!

These exciting, love-filled, full-length novels are yours *absolutely FREE along with your Folding Umbrella and Mystery Gift*...a present from us to you. They're yours to keep no matter what you decide.

...be delighted!

After you receive your 4 FREE books, we'll send you 6 more Silhouette Special Edition novels each and every month to examine FREE for 15 days. If you decide to keep them, pay just $11.70 (a $15.00 value)—with no additional charges for home delivery! If you aren't completely delighted, just drop us a note and we'll cancel your subscription, no questions asked. EXTRA BONUS: You'll also receive the Silhouette Books Newsletter FREE with each book shipment. Every issue is filled with interviews, news about upcoming books, recipes from your favorite authors, and more.

To get your 4 FREE novels, Folding Umbrella, and Mystery Gift, just fill out and mail the attached order card. Remember, the first 4 novels and both gifts are yours to keep. Are you ready to be tempted?

Even as she watched it happening, Summer didn't believe it. She imagined herself screaming at Harris to stop, but all she did was stand there, speechless.

Over the furious curses of the boy, Harris said with a perfectly straight face, "Officer Sonny Crockett, Miami Vice. You ever hear of me?"

What? Summer hardly knew whether to laugh at Harris or cringe for the boy. She pressed her fingers over her mouth to keep from smiling, but the boy wasn't finding it at all funny.

"N-no, man," he sneered and flailed helplessly behind himself, which was a bad mistake on his part for Harris grasped his right arm and twisted it back into a hammerlock.

Things were no longer amusing, and Summer closed her hand frantically around Harris's wrist. Harris pushed her away with a flashing warning not to interfere, and the boy finally quieted down. Summer grimly watched Harris go about the business of frisking him down. When he found the wallet in a back pocket, he fished it out and threw it open with a snap of his wrist.

"Emilio Ortega," he read and handed the wallet to Summer. "Here, hold this. Well, Emilio, tell me. What's your address, the great city of Miami?"

"None of your business."

The pressure Harris exerted on the hammerlock was persuasion enough.

"Twenty-four, thirty-seven Wabash Street," Emilio yelled. "Hey, man, let up, will ya?"

Summer glanced at the driver's license. It didn't agree with the address the boy had given.

Harris laughed nastily. "Well, I would let up, Emilio, except we've got ourselves a little problem. Seems like your license and you don't agree. Now, that's not nice, is it? Hmm,

Emilio? Telling little fibs like that? Didn't your mother tell you that nice kids don't tell fibs?''

Emilio groaned.

"Say, 'No, that's not nice, Officer Crockett.' "

The boy went limp across the truck door. "No, Officer Crockett, that's not nice. It's my brother's license, man."

Here followed a stream of Spanish that Summer couldn't begin to follow, but Harris apparently had no difficulty. Emilio himself was no mystery, however; she'd seen hundreds of boys exactly like him in her job. She'd also seen hundreds of detectives and policemen interact with these same rough boys who grew up into rough men and populated the state's prisons.

Harris gave the boy a shake. "Hey, Emilio, hold up. I can't understand it as fast as you talk it. Tell me about the truck. In English. Is the truck your brother's, too?"

"Oh," groaned Emilio. "I'm dead, man, can't you see that?"

"What I see, sweetie, is that you're spaced right out of your gourd. Junkie talk doesn't impress me."

"Wait a minute, man," Emilio began to blubber. "Now, you—you just wait a minute, see. I'm gonna—"

"No waiting a minute to it, Emilio," Harris's voice was raw and acidic. "Where'd you get the truck?"

"I borrowed it, man. From a friend."

Harris slammed his knee into the back of the boy's right leg and made it buckle. "Tsk, tsk, tsk. Shame on you, Emilio."

"All right, all right. It's . . ."

"Stolen," Harris supplied crisply.

Emilio didn't answer. When Harris used his knee again, he yelped, "I don't understand."

"You understand three years in slam, don't you, Emilio? Hmm? Do you know, all I've got to do is snap my fingers, and you're gone, Romeo. History. Why, every chick on the

East Coast will be gone by the time you get out. Come clean with me. What're you doing this far from Miami? What's this? What is this in your pocket, Emilio?'

"Oh, shit."

Summer watched Harris find the handful of pills. He dumped them out into his palm and poked them inside the truck and held them under Emilio's nose.

"What I want to know, Emilio," Harris said, "did you get these from your brother, too? Or did you get these from your friend?"

"I don't narc, man," Emilio said in a frightened whisper. "You can beat me to hell and back, but I don't narc."

"Ah, Emilio, I suspect the old pills are letting you down about right now. Now, you listen to me. My partner and I've been watching you, see? You're in big trouble, Emilio. Why, there may not be an East Coast by the time you get out. Dealing? That has a bad rep, Emilio. Real bad. Only one thing worse. Lyin' to a Miami vice cop."

Harris was going too far, Summer thought, and she kicked the side of his shoe. He glared at her, then, returning to the boy, said more lightly, "Hey, maybe you're in luck, Emilio. My partner thinks I should give you a break."

"Wha—"

"If you tell me where you got the pills, I might just consider letting you go."

"Oh, man." Emilio lay limply across the truck door. Harris would have released him, Summer thought, and he would still have lain there.

"Hey," Harris barked. "Who'll do easier time, farm boy? You or the dealer?"

"I was jus' holdin' for someone, man."

"Who?"

"Somebody small. I don't know anybody big."

"Give us a small name, then."

"All I know is Paulo. I swear, that's all I know. He wanted me to do this favor for him, see? I was supposed to drive this truck up to West Palm and leave it on a parkin' lot. He said he'd give me a little junk. That's all. I was doin' what he said. I swear that's the truth, man. Hey, he's little. He's nothing. But he'll wipe me out. You don't let me get out'ta here, I'm gonna get caught in a big squeeze, man. I'm not kiddin'."

"Paulo?"

"That's what I said, pig."

"Hey! Watch it, Emilio!"

Emilio instantly watched it. The look Summer exchanged with Harris was one she might have given one of the detectives she worked with. Emilio was a negligible statistic, for, unless she missed her guess, something of considerably more value was planted somewhere on the old truck. Paulo, little man or not, was someone to look up.

She motioned to Harris, but where she was thinking of the larger picture, he was thinking of the smaller. He was asking her with a gesture if she had a pencil and paper in her tote bag. Wondering what he was about, she fished it out. He scribbled a telephone number on the paper, and before she could question him with a look, he stuffed the paper into Emilio's back pocket.

"Okay, Emilio," he said with rough authority, "I'll tell you what we're going to do. We're going to let you go."

"Hey, I can't go back if you bust Paulo. He'll know I squealed?"

"Of course he will, Emilio. But I've thought of that. Now listen good, 'cause you're plastered. When you sober up enough to know what a great favor I'm doing for you, you look in your pocket, because I've put a telephone number in there."

"Why—"

"Because I'm a great guy, Emilio. Now pay attention! What I want you to do is to walk off this parking lot and down the street. If you look back, just one time, I promise I'll haul your butt in so fast, you won't know what hit you. You got that?"

Emilio groaned again.

"You get yourself straight. Then, if you don't want Paulo to kill you, you call this number. It's long distance. You know how to call long distance?"

He nodded.

"You call that number. Tell the man that answers that Harris said to call."

"Harris? I thought your name was—"

Harris slammed Emilio's knee against the truck door again, and Summer winced. "Did I tell you to think, Emilio?"

Shuddering, Emilio shook his dark, curly head. "No, man."

"Now." Harris glanced around at the parking lot. "You call this number. The man you'll talk to will be a tough guy, but he's okay. He makes deals with kids like you."

At the word "deal," Emilio's spirits rose noticeably. And Summer, gazing up at the anxiety on Harris's face, understood. It was how they worked, Harris and Bud. Harris wasn't being harsh; he was speaking the only language that Emilio knew.

On Harris's hard, brooding features, was none of the ex-convict. Not even the working man who labored in the hot Florida sun to make money for a school because nobody else would do it. Summer saw a kind man, a lonely man, who thought little about himself but a good deal about boys on a downhill road.

Harris spoke so abruptly that she started. "Okay, space cookie, get your butt out'ta here. And you remember what I said."

When Emilio realized that he was free, some of his cocky brashness returned. He lifted his shoulders with a swagger and combed through his black curls with his fingers. He went through the motions of being about to turn around, but he didn't quite see it through.

"And what if I don't remember what that was, man?" he asked, testing, his eyes on the asphalt.

A bleak unhappiness claimed Harris's face, and no trace of the facade was left. Softly, he said, "That's a chance I guess I'll have to take, Emilio. Maybe you're worth it. We'll see."

Emilio appeared to try to think, but his brain wasn't tuned in. His saunter across the lot, however, wasn't quite as brassy as it had been the first time. With his hands stuffed into his pockets, he did as Harris said and didn't look back. Once Summer thought he might, but when he hesitated, Harris yelled out, "Emilio!"

After Emilio had disappeared, Harris looked at Summer and shrugged without emotion. He said, "I guess I'd better make an anonymous call to the Feds."

"I guess so."

"And you'll have to make an extra report when you get back to your office."

How had he done it? Summer wondered. How had he tipped her world on its axis with no warning?

"I suppose I will," she said softly and slipped her fingers into the cup of his hand. "Do you think Emilio will make that call?"

"Who knows? You never know, Summer. Not on my end. Not with kids like that. If he gets scared enough...desperate enough..."

Something good and warm unfolded inside Summer when he placed his handcuffed hand to the small of her back. She paid him her finest compliment. She hoped that her son, if Tom ever found himself in trouble, would have the good fortune to fall into the hands of a man like Harris Chandler.

Chapter Seven

Three television stations and four newspapers sent reporters to cover the derailment. Four fire departments put trucks on the premises. Heavy equipment was already at work with cranes and winches in an attempt to right the toppled coaches. Policemen, hectically rerouting cars, made the ground almost as deafening as the sky, which was speckled with helicopters.

The cleanup would take weeks, authorities were saying. And the reason for the freak accident? Insurance investigators bleakly admitted that it might never be known.

Arthur MacLean parked as close to Industrial Boulevard as he could. While Pat and Tom waited at the Seville, he approached the hastily constructed cordon on foot.

Over the years, Arthur MacLean had never really cared for Summer all that much. As a statement of his disapproval he had pointedly insisted on calling her Jacqueline, and he secretly blamed Martin for bringing Summer into their lives. Martin had been a brilliant, popular man. He could've had his choice of any number of women. Why a nobody? The daughter of a man with "no visible means of support."

He'd been extremely disappointed. Jacqueline wasn't one of them and never would be. Even after she and Martin were married, she refused to hire a maid, and she never learned the art of intimidation. There was a certain image that having money and power necessitated, and she never caught on. When Martin's house in Coconut Grove needed a new roof, she had had the appalling taste to suggest that they do the work themselves.

Jacqueline aside—he admitted it now—his life had stopped with Martin's death. There had been times when he thought he would die himself. What was there to live for? What could he do that someone else couldn't do? Better? To Pat, he was someone who interrupted her schedule. To Tom? He wasn't sure.

Once he reached the site of the disaster, Arthur was surprised. Almost as if by magic, doors opened whenever he mentioned that Jacqueline MacLean was his daughter-in-law. What's more, they opened readily. He was escorted right up to the tracks.

"This is the A.P.A.'s father-in-law," the officer said to his partner. "Give him what he wants."

Martin's wife had built herself a reputation of sorts, Arthur admitted with grudging respect. But then, if she hadn't been Martin's wife, she wouldn't have been Neil Jarvis's assistant to begin with. And if he and Neil's father hadn't been fraternity brothers....

He collared a policeman climbing out of the wreckage. When he identified himself, the officer said, "Oh, yeah, Mr. MacLean. You see that television lady over there? I think she'd like to speak to you."

"Me?" Arthur was immensely flattered.

"And if I can help you, let me know."

"Why, I appreciate that, officer. Thank you. Thank you very much."

By the time he returned to the Seville, Arthur almost felt pleased with himself. He had received respect, and not because he was a millionaire. Who noticed millionaires around Palm Beach, anyway?

Pat was leaning back against the hood, fanning herself with her hat. Tom, watching the emergency teams at work, was gnawing on his fingernails—a habit he'd inherited from his mother, Arthur noted dourly, remembering Jacqueline's nails after the accident.

"Police helicopters have been combing the area looking for her," he told them both. "They think that she . . ."

"They think what, Grandpa?" prompted Tom, coming around the car with fear wide in his eyes.

Arthur studied his grandson across the hot expanse. Tom was a bright twelve-year-old, and trouble was nothing new to him. But how could he tell the child that his mother's life could be in danger? Fixing Pat with an unhappy stare, he replied, "They think she left with a man."

"Arthur!" gasped Pat.

Tom digested this news without comment. No one spoke until a siren faded away from a passing ambulance.

"But how do they know?" Pat protested. "Maybe there's a mistake. In all of this confusion, it would be a miracle if they didn't make a mistake."

"One of the women in the coach remembered seeing her." Arthur lowered his voice to the level of secrecy with Pat. "I also talked to a policeman who recalled seeing a man and a woman, and he thinks the woman could have been her."

Overhearing, Tom asked, "What man?"

Arthur considered the lavish diamond upon his pinky finger and felt protective. "No one is sure, son. The man—who's also missing—it seems that he was handcuffed to a deputy sheriff. Your mother was seen talking to the deputy in West Palm before the train left.''

Pat asked, ''What does the deputy say?''

''Nothing. He's on his way to the hospital, unconscious.''

When Tom withdrew into his own distant thoughts, Pat whispered from the side of her mouth. ''Arthur, I think Tom would be better off if he stayed with us until this whole thing is cleared up. Down there in Miami—it's bad enough with only Summer now that Martin and Bobby are gone. Now with this—we have to convince her it's best, Arthur. She wouldn't deprive her son.''

''Why don't we see how things turn out with Summer first.''

Pat MacLean reared back as if struck. Had she heard Arthur right? He had actually called Tom's mother ''Summer''?

Tom walked up, chewing the skin around his cuticles. ''Are they sure it's Mom?'' he asked. ''Maybe it was someone who looked like her.''

''Her attaché case was found on the train, son,'' Arthur said gently. ''If she'd been going to the hospital or back to West Palm in one of the official cars, she wouldn't have left it behind.''

''Do they know the man's name?''

''Chandler. Harris Chandler.''

What Arthur intended to tell Pat once they were alone was that the police had already put out an all-points bulletin on Harris Chandler. Chandler was considered to be dangerous, though the police did admit that the deputy still had his weapon when he was taken to the hospital.

Pat was planning a strategy to convince Summer that Tom would have so many more advantages with them.

''Anyway,'' Arthur said in an effort to be optimistic, ''we mustn't fret. Any of us. Summer is a very spunky lady, I've always said that. I'm sure we'll hear from her soon. Until then, I think we should get some lunch somewhere and take out the boat. We'll have the radio and the portable television on board. It'll be better than sitting at home chewing our nails."

Tom didn't catch the hint to take his fingers out of his mouth. He was glad that he'd hugged his mother before she left. He'd wanted to do it for a long time now. Almost to himself, he murmured, "He looked like Dad."

His grandparents telegraphed messages they wouldn't have dared to have spoken aloud. Pat turned around to arrange the lock of hair that had fallen across Tom's forehead. "What did you say, dear?"

Tom's face had the transparency of innocence. "I saw the man. At the train station, I saw him in the police car. I thought he was Dad."

Pat's color washed away, and when she tremblingly touched her husband's arm, it was a gesture that pleaded for comfort. "Arthur?"

"Well, Tom," Arthur said in his bolstered-up grandfatherly voice, "in the first place we're not sure she left with him. And just because he might have resembled Martin ... well, I mean ..."

Tears misted Arthur's fading eyes. Keeping his gaze fixed upon Pat, he said to Tom, "Did you see him very clearly, son?"

"Yes," Tom said.

Arthur shook his head at his wife. "He has to give the police a description, honey. They need one—what Chandler was wearing, anything. They told me they did."

It was all too much. Pat bent her head, and her words were muffled against her palms. "Not again. Tom's too young to go through all this again."

With an uneasy attempt to comfort people two generations older than he was, Tom laid his long, thin fingers upon

Pat's shoulders and shook it gently. "Don't worry, Gran'Pat."

"Don't worry!" Immediately regretting, Pat held out her hands and took Tom's face between them. "How can I not worry?"

"He won't hurt her."

"How can you know a thing like that?"

"Because I saw his face," Tom said with a logic that was completely beyond the two adults to understand. "I know he wouldn't hurt her."

Once again the older eyes exchanged a message. To be young again and believe in such fantasies. Well, let him believe to the last possible moment. Disillusionment came quickly enough as it was, God help them all.

"No!"

"Yes!"

"I can't."

"You haven't tried."

"I know already that I can't, dad-gummit. Do you have the vaguest idea of what you're talking about?"

"You said you'd chew these things off before nightfall."

"Gee, grandma, what long teeth you have."

"It's nearly dark, and they're still on." Summer rattled the handcuffs as evidence. "Your witness, counselor."

"So they are. And so it is. Nearly dark, I mean. Hey, I must have lied."

The sunset was going to be one of those brassy, gorgeous splendors that only Florida could have when spring was creeping into summer—a sunset with fragrance because the night was sprinkling dew upon hot, dusty blossoms and sandy grasses and scrub pines whose needles were dry and rusty with heat.

For hours, Summer had watched her shadow elongate until it was a spindly replica of E.T., and she'd tried to arrange everything neatly and logically inside her head. But only two things were real now—the magnetic force of the man locked to her wrist and a few slender books lying in a safe somewhere in Palm Beach County.

She didn't belittle the importance of the record books now. The lawyer in her was probably more desperate to get them than Harris was. But between the books and themselves was an interminable stretch of land.

The western flange of Palm Beach County had to be the margin of hell. With darkness coming on, the wind was picking up and tearing the few clouds into pieces of tissue paper. The insects started their frantic chirping, blaming Harris and herself for intruding. The mosquitoes took vengeance. Then, there was the saw palmetto.

Ah, yes. The palmetto. The saw palmetto wasn't an evil-looking plant; it had the kind of spiney blades one could find in pleasant little rock gardens outside service stations and fast-food establishments. But the green spines Summer encountered were demon possessed. They took a fiendish pleasure in chewing at her flimsily-shod feet like barbed wire. They gouged and poked and scraped and pricked.

Finally, in desperation, with her toes bleeding and her ankles shredded, Summer whimpered. "If we're not lost, how much longer?"

Harris leveled a stare at her over the slope of his shoulder, trying to trick himself into thinking that another glimpse of that stubborn chin would cauterize his need to stop all this and take care of her. He should have stolen the truck, taken her to his house in Miami, sawed through the damned chain and taken her home.

Regret rolled over him like a breaker. "Another four, max," he said with enthusiasm. "Maybe less. We're on some guy's land southeast of the development. Don't you need to rest?"

"Me?" She laughed a completely ridiculous laugh. "Of course not."

"Well, if you'd worn some proper shoes..."

"I didn't know I was going to enter a marathon, Harris!"

Harris smiled with satisfaction. Anger was an energizer. She slapped at a mosquito on her neck.

"Put your mind on something else," he advised blandly.

"Like what? Murder?"

"That's getting warm." He chuckled. "Heap curses upon my head."

She smirked at him. "Even that pleasure, Harris, has sadly begun to lose its charm."

"Count your steps, then. It's therapeutic. When you reach a thousand, let me know."

"I don't think I'll reach a hundred."

"Weren't you good in math?"

"That isn't exactly the problem, Harris."

Though he would never have admitted it, Harris was finding her complaining comfortably like that of a wife. He was loath to lose that. He stumbled into her for the hundredth time, striking her hip with his. He took her arm for the... he'd lost count.

He said, "Are you going to tell me or leave me in suspense?"

Her look was a cross between a dagger and a laser beam. "I've got to go to the bathroom, Harris!" she snapped. "Did it ever occur to you that human beings occasionally have to be human beings?"

Laughing, Harris poked a finger into the questionable depths of his soggy hair. "Thank God. I was beginning to think you never would."

Her glare reached the flash point.

"Well," he said, lifting both arms in a sheepish explanation, "I'm shy."

"In a pig's eyes, you monster."

Spotting the most face-saving undergrowth she could find, Summer stomped doggedly toward it with Harris in tow and tediously accomplished the unbuttoning of her own jeans.

"You can do me the courtesy of turning your vile head," she ordered when he stood staring at her.

"Only because you ask so nicely," he retorted and swiveled around to squint at the blaze of sunset.

"I swear, Harris," Summer promised through her teeth, "I'm going to personally see to it that you get life imprisonment."

Chuckling, he yielded her the small tidbit of needed privacy; he could afford to be generous.

By nightfall, however, nothing was funny; nothing was remotely amusing. Even their scrapping stopped, and walking became a test of faith. Summer lost track of time, and as much as she despised skittish, jabbery women, she found herself turning into one. It was either that or burst into hysterical tears.

"When I was a little girl," she said, hardly caring at this point whether he listened or not, "my mother used to recount all the things she had to do to get along. 'Get along'— that was her favorite expression. 'I've done a lot in my time to get along,' she'd tell me. Then, when she had my attention, she would recite her list. My mother was a great maker of lists. To her they were a tranquilizer."

He shot her a moody look. "The agenda of the future will save you from the failures of the past."

"You make lists, too, I see."

He neither agreed nor disagreed. "And did you?"

"Give her my attention?"

"Do everything on the list."

The chain clinked its soft melody between their wrists. "She was my mother. What girl listens to her mother?

Martin taught me more than anyone about how to get along."

Martin was an open wound between them.

"Yeah," Harris muttered glumly. Good old Martin. "Martin throws a vast shadow, all right."

Appreciating Harris's prejudice where her husband was concerned, she said, "Do you think that's fair?"

His cynicism was a sound from deep in his throat. "How could I know? Fairness is for the rich of this world. Rich, fair—all third-degree, four-letter words."

"Your contempt makes me furious, Harris!" she countered with a hot loss of control. "You're talking about yourself, you know. You'd have all the money you want if you didn't pour everything into the school. Don't pretend ignorance about success, either. You've made a career out of dodging success."

Her speech placed a few more lines onto Harris's face, and in his heart he agreed with her more than he wanted to. "Don't confuse my attitudes about the system with success. I'd like success. Who wouldn't?"

"Then why're you building houses instead of men?"

The ease with which she judged him rankled Harris no end. Who was she to stand back and criticize? "What d'you want me to do?" he snarled at her. "Start a campaign?"

"Would that be so terrible?"

"It's no one's business what I do with my money. First thing, when they find out, people are giving you advice, bossing you around."

"You could handle that."

"No I couldn't."

"Then let someone play devil's advocate. Let someone else bring in the money, Harris. There's plenty of it around. Do what you were meant to do. Work with minds. I saw what you did with that boy. You're probably the only chance he's had in his entire life. Do you realize what a rare gift you're hiding under a bushel, Harris?''

Harris found her words intolerable, especially since she was right. Stopping dead in his tracks, he jerked on the handcuffs and brought her around so he could search for condescension in her eyes.

"You seem to have my life all worked out," he said with a grave scrutiny. "Neatly boxed and tied with a big red bow."

Summer could feel his pulse beat in his hands—racing too fast, like her own, and she had, suddenly, an unwilled, visceral need to pull that stubborn head to her breast. Fearing suddenly that her need would show in her eyes, she looked away, spied a clump of rocks half-buried in the white sand.

"There!" she exclaimed and began dragging him toward them. She dropped down into the sand on her knees and pulled the chain between their wrists.

With a deep crevice gouged between his brows, Harris stooped to one knee and watched her dig through the sand to find a smaller stone.

"Here," she said and thrust it at him.

Eve couldn't have offered the apple to Adam with more hope on her face.

Harris slumped. "Summer, I'm telling you—"

With no warning, the need to cry was suddenly burgeoning behind Summer's eyes and knotting in her throat. He was so damned sure of himself, kneeling there on his folded legs that were so much longer and stronger than her own. All afternoon she'd been thrashing around in her brain, trying to come up with some magic solution to a problem that had no solution, and he simply knelt in the sand and looked at her—the wronged hero. Typical male!

"You just don't want to!" she raged and wanted frantically for him to at least equal her misery. "Don't you want anything, Harris, except to hide in your nice, dark corner of the world? Oh, you don't care. I don't want to hear any of this talk about how you care. People besides juvenile delinquents need things."

Yes, he wanted things. Up until he'd known her, he had simply denied himself. But now he wanted it all. He wanted her. He saw the way her hair was flying around her head and accentuating her face like a cameo from some timeless era.

Softly, urgently, he said, "Do you need things, Summer?"

It was in her to understand. Mixed with all her fears and griefs and sorrows and guilt and resentment of life was the equipment to understand exactly what he was asking her.

But she deliberately passed over it. "Of course I need things. Everyone does but you, Harris. You have your great pride. Well, take it to jail. Sit there for the rest of your life. Let it keep you company. You may find it a bit crowded in a cell—you and your complacency take up a lot of space."

The outburst was totally unfair, and Summer knew it. Her embarrassment made her want to hide her face. "Oh, give me that! I'll do it myself! I'll—"

In a frenzy, she jerked the stone from his hand and began banging at the high-tensile steel that mocked her feeble blows by not even accepting a scratch. The harder she slammed, the more it mocked—tearing at her nails and barking her knuckles, and when she looked down through the glassy prism of her fury, it twinkled sadistically in the light of the rising moon.

"Why won't it break?" she shrieked and squeezed her eyes tightly shut for she was at her wit's end, really, and she would never understand the ability of a man to stand silently by and watch a woman go to pieces and make an utter fool of herself.

Harris's hard, strong fingers closed over her own. He pried the rock out of her fist. Letting it go, Summer wretchedly hugged her middle, and dropping her head, bent until she was touching her knees.

"Because it's stronger than we are, Summer," he said with infinite patience to the top of her head. "It was never meant to break."

No matter what allusive mask he put on the words, Summer knew exactly what he was talking about. She couldn't pretend to misunderstand.

"Enough is enough," he said, taking her into his arms and rocking her like the spent child she was at this moment. "We'll walk over to the highway and catch a ride back into West Palm. Damn the books."

Somehow, Summer thought, as she gladly accepted his comfort, a domino had toppled over the others. Her nice, professional life would never go back to what it had been before. How had it happened? Everything she would ever think or do after today would be colored by Harris Chandler's impact.

Perhaps that was the real anguish that was pouring out of her: she didn't want to love again. It hurt too much to lose.

"No," she said quietly and, keeping her head bowed, flicked her fingers over her lashes and dislodged the unshed tears. "We'll get the books. We have to get the books." Straightening, she sniffed. "I'm sorry. I'm all right now. It was a..." She tried miserably to smile. "A transitional phase. I'm in control again. Why are you looking at me like that?"

Harris's crooked smile was no more of a success than her own had been. The sky was an inkblot behind his wildly disheveled head, spreading everywhere. The insects were filling the night with a lulling cadence. The moon was coyly hiding one eye.

Summer's single word came out all silvery and thin. "Harris?"

Still on his knees, he leaned over the jutting stone that separated them and took her hands in his to tenderly kiss the scrapes and roughened red places.

Weakness traveled up from Summer's shaking fingertips to her lips. She bit them hard, then whispered a subterfuge, "I'll help you, Harris. I can help you. Really—"

When he lifted his head, the moon was reflected in the blue of his eyes. He leaned nearer and caught her lower lip gently between his teeth.

"Then help me," he breathed as his hands slipped into her hair. "Help me do this."

As if it were choreographed long before either of them knew about the other, Harris unfastened her bag and dropped it. Summer clung to his neck. The wind blew tiny flecks of sand over their feet.

"You make me afraid to want this," she confessed as his lips covered hers.

"Want it," he muttered into her mouth, for it had been long enough in coming. "Want me."

Harris thought he could have kissed her forever. Hypnotized by her contradictions—she wanted so much but took so little—he was careful to prevent her tears this time. He tested her with ever-deepening sips, parting her lips, tilting his head, shifting again and tasting deeper and deeper until he was past her inhibitions.

Her hunger grew slowly, but as it grew and her fingers tightened in his hair, wanting, demanding, the more uncertain Harris became. She wasn't a girl to be toyed with, and she had no way of recognizing the permanency he was offering with his mouth and his breath and his body.

He lifted his head, meaning to speak, but she protested with a whimper and lightly strewed kisses over his face. "I've forgotten what it's like," she whispered. "Was it really like this?"

Success made Harris greedy. It was such a fleeting thing, that exquisite rush. He lifted his chin and accepted the kisses she rained there. He coaxed her with the rounding of his shoulders and the aggression of his hips.

Summer drifted through the feverish memories of a night almost lost—of the back seat of a car when she'd been fifteen years old. He had been . . . she couldn't remember the boy's face, but his name had been John. Then there'd been the heartbreak of a professor at the university when she'd been in her first year: brief, disastrous.

Now, from the mist of her spinning senses, she wished that she could explain to Harris that though she was a wife and a mother, she was different from the women he had to have known. But what words did she use for a confession like that?

His lips moved leisurely from her mouth to her ear, and she could feel the now-familiar assertion of his desire. She wanted to learn about his body, but she hardly knew how. As his hand moved over her breasts and down her length, exploring its hollows, each nerve and vessel and quick, silky secret opened to him.

She tucked her face against the curve of his neck, grateful that he knew all the things to do.

"Easy, sweetheart," he murmured when she shivered. "It's all right. I won't do anything you don't want."

"Oh, Harris," she begged, for now his fingers were working buttons and zippers. "Don't be disappointed in me."

Disappointed? Harris marveled that she could think for a moment that all he wanted from her was sex.

"I would want you as much," he whispered, "if I couldn't touch you at all."

So he indulged his adoration. He worshipped at the shrine of her goddess-ivory breasts and pearl-flecked thighs, himself a pagan, furious in his prayer as he slowly dropped to his knees before her.

Her white shadow merged with his seeking mouth, and she clung to his hair as if to a ballast, moaning and whispering his name. Her purr, when it came, was music to him. She closed her eyes as he stood at last to kiss her hair and her eyes and her lips. When he stroked between her thighs again, feeling the heat spread over her, he swallowed his own moan of urgency and sank his fingers deep inside her.

Harris thought that if he'd had the control of any sane man, he would've stopped right then. The tightness! The incredible tightness! But women were such mysterious creatures. What man knew the secrets of any woman?

For a few seconds he stood there, consumed by a deranged logic. "Summer, sweet," he muttered.

"It's all right," she said, and he, dulled, passion-drugged, fumbled with his clothes.

Harris's passion moved through Summer like a rush of quicksilver, and her senses were unbelievably attuned to everything around them—to the lowings of pine trees and the glissade of the darkness. Then he was falling with her, and the sand was at their backs and his mouth was open upon her nipple. Their blood and bones and hair were surpassing boundaries.

As her legs splayed in that eternal invitation, excitement tightened unbearably in Harris's groin until he thought if she didn't touch him he could not go through with it. But something was wrong, something he didn't understand, and he felt as if he were violating some sacred shrine.

He removed his hand that was moist with woman's desire.

"No!" she cried out, and in the darkness her face caught the moonlight like the cut face of a jewel. "Please." Softer, "Please."

Harris was at an agonizing impasse. She pulled up on his shoulders and buried her nails into his flesh.

"What have I done wrong?" she moaned, defeated.

Reaching beneath his clothes, she gripped him with a savagery that brought Harris the most excruciating pain, and when she lifted herself up, he felt as if he were dragged over a madman's thin line by some terrible demon. No surgeon's knife could have made so clean a stroke as he when he entered her.

He thought he would remember her cry for all eternity. God! His heart stopped. Driving force scorched the backs of his eyes.

She groaned through teeth gritted against the pain. "Don't stop. Don't stop."

He couldn't. Every blood-red fantasy he had ever dreamed spilled over him now. He choked out her name in some wretched plea, and the sound traveled through him like an arrow, speeding to every part of his body until he found her mouth and kissed her as he had never kissed a woman. He was drawn into the center of her soul: Dante into the flames. His release came with savage swiftness, starting at the small of his back and putting his bones on the outside of his flesh.

When he lay depleted upon her, despising himself and hardly able to breathe, he said the words he'd been trying to say from the very first.

"Damn you, Summer MacLean," he muttered as she slipped away from him and began disappearing into the misty forests of sleep. "What have you made me do?"

She roused once, deep in the throes of the night. Harris nestled her deep into the cradle of his body. She jerked against him, whimpered in her sleep.

"Shh," he whispered against her temple. "It's all right, Summer."

"Martin," she mumbled, turning toward his kiss, pressing closer. "I dreamed you were dead."

Long after that, just before dawn, the bruise upon Harris's heart gave him enough peace to let him sleep.

Chapter Eight

During his stint in prison, Harris had learned the fine art of awakening. Like some fabled Indian scout out of a James Fenimore Cooper novel he would lie perfectly still as he swam up to consciousness. He would familiarize himself with the feels, the sounds, the dangers of being alive—all without opening his eyes or moving a muscle. More than a few could have testified, first-hand, that in those first few seconds he was a perilously dangerous man.

Summer, on the other hand, was a fragile Southern blossom that slowly unfurled, one dewy petal at a time. Her best thinking was done in that dreamdust interlude after the alarm had gone off. On occasion she'd been known to fix Tom's breakfast, dress and get in the car before she woke up.

Her first thought now, as she felt Harris stirring beside her, was that they had stopped to rest and that she had just experienced the most wonderful, lusciously erotic dream in a long time. She could literally taste Harris and feel him on her skin. She was in the process of stretching and realizing that one of her arms had gone to sleep when pain, some *terrible, terrible* wound between her legs, made her draw in her breath in a little cry.

Dear God! She tried to move, but branches of crucifying hurt shot upward and downward, stunning her with the brightness of their intensity.

Summer compressed her mouth tightly and opened her eyes. The sky, instead of being black and velvety and pinpointed with stars, was sultry and purple. A blood-red dome was struggling to burst through the crust of the horizon.

She steeled herself for the ordeal of sitting up, but before she could move, she felt herself grabbed brutally by Harris and practically smothered as he flung himself across her waist and twisted around until he was half-kneeling, half-crouching—all this in less time than she could think it.

To the day she died, Summer guessed, she would not forget Harris's savagery as he twisted around to see how she fared. One of his arms was flung wide like a street brawler, his hands weren't fists but worked themselves open and shut, his color ghastly, and his chest, heaving with fury, almost a match for his eyes that shone like wet, blue stones.

"Oh!" She groaned as she struggled to her knees and heard a strange sound behind her head. Hooves?

Hooves! They were attached to the largest animal she had ever seen—a huge, picture-book stallion with incredibly dainty, prancing feet and a magnificent, highly arched neck and glittering black eyes.

Seated upon the stallion's back, glaring at Harris, was a black Conan the Barbarian, also the largest thing Summer had ever seen. Denim pants were taxed to cover the lower half of him, and his riding boots glistened with a fresh shine of wax. The upper half of his body was bare; the sun glinting off the fine sheen of sweat on his chest made it appear to be carved out of the finest, polished ebony. In the crook of his great arm was balanced a gun. Its barrel gaped at Summer like the grim, business end of a cannon.

Summer screamed. She closed her eyes. It was a dream, a horrible dream.

"Ma'am?" Conan's voice rumbled out of the sky. "Are you all right?"

"I'll be damned," Harris said in a wondering voice that bewildered Summer even more. "Titus Little."

The sky rumbled with thunder again and Summer's eyes flew open. The horse thrust down his nose in an explosive snuffle.

"When I want to hear from you," the thunder declared, "I'll give you the sign. And if you make one move without me tellin' you, I'll part your hair right down to your navel. You got that, lowlife?"

Summer had never heard the oath that came out of Harris's snarling mouth.

The barrel of the gun raised a notch, and the stock slipped into place against a shoulder as big around as her thigh. And God knew she didn't have skinny thighs!

Rising warily to his feet, Harris extended Summer a hand and pulled her behind him, at least as far behind him as the handcuffs would allow. Summer guessed, as she clenched her teeth in agony, that Harris would never know the pain the movement cost her; she had been loved thoroughly and well for what technically had to be called the first time in her life.

"Just a minute, friend," Harris said with a careful, deadly courtesy to Conan.

The black man growled. "I ain't your friend, jailbird."

The smile disappeared from Harris's face altogether. In its place was a frigid dislike. His words were a lazy, challenging drawl. "And you ain't gonna be on that horse much longer if you call me jailbird one more time, Mr. Little."

No, Harris, Summer wanted to say, *this isn't hero time. Harris. This man is Arnold Schwarzenegger.*

The giant swung a great leg over the saddle horn and prepared to dismount. "Look!" he shouted. "I got the gun, see, and that makes me the boss. Now, stay right where you are, and maybe, just maybe, I won't kill you."

Here he took a breath and his voice changed drastically. Leaning down, he said with sweet, boyish concern, "Did he hurt you ma'am?"

The innocent irony of his question was too ludicrous even to consider. Summer shook her head and asked Harris from the side of her mouth, "Who is Titus Little?"

Harris kept his conversation riveted to the man on the horse. "Mr. Little, in case you don't know who we are—"

"I know exactly who you are, huckleberry. I ain't seen nobody else's face on the television for the past twelve hours. You're in bad trouble, you know that, Chandler? Mrs. MacLean, ma'am?"

Starting, Summer squeaked her reply like a child. "Yes?"

"Did this man lay a hand on you?" The gun barrel swept around to point at Harris like some righteous finger. "You say the word, and I'll blow him away right here."

Actually, it was the kind of moment Summer excelled in. Being a good lawyer, Martin had often drilled into her, was often nothing more than being a good actor. People were only human beings, after all, composed of thoughts and feelings that weren't immune to what their eyes viewed and their ears heard.

Peering up with honest concern at Titus Little, she drew her hair from her face and said to Harris, "Mr. Chandler, would you kindly introduce me to this gentleman?"

Before his life had begun to disintegrate, Harris thought he knew most of the properties in this side of the county. Obviously he didn't, and he looked at Titus Little with an eye as jaundiced as when he'd regained consciousness on the train.

Though he spoke to Summer, his sarcasm was aimed at Titus. "This is Titus Little, Mrs. MacLean. Ex-fullback for the Miami Dolphins."

"Retired fullback," Titus Little blithely corrected as he slid to the ground.

Fumbling in her memory, for football was an expertise she eagerly left to others, Summer found her hand in the huge black one. "I'm Mr. Chandler's attorney, Mr. Little." She added with a hopeful smile, "We're glad to see you."

The man waited for a moment. Summer expected a barrage of questions, but he merely cleared his throat.

"Yes, well," she said and commenced upon one of the most impelling opening statements of her entire career.

Titus had left home at the crack of dawn. His sleeping wife had rolled over in the bed and groaned, "Where are you going at this ungodly hour, Titus Little?"

"To look for Sal," Titus had told her, Sal being his son's horse who had wearied of the pastures on her side of the fence.

"You're insane."

"Go to sleep. Maybe I'll run across those two the police are lookin' for."

"You're still crazy."

This would show Nita who was crazy, Titus thought with a private vindication. He wasn't exactly sure, now that he actually had found them, what he'd expected to exist between the two of them. He had a definite opinion about what they should look like—a dastardly, suspicious-looking fugitive and a battered, hysterical victim.

Instead, he was staring at a rumpled but gracefully dignified woman and a tough and surprisingly sophisticated man. He listened politely as the assistant prosecutor explained all the questions raised on the television. She finished her discourse with an explanation of how they had intended to pick up Chandler's records, copy them, then call the police. For a reason he didn't quibble with, though he couldn't have explained it, Titus didn't doubt a single word she said.

He grinned, "Well, seein' as how you've explained it all, ma'am, there's no need for this, I guess."

He shoved his rifle into the scabbard attached to the saddle. "You'd best come on up the house. Nita—that's my wife—she's in a motherly way right now and has a fuse about as long as a bottle rocket. Anyway, she'll just about have breakfast ready by the time we get there. If you don't mind my sayin' so, you both look like somethin' my hounds sometimes drag home. I guess you can ride Upper Cut, Mrs. MacLean."

In all the pressure of making herself believed, Summer had almost forgotten about the big stallion. At the mention of his name, Upper Cut stretched out his head to nibble playfully at Titus's back pocket for the sugar he wanted.

Without so much as a glance backward, his smile not faltering for a second, Titus reached back and wielded the animal a bright, backhand clip across the nose. Outraged, Upper Cut whinnied and reared up on his hind legs, thrashing the air with fury.

Summer clapped a hand over her breast to keep her heart from leaping out. A silly smile spread across her face.

"Oh, that's all right, Mr. Little," she said hastily. "I don't mind walking the least bit. In fact, I've grown rather fond of it. Besides, you forgot about these."

She held up the handcuffs and breathed a sigh of relief. Walking was painful enough, but straddling a Western saddle? On a horse descended from that of Attila the Hun? Forget it.

Titus's black brows lifted in amusement.

"Really," she repeated and nodded with a vigorous effort to convince him.

"Aw, you're not afraid of Upper Cut, are you? Why, this li'l old fellow is as gentle as a kitten. See?"

Titus proceeded to prove the fact by ruffling Upper Cut's mane and kissing him noisily on the nose. The stallion obligingly snuffled forgiving love noises at his master.

Summer shot a pleading glance to Harris.

Without warning, either to Harris or to herself, Summer caught Harris in one of those cloudy disjointed moments of introspection when a person doesn't think to mask his face. And Harris's, she thought, was all too easy to read.

With his head tilted and the shadows giving him a heavy gravity that made her lift her hand to her mouth, his eyes were saying all the words they had not said the night before. *So, it's ending.*

Summer stood helplessly, her surprise fueling her sense of unreality.

Necessity will separate us now, and what happened between us will be memory. What are you going to do with that memory, Summer MacLean?

You're borrowing trouble. We've planned what we'll do.

How will you feel when you see me made a prisoner, Summer? How will you feel when you see me maligned in the press? Will you wonder if I'm not the thief they call me? Will you want my kisses then? Will you want me to hold you? Or will you go on treasuring your woman's secrets and keep your sensible life?

So that was it. Because he had stumbled upon her pseudovirginal secret, he now wondered how many more secrets she had tucked away. Couldn't he do for her what he had asked? Couldn't he put himself in her place and see that she had been a woman living only on the fringes of the sexual revolution? That she was modern, with modern needs, but that she was still years behind herself?

He turned his head briefly in disappointment, then back, rigid with thwarted hope. *Well, treasure your woman's secrets, and keep your sensible life,* his retort slammed into her. *But I'm going to learn what those secrets are, and I'm going to break you down and wear you down until you'll sell your soul for the sound of my name. I'll make you want me as you've never wanted anything in your sensible life, Mrs. Sensible Summer MacLean!*

Summer's breasts rose and fell with bafflement. No one could live in this decade and call sex love. It might turn into love, but what Harris was asking for was commitment. How could she commit the rest of her life? She couldn't even see the end of this day.

"I'm lost," she whispered, praying that he would understand.

Then, because she couldn't bear to see the bleakness of Harris's face, she smiled lamely at Titus.

Stepping forward, Titus reached out to finger the steel links. He said to Harris, "Nasty looking wrist you've got there, Chandler."

Harris tore his eyes from Summer, feeling as if the breath had just been knocked out of him. "Yours would be too if you'd had a train try to rip off your hand."

Throwing back his great head, Titus laughed and placed Upper Cut's reins into Harris's hands. Without a by-your-leave, he reached for the gun he'd just placed in the scabbard. Swinging it around, he took two steps backward and fit the end of the barrel firmly against the centermost link of the chain. He indicated with a jerk of his head that he wanted them to stand as far apart as possible.

"Hang on, there!" Harris's roar made Summer gasp.

Titus Little blinked and reproachfully lowered the barrel. "I wouldn't miss."

"Yeah, well..." Harris's brows jerked together. "I'm not ready to find out if you flatter yourself as a shot, Titus."

The huge man shifted his weight and smiled sheepishly at Summer. In a wry, black dialect, he said, "Some people is so picky." He considered the steel chain again. "Wrist pretty tender, you say?"

In an equally exaggerated black dialect, Harris said, "You gets de' high score."

Titus bubbled over with giggles, and Summer wasn't quite certain if some of his football years hadn't scrambled his brain. She gently shook the chain between Harris and herself.

"We can live with the handcuffs a little longer," she said hopefully.

Mischief twinkled briefly in Titus's eyes. He made as if to turn away. Then, with one of the agile moves that had made him famous—miraculous, considering how big he was—he closed both meaty fists upon the short length of chain. Before anyone could say or do anything, he swung his arms straight out to his sides with a blood-curdling yell.

"Aaeiii!"

Summer didn't know which pain was worse, that which stabbed brilliantly through her wrist or the one deep inside. "Oh!"

Bending, cradling her arm against her middle with a rocking motion, she felt the broken end of the chain dangling in her fingers, its fragile jingle like gay, rippling laughter. Incredulous, she straightened and shook the piece of chain.

"He broke it," she said in amusement to Harris. Then she shrieked and threw away her composure in a little twirling dance. *"He broke it, he broke it!"*

"I'll be damned," Harris said with comical equanimity and scratched his head.

Catching Summer as she spun past, he laid her back in his arms in a swoon. "You see," he said with facetious triumph glittering in his eyes, "I've caught you already."

The laughter between them transformed into gravity until it finally ceased to exist. The words were very real, very feelable.

Flushing, Summer lowered her lashes, not because her length was molded to his, but because he was falling in love with her, and she didn't know what to do. "If you don't put me down," she whispered, her body melting, "neither of us will escape."

He moistened his lips. "And then what will you do?"

"Sin?" she said quickly, making the outrageousness of truth to be a joke.

Her acting didn't trick Harris. He set her on her feet. "You'll talk to me, Summer," he promised her hoarsely. "I promise you that."

Until he moved away, Summer wasn't physically aware of what being separated from Harris truly entailed. Her life with him had been unbreakable, but now he could walk as far away as he wanted to. He could walk so far, she might never see him again.

She felt as if part of herself had become dislodged, had ceased to work properly. She blurted after him, "The books first. Then ... then we'll talk."

"I'll get my own books, Summer. You're not getting any deeper involved in this than you are already."

Titus and the horse were forgotten in that sudden swelling pause. Summer followed Harris as he strode away. Every step cost her agony.

Catching up, she buried her fingers in the hard ropes of his arm. "What're you talking about?"

"I'm having Titus take you into West Palm."

"I'm your attorney, Harris Chandler." Fury tightened around her throat like a wrench. "Are you telling me you'd like to make a change? Am I fired?"

"I'll call you first thing, counselor. You can come with me when I turn myself in, see them put on the old cuffs."

Damn him! Summer wrenched her look to the black man who was standing silently by, holding Upper Cut's reins and watching the puzzling theater going on between them. She despised quarrelling in front of the man, but Harris was being unreasonable now. Just because she hadn't fallen blindly into his arms.

She threw back her head.

"Look," he said, throwing his weight to one hip and slouching, "I'm not going to argue with you about this. I meant it when I said I wanted you as far away from me as possible. You're a free woman."

"A free woman?" she taunted him softly. "Don't you mean to say, 'a consenting adult'?"

His reply was the sudden weariness that fit upon his shoulders, and hot tears pressed against the inside of Summer's eyelids. Her fragile facade crumbled. She was behaving like a spoiled child; relationships were made up of giving and taking. It was her turn to give.

She lifted her gaze to find Harris caressing her with a patient, weary smile. Tilting her head, she smiled back. She could never seem to hold out against this man.

Keeping her smile his prisoner, Harris called over his shoulder, "Titus Little?"

"Yo."

"Does this pussycat of an animal ride double?"

"Harris, my man," Titus slapped his sides, "he'll even purr."

With an agility that Summer found quite tactless, if not downright rude, Harris walked effortlessly to Upper Cut's stirrup and fit in a foot. He swung himself limberly up into the creaking saddle.

He would look dashing, Summer thought nastily, with his hair flying in the wind and his strong, sexy biceps on display, his flat belly and his tall, erect back. He motioned for her to come.

"Let's go eat Titus's food," he said heartily.

Summer walked over with painful steps and said with a meaningful intensity to Harris. "There's no need to tax this animal, Mr. Chandler."

Titus was hooked. He threw a glance to Harris to see what move the man would make now.

"He won't even know you're here, featherweight," Harris said to Summer and laughed. "Come on."

The lady's smile, Titus thought, wouldn't have passed for a sneer. Through her teeth, he heard her hiss. "That isn't the problem, Harris."

Titus smiled to himself. So that was the way of it, eh?

Harris coaxed Summer with a deep-throated urge. "It's okay, sweetheart."

The black man discreetly pretended not to be eavesdropping, but when Chandler cleared his throat, he looked up.

"Ah, Titus...would you..."

Summer had always suspected that men possessed a language unique to their sex, as women did, only more so—one that could transcend language and continents, a brotherly conspiracy with no questions asked. Even while she watched them, Harris and Titus spoke that wordless language.

"Sideways, I think," Harris said.

"You got it," Titus replied.

Which meant, interpreted: *it has to do with that weird woman thing, Titus. Like P.M.S. or pickle-craving. Trust me as I would trust you. If you ever need the favor returned, you've only to ask.*

Summer suspected that Titus was secretly indulging one of those chauvinistic snap judgments, and that he would like to ask her if she hadn't overdone it a tad, honey.

"Ma'am," he politely inquired. "With all due respect..."

The next thing Summer knew, she was being lifted beneath her arms as she had so often lifted her boys when they were small. With utmost care, Titus positioned her upon Upper Cut's neck as if she weighed nothing at all. Taking her hands, he placed them firmly upon the saddle horn.

"We'll go real slow," he promised her, but Summer knew he was speaking to Harris.

Embarrassed she mumbled, "Thank you," but he was already taking his place at the horse's head and gathering up the dangling reins. As he led the animal out across the dry sandy stretch of Palm Beach County, he called back to them.

"Oh, by the way, Chandler, that Delaney guy?"

But Harris was absorbed with studying Summer's profile as she perched unsteadily in front of him. One of her hands was angled tenaciously in the horse's mane and with the other she balanced herself upon his thigh. An oblique shaft of sunlight had cut its way through the wild tangle of her hair, silhouetting her with brightness, much as a photographic lens could place an ethereal mist upon a subject.

She had no idea of how exquisitely beautiful she was, not just a physical beauty but one that had to do with the inside of a person—her age, her sadness, her haunting mysteries. It was so simple, it staggered him. There would never be anyone but her for the rest of his life.

"Yeah?" he said sluggishly, dragging himself from the weight of his own destiny.

The black man looked back. "He died."

Chapter Nine

The sun glinting off Titus Little's whitewashed adobe ranch house reminded Summer of old Westerns where the hero was saved by sunlight reflecting off a rifle barrel. Or a Scot warrior returning home from the war and being met with messages sent from the castle with mirrors. Set out in the Florida Grass Prairie—not exactly no-man's-land but not missing by much—the bright red tile roof twinkled like a ruby, and the luscious green lawn glimmered like an emerald carelessly dropped by a passing god.

When they were a long way off, Titus put both hands to his mouth and gave a tremendous yell. Down the driveway, barely visible, sped four children of assorted sizes and shapes with brightly clad balls bouncing and skimming toward the black iron gates with the letter *L* welded onto the arch.

"What I should do," Titus said happily over his shoulder, "is get my own television show like Bill Cosby. He thinks he's got kids? Hell, he's just gettin' started."

"Some layout," Harris remarked in a pensive tone that made Summer know that his thoughts were running in the same channel as her own: Hank Delaney, dead! It wasn't right. It wasn't fair.

Her statement to the police would clear up any manslaughter charge made against Harris, of course, but public opinion was so fickle. Already Harris possessed enough bad press to last him a lifetime. Some people would believe to their deathbeds that Harris caused Hank to die.

"He was married, you know," Harris said sadly as his arm tightened around Summer's shoulders.

Summer spread her hand wide upon the span of his chest. They had survived a crisis together. They were creating a history. "Do you remember," they could ask each other at some point in the future, "how we felt when we learned about Hank Delaney?"

"A few more hours and this will all be cleared up," she told him, relishing the peace she was feeling, despite the news of Hank.

His smile disagreed. "I only wish it would be."

He was right. Once the charge of manslaughter was cleared up, trouble would just be beginning.

The gait of the horse jostled Summer, and Harris took the force of her weight. It brought him enormous pleasure, and he cushioned his chin in her hair. The dawn was staining everything now, turning it all beautiful, even the monstrous saw palmetto. The birds were coming alive, and their mad tweeching filled the morning sky, and the sawing of insects, the hush of the wind moving gently in the pine boughs.

"Everything is lovely just now, isn't it?" she said contentedly against his jaw, completely unaware that tears had collected in Harris's eyes.

The sense of rightness that filled Harris threatened to burst his lungs. He could have been a boy again, sitting on the shore of Lake Michigan and smelling the odor of apple trees and summer and fish and wild blossoms, ready to take it all just because it was there to be taken.

"Someday," he murmured into her hair, "when this is all over, I want to take you to meet my dad."

Summer's glance upward teased him. "That's pretty old-fashioned for an old rebel like yourself, Mr. Chandler."

"I'm trying to get you in my clutches."

"Evil clutches."

"Do I look evil?"

"Decidedly."

"Then, would you please do me a favor and kiss this reprobate?"

She made her eyes wide. "Titus is only a small distance away."

"I only want a small kiss."

Swallowing her laughter, Summer reached up to peck Harris on the lips.

He didn't move but continued to stare down at her. "That's it?"

She sucked in her jaws for a reproach.

"Heck fire, Summer, Upper Cut could kiss better than that."

"Kiss the horse, then."

"Summer, why can't you be more selfish and despairing?"

The children were skidding to a stop at the ranch house gate and climbing on to wait for their father and the unexpected appearance of two strangers.

The immediate present was like a creature stirring in Harris's gut, and he saw his chances with Summer being trampled underfoot. He gripped her so hard, she made a sound of protest.

When she turned, he said, "I don't know if we'll be alone again."

Her stricken face disagreed. "Of course we'll be—"

He stopped her with the thrust of a look. "Hush, Summer, and listen. If something happens, if something prevents me from seeing you for a while..."

Tears brightened her eyes, and she slowly shook her head back and forth.

Harris spoke so quickly, his words spilled over each other. "Summer, all my life I've looked at people in love and thought they were cowards. Or selfish, at the very least. Addicted to lust or something, I don't know. But I know in my heart that for any kind of relationship to last, someone has to give more. I don't care what they say, there's no such thing as fifty-fifty in the beginning. Nothing is equal and survives."

Harris glanced at the gate where the children waited. He remembered her calling him Martin in her sleep. He shouldn't be saying these things to her.

"That power is exchanged many times when two people stay together, Summer. It has to be. And if you love someone... Am I a fool to use that word? If you love someone, you accept the changes. You grow. But in the beginning someone has to go first. Someone has to bend, to ask." He shrugged a shoulder ruefully. "Hell, more like get down on their knees and beg."

From his angle, Summer knew that Harris could not see her stolen glances. This man, this dangerous, rebel man was speaking tenderly to her of love. Not even Martin, in all his persuasion had said words like that, words not of a love affair, but love—richer, poorer, sickness, health, death.

She wanted to reach out and stop the words she could not shut her heart to, but she couldn't find anything to grab hold of. So she was honest. She tightened the grip she had taken of his shirt. "I know what you're saying, Harris. I've been there."

His eyes were a dark cobalt color when he gazed down. "I'll go first. I'll love you more. I'll give you time. I'll get down on my knees and beg."

They were being descended upon. The smallest of Titus's children, a girl of five, rode a swing as it swept out in a great inviting arc. Two more girls, seven and nine by Summer's guess, stayed just inside the yard, their eyes like saucers.

Titus motioned the oldest, a boy, forward to him. "Here, take Upper Cut, son," he said, "and rub him down good."

Kyle Little had to be about Tom's age. Summer smiled at him. A puzzled query passed over the youngster's face when he saw her, but Titus grabbed his shining black ringlets and ruffled them.

"Didn't you find Sal?" Kyle asked with disappointment.

"She can't get far. We'll go out again after breakfast. Where's your mother?"

"She's out on the veranda," one of the other girls called from the gate. "She's got the broom, Daddy."

"And the can of Raid," added Kyle as he flicked his eye in a not-so-subtle inquiry about the riders.

Titus was gently grave with the boy. "Don't believe everything you see on television, son."

"Boy, are you in trouble, Daddy," chirped another elfin girl, Emily.

Another sister chimed in, "You didn't take down the wasp nest."

"They chased Mama."

Titus puckered his mouth and met his son's wide eyes in a commiserating male look. "That true?"

Kyle showed a mouthful of sparkling teeth. "Every time she'd swat the broom, she'd say, 'Take that, Titus Little.'"

Behind her, Summer felt Harris's laughter from deep in his chest. She twisted around. "What're you laughing at?"

Harris wiped the smile from his face with prudent haste. "Nothing, love. Not a thing." He held up a palm. "I swear that the testimony—"

"Shut up." Summer gave all her attention to the figure who was heavily descending the rank of steps from the house.

As he walked, Titus extended the reins to his son. "Boy, oh, boy, if it's not one thing, it's ten others."

Having been momentarily forgotten, Summer exchanged a look with Harris, and his gesture for her to slide off the horse made her narrow her eyes.

He grinned sheepishly. "I forgot." Then, with a doubtful squint, "I really did that to you?"

"I don't want to talk about it."

Chuckling, he swung a leg up and over her to dismount. With more enthusiasm than Summer thought was required, he helped her slide to the ground. Once there and shielded momentarily by the horse, he too casually grazed the swell of her breasts.

He murmured, "It's much more convenient having two hands, isn't it?"

"If thine hand offend thee, Harris," she warned and smiled at Kyle as he made clucking sounds to Upper Cut and led him away.

"So, Titus Timothy!" The loud command brought the girls scampering from the gate back to the house. They lined up on both sides of their mother.

Harris, meeting Summer's eyes, laughed and lifted his eyebrows. "Titus Timothy?"

"And I can do without any of your lip," Titus called back, not taking his eyes from his very pregnant wife for a second. Stepping forward, he kissed her meekly on the mouth. "How're you doin', sugar babe? Uh, one of the kids said you had a little trouble."

Summer knew on sight that she and Titus Little's wife would be friends. She was a tall, strikingly dignified woman. Beneath the long flowing shift that swept the steps, protruded a belly heavy with child, and she had her hair wound up in a perky, Aunt Jemima bandanna. But her widely set brown eyes sparkled with intelligence. No one could have guessed that she was the mother of four-going-on-five. She didn't look a day over twenty.

She hammered the handle of the broom onto the steps like an ancient sage calling for order among the people.

"Don't you 'sugar babe' me, you Jolly Black Giant. It's a good thing I didn't get stung, that's all I can say, or this would be a shotgun waiting for you instead of a broom. Hello, I'm Anita Little."

To be as bizarre as it was, the explanations of how and why they came to be upon the Little property was accomplished with a miraculous economy, Summer thought. Titus simply picked up his wife and twirled her around in a billow of brightly colored skirt, replaced her to the huge, sprawling porch, and bent to whisper a few words in her ear.

Instead of puzzlement or disapproval, Summer saw merriment and graciousness on the woman's face. Anita waved them forward. "Breakfast is ready. I promise there are no wasps in the kitchen."

"Oh, Mama," the girls groaned affectionately and raced ahead to open doors.

"Very neat," Harris murmured to the top of Summer's head as they moved forward to accept the Little's hospitality. "I wonder what he told her."

Through her smile, Summer said, "Don't look a gift horse in the mouth. We're talking food here, Harris. Real food."

Anita Little kept up a steady narrative as she ushered them through a house that looked more like a football field with a few walls and wide open spaces, all carpeted with heavy duty, indestructible turf.

"Titus goes out on these terrible jaunts before breakfast," she explained as she motioned them into the kitchen that exuded marvelous aromas of fresh coffee, scratch biscuits, scrambled eggs and sizzling bacon. "Actually, it's selfdefense. He can't brave all the children running around demanding the bathroom."

By the time Anita instructed the children to push another table to the existing one—the kitchen furniture consisted of a monstrous picnic table painted brilliant lime green and oddly decorated benches—Summer and Harris were in love with her. Anita wiped her hands on a tea towel and invited them to wash their hands at the sink.

"Life around here is in the informal mode," she said, "and we'll hear no talk about baths before eating. We're old ranch hands, and when we talk dirt, we mean dirt. Mr. Chandler, you may sit there. And Mrs. MacLean, I suppose you should sit by me."

"Women feel the need to stick together," Titus blandly observed as Kyle slammed the back door and took his place at the table.

"And if we didn't?" Anita challenged her husband in a friendly combativeness that made Summer feel good.

Titus winced. "There might be a few more mouths around here to feed."

"I don't eat much," the youngest girl protested with a pretty sulk.

"Neither do rattlesnakes," Kyle observed gravely, "but they're a bitch to get along with."

"Kyle!" scolded his mother.

Over the table, as the food went around and around in confused circles, Harris met Summer's look. *It's nice, isn't it?* his eyes asked.

Life like this has a high price tag on it, she told him.

It's all right. I'm buying.

But their presence did cause a disruption in the Little household. When Anita shooed the children out to play and insisted that she and Titus would clear up the breakfast things while Summer and Harris showered and changed into some clothes she could scrounge up, Summer wondered if it wasn't all a ploy to occupy them so Anita and Titus could talk.

Anita laid out a supply of fresh towels and laughingly remarked, "I'll find you some clothes, Mrs. MacLean. Believe it or not, when I'm not this way—" here she exaggerated the shape of her extended belly. "—I'm about your size. With a few added inches in length, but you can roll up the jeans."

Summer smiled wearily and slumped down onto the chair of the big master bedroom. "I'll start a fashion."

"Maybe you already have," the other woman admitted, smiling more gently. "This is the most excited I've seen Titus in years."

Not sure if she should smile back, Summer asked, "Is that bad?"

"It's not every day you find people with all-points-bulletins out on them."

They had disrupted things. Summer was embarrassed and wished she could think up an excuse to leave suddenly.

Realizing, Anita hurried over. "Please, don't take that wrong. That's not it."

"Oh?"

She sniffed the fresh bar of soap. "I don't know if you remember all that ruckus in the papers about Titus and the drug charges."

Summer admitted her ignorance of the sports page.

"Titus was ready to fight, take every team authority to court. I mean, the man was primed." Anita hesitated, then said, "I was pregnant with Janie, and I got down on my hands and knees and begged Titus to let it all go. All this—" she threw out her arm in a gesture to include everything "—is a panacea. But when Titus came walking into the house with you two, I saw the gleam in his eye. Oh, he's had it before—championing the cause. He's done commercials for mental health, all that, but this time he's caught the bug. I can feel it."

Summer's hand trembled at her throat. Somehow she knew some of what Anita Little was trying to tell her— women had their language, too, after all—and she didn't know if she should be happy or sad.

"Harris is a fighter," she admitted to Anita. "Titus couldn't help but feel a kindred spirit. But Titus doesn't have to be involved with this. He's not harboring a fugitive. Please don't worry about that."

Anita smiled unhappily. "Titus would probably relish it if he were. I took the fight out of him. At the time I thought it was best, but I've never really known."

Bending her head, Summer said slowly, "Harris is a very complicated man. You know? He's also enormously talented, and his interests are so complex, they're staggering." She laughed. "Anita, I guarantee that you've never met anyone like Harris Chandler."

Then she pled a different kind of case than before. She told Anita about Harris's father and the school.

"So you see," she concluded with a shrug, "if Titus really wants a cause to champion, I know these boys..."

Anita left Summer adjusting the nozzle of the shower. Summer sighed with bliss as the spears needled into her scalp. She looked down at her lathered body, and for the first time that she could remember, she actually liked all those functional parts of herself. She touched her breasts, and the memory was there of Harris's insatiable desire.

She grew absorbed with soaping the handcuff and trying to slip it off her hand. But her wrist was simply too tender.

The noise of the bedroom door opening and shutting intruded vaguely into her efforts. Over the noisy stream, she called out, "I'll be finished in a minute, Anita. Just put the clothes on the bed." As an afterthought, she poked her dripping head from behind the shower curtain. "And thanks—"

Summer couldn't have taken her eyes off the sight of Harris stripping off his clothes if someone had slapped her face. In the darkness the night before, she hadn't thought of him as Martin at all, and once in the light of day and past the clothes, he was his own man entirely.

How did he keep so fit? His legs, as trimly tapered as an athlete's? His waist as finely muscular as a youth's?

"Harris!" she gasped as he met her stare without the least abashment at his unaroused state.

"Summer," he retorted and stepped past the curtain, jerked it shut, and moved her boldly aside to stand with his face lifted against the hot, steaming spray.

Out of a rather ridiculous sense of modesty, Summer crossed her arms upon her nakedness, but if Harris noticed the misplaced gesture, he made no remark about it. He proceeded to soap his face and scour his stubble of beard. When he was finished, he spat water onto his feet and turned as the soapy water sleeked down him in sheets.

"Titus and Anita have their heads together over something," he said pleasantly. "I thought I might as well save messing up another shower. Turn around and I'll shampoo your hair.''

The connection between Summer's brain and her tongue finally activated. Taking a breath, she said exactly what she did not mean. "Shower stalls don't get messed up, Harris.''

"Really? And all these years, I've thought..." Reaching across her, he lifted a bottle filled with green liquid from the rack that hung in the corner. "Hold still," he said and calmly poured some upon her head.

Standing before Harris Chandler with her head tipped back and the whole of her body naked between them had to be one of the most difficult of all ego trials. He scrubbed her head as if she were a poodle. When he was finished and she was rinsed, he slapped the bottle into her hand as a surgeon's assistant would pass a scalpel.

"Return the favor," he ordered.

Not until they were both scrubbed, shampooed, and rinsed did he lean back against the slick tile and turn his attention to all the parts of her that he had only half seen in the darkness.

"I approve," he said heartily and grinned.

Summer was violently aware of the metamorphosis from non-arousal to passion. It happened before her very eyes, soaring out of his groin and swaying, seeming to reach her before the rest of him did. When he took her in his arms and kissed her beneath the warm, hypnotizing spray, it nudged her belly.

Summer swore to herself that she wouldn't be self-conscious, yet she trembled. Thirteen years of ingrained habits. She looked down at the swirls of soapy water rushing around her feet and wondered what to do.

But if she didn't know, he did. He kissed her leisurely, a long, lingering kiss. His tongue slid to her eyes and her ears and her neck and her breasts, her waist. He toured every part of her and she loved it. But still she trembled.

"Sweetheart," he murmured, "why are you so afraid? I won't hurt you again, I swear it. I wouldn't have hurt you for the world, Summer. I'm not a beast that can't be reasoned with."

Couldn't he see that she wasn't ready for this kind of a confidence? She was prepared to step out of the shower, but he placed both hands at her waist. The steel of the handcuff gouged into her flesh, adding memories to the spray that stung them.

"Talk to me, Summer," he said and cupped her hips, bringing her up to the passion in him.

"You want me," she said, her helplessness mixed with awe.

"God, lady," he said as his head bent to claim her quivering lips, "what have *I* done wrong?"

There was no time for Summer to rally her defenses. She supposed that she didn't even want to. The fierce aggression of his lips upon hers was the picking up of a thread that had spun out from his shock the night before. As if in warning that he meant to have his answer now, he thrust his tongue boldly into the sweetness of her mouth.

Summer wondered how she could be less than honest with him. She tore her mouth from his and buried her face in his neck.

"You haven't done anything wrong," she gasped. "Neither of us has."

The telling of her secret took so long that Harris reached over her head and twisted off the water. "You mean," he said with surprise deepening the wet creases of his face, "that Tom is not Martin's son?"

She turned to face the corner of the shower and dropped her head against the tile. "No one knows. Well, Angelica knows. Sometimes when Pat MacLean hints how Tom should come and live with them, that she could be a better mother than me, Harris, I want to take her by the shoulders and just tell her the truth. No, Tom is not Martin's son. I never had sex with Martin. No woman ever did.''

Without warning, he bent and lifted her in his arms like a child and walked with her to the great, unmade bed that Anita and Titus had shared with such prolific results. ''I don't think they'd mind,'' he said as he fell with her to the pillowed haven.

She protested with a hand slipped between their mouths. ''Harris . . .''

''I can't go away now, Summer. Can't you see? Let me be the one. Even if you never see me again, let me be the one.''

His dread of the future was so heavily marked upon his brows and in the lines of his face still covered with their lengthening beard, Summer pulled up on her knees. A smile found her mouth, and she leaned over to kiss his cheek.

''Do you see me as a virgin, Harris? Because I'm so naive about . . .''

His smile was more wicked than innocent as he grasped her hand and closed it upon the hot, throbbing shaft. ''I don't suffer from any delusions, my sweet. I'm simply a man, and I've ego enough that I'd like for you to sample the good about it rather than the hurt.''

Just touching him made goose bumps rise all over Summer's body. He leaned down to touch the tip of his tongue to her nipple, and she let her head come to rest against his hair. He closed his hand over hers and began moving it, and the sensation was exhilarating to her, and terrifying and unspeakably arousing.

In a blaze of desire, Summer hardly cared if he reciprocated or not. She wanted it all, everything she'd ever heard about or read about or accepted Martin's apologies about. With her wet hair falling coldly about her shoulders, she bent her head to his lap. When she closed her mouth upon him, she felt his control wage war within its borders. He made a sound of helplessness deep in his throat and held her head trapped in his hands for long, interminably tortuous moments.

The awareness Summer experienced in those moments was cataclysmic. Her life was changing. She didn't know where it would go, or how it would end. But this man who would never fit into her circle of friends, who would never be accepted by people like Pat or Neil Jarvis—this man had to be a part of her life. If he weren't, what point was there to any of it?

He tipped up her head and held it cupped in his hands. With his eyes glistening, he bent to kiss her. As gently as if he were handling a newborn, which in a sense she was, he drew her up into his lap where he knelt. Again he guided her hand so that she could do as she willed.

"I can't bear to hurt you," he whispered as she slowly and carefully lowered herself onto him.

Reality was a tension in Summer's stomach. As Harris closed his arms around her and rose up inside her, fastening his mouth to hers, she muttered into his kiss, "Harris, don't get me pregnant."

Tension rippled through Harris like the sudden entrance of cold wind, and he looked up, his eyes still dazed with desire.

"You mean," his words came sluggishly, "that before, you..."

"There's been no need for me to take anything, Harris. I haven't been playing around."

"Then you could already be pregnant."

She knew there was the chance of that, but it was unlikely. This was all going badly. Reality was cruel.

When he pulled away, Summer clung to him, shivering. "I'm sorry. I'm not skilled at this. I'm clumsy. I'm—"

He took her urgently by the shoulders. "You're none of those things. Oh, hell, I should have known. I should have guessed."

He was upset with her now, and she found it unbearable and grossly unfair. Flinging herself off the bed, Summer grabbed up a towel and wrapped it around herself. It had been good, wonderful. But now what?

Moving to the mirror, she began working the tangles out of her hair, aware that he was studying every move she made. She didn't dare turn to say anything, for he had made no move to dress or cover himself.

"Have you stopped to think what this might cost us?" he asked.

Her words were muffled. She didn't like his tone. "Cost *me*, Harris. *Me*. I'm a big girl, even if I don't appear to be."

He snorted his disagreement with that statement of fact and swung his legs off the bed. Having no other clothes, he stepped back into his pants without any briefs and buttoned the stretchy waistband around his middle.

"If you were pregnant..." He hesitated, and Summer, realizing that this issue was tearing him to pieces, whirled around.

"I'm not asking you to marry me," she snapped.

"Well, how could I?"

"What d'you mean, how could you?"

"I'm the pauper, Summer, pining after the princess." He dragged his hand through his wet hair and left it standing out in spikes. "Pauper nothing, I'm a convict."

It had never been on Summer's mind to wrangle a proposal of marriage from Harris. Not once since Martin had she even conceived of marriage with anyone. But now that the issue was raised, she felt she was being slighted and cheated.

Outrage pinkened her cheeks and flowed through her veins. "You mean," she demanded, stepping before him and planting a fist on one hip and pointing the comb at his nose, "that if I turned up pregnant, you wouldn't marry me?"

"I mean," he came back at her, "that we should be careful."

How dare he cheapen what they had done? How dare he attribute such motives to her when what she felt for him was respect?

A sneer curled the edges of her mouth, and she blurted the first cutting words that came to mind. "Don't make any sacrifices of yourself, Harris Chandler. We wouldn't want that. No sacrifices."

His face darkened. "What're you saying? You're taking this all out of context, Summer." His chest rose and fell. "I only said—"

"You said!" she cried. "You said that you wouldn't marry me if I were pregnant. That's what you said. Well, I believed in you, Harris. I believed in you as a decent man. I put myself on the line for you, damn it. I threw away a career for you!"

Chapter Ten

Summer had never been a pouter. Angelica was a pouter. Martin had been a pouter. Perhaps, she thought, she wasn't skilled at it because she had never had the misfortune of knowing Harris Chandler.

He was the best excuse she would ever have, so she avoided Harris's eyes and talked silly nonsense to Anita. Harris—she couldn't quite say he was pouting—avoided her eyes and talked nonsense to Titus.

Titus and Anita didn't avoid anyone's eyes; they looked at each other as if to say, "What in hell happened?"

Summer made her phone call to Arthur and Harris made his to Bud just before early morning news came on Channel Two. At least two sets in the area were turned on for the news, the kitchen set in Titus Little's house and a portable set Lila Dean had set up on her bedroom vanity so she could get a head start on the day while she tried to do something with her hopeless face.

"The search for Summer MacLean and Harris Chandler continues," the reporter was saying as Lila flicked on the knob.

"According to authorities, the assistant prosecutor of Dade County and the Miami developer were last seen in the western quadrant of Palm Beach County. Harris Chandler—" here a photograph flashed onto the screen "—has been charged with grand larceny in the recent Pinnacle Bank investigation and is now wanted for questioning in the death of Deputy Sheriff Henry Delaney. Summer MacLean, allegedly handcuffed to the man wanted by Dade County officials, is the widow of the late Dr. Martin MacLean. It has been expected that Mrs. MacLean will announce her candidacy for the office of state prosecutor in the upcoming election. Chandler, a twice-convicted man, is not thought to be armed but should be considered dangerous. Anyone knowing of his whereabouts should contact the Dade County sheriff's department immediately."

Deep in thought, Lila Dean sat holding her mascara wand. On impulse she rose and walked to the phone. When her editor answered she told him she wanted two days off. When he asked her why, she told him she was going to Lansing, Michigan.

"For what?" he wanted to know.

"I want to see what I can find out about Harris Chandler."

"You're carrying this too far, Lila. I don't think it'll be worth it."

"I'll pay my own way," Lila told him. "My nose itches on this one, Josh."

Josh wasn't quick to disregard Lila's nose. "You think he's innocent, don't you?"

"Well, I certainly don't think he killed Hank Delaney, if that's what you mean. I'm getting quite a file on the man, Josh, and it's all copy material. Book material, even. I'm telling you, this thing would already make a pretty good TV movie.''

''All right,'' Josh told her slowly, ''but the paper'll buy your ticket. And if you call your friend at *People* magazine, you're fired.''

The four adults in Titus Little's kitchen exchanged a dozenth, wondering glance when the spot was finished. Harris was slouching moodily near the door, smoking one cigarette after the other. Summer, after slamming one of Anita's ashtrays near him, moved to the opposite side of the room and continued practicing her sulk.

Titus, walking over and thoughtfully turning off the set, said, ''I guess someone should call the sheriff, now. To set them straight about Delaney.''

Feeling the pull of Summer's stare, Harris threw her a glance that said. ''Be my guest,'' and pushed through the back door and went to stand on the porch.

Summer compelled herself to stay where she was, but she saw herself going to him and either beating her fists against his back or slipping her arms around his waist.

''Not quite yet, I think.'' She avoided Titus's visual query and walked to where her tote bag lay crumpled on the end of the counter.

From her bag she fished out a small book from beneath the clutter and flipped through the pages. Pressing it open, she returned to the telephone and dialed a number.

''Hello, Lila,'' she said when the telephone was jerked up on the first ring.

''Make it quick, lady,'' came the brusque reply. ''I'm on my way to catch a plane.''

''This is Summer MacLean, Lila.''

A breathy pause occurred on the other end of the line. Summer turned her back to the room so she could hear better, but Harris, overhearing, walked through the back door and came to stand quietly behind her.

"What're you doing?" he muttered.

Summer pushed him away as Lila swiftly rejoined. "I've got time enough for you, Mrs. MacLean. Do you know that half the state is looking for the two of you?"

"Lila," Summer said and held up a forearm to keep Harris from taking the receiver, "how would you like a story?"

Another pause. A breath. Then, "About Chandler?"

"I'm his attorney."

Lila gasped. "Do you know I was just on my way to Michigan to talk to his father?"

"When will you get back?"

"I'll hold off going if you'll give me the story today."

Summer consulted her wristwatch. "I should be back in Miami sometime late this evening. Mr. Chandler and I have a small errand to run. Then we'll be calling the sheriff."

Harris grabbed at the receiver. "You're not coming with me. Damn it, Summer."

For a moment Lila was silent. "Is that Chandler I hear? Where are you, Mrs. MacLean?"

"I'll talk to you in Miami later tonight, Lila."

"This had better be good," Lila said before she hung up. "The state prosecutor is frothing at the mouth for Chandler's hide."

Which raised the question they all had asked: Why? Why all this?

There came a time, Summer knew, as she carefully hung up the telephone, when the handwriting was simply on the wall: zero hour, bottom line, nitty gritty, angel wings. She knew the way a woman knows when a man's been cheating, that Neil Jarvis's involvement in Pinnacle's collapse was unhealthy. And so was Herschel Starky's.

In all likelihood, Harris's first conjecture—that Starky had an account at Pinnacle State Bank, that he had made the false notes himself—was true. For Neil to be so unreasonably determined, he had to be protecting the good judge.

Summer supposed she had considered going after Starky before this. She knew now why Harris kept the world at bay. It left him a free man. Well, without the state prosecutor's position dangling before her nose, she was a free woman, too. She shuddered. She'd never taken on anything this heavy.

Everyone was walking out onto the back veranda now. Titus and Harris stood apart from everyone else, the coffee cups in their hands sending up brief swirls of steam to dissipate quickly in the hot morning air.

To break the tension, Summer said with a tiny, modelish pose to Anita, "Well, how do I look in your clothes, Anita?"

Anita's dark eyes twinkled. "A whale of a lot better than I do, but that's not saying much. I look like a whale."

Summer laughed. She inclined her head to the men. "What's going on over there?"

When Kyle strolled up, Anita drew him to her side. Bending, she kissed him. "I think Titus is trying to convince Harris to turn the ranch into a boys' school."

"Aw, Mo-om," Kyle singsonged.

"Sounds like someone at my house," Summer said. Both mothers laughed. Summer stopped, cocked her head. "You're kidding about the school, right?"

Eyes wide, head shaking, Anita drolly said, "No, I'm not. Titus worked out the whole remainder of Harris's life while you were showering."

And screwing up the rest of my life, Summer could have added.

"Just make sure the old clunker has oil." Titus was explaining about the pickup he was preparing to loan Harris. "Return it when you can. No big deal."

Still shirtless, Harris watched as Titus worked to pick the lock of the handcuffs. They were both quickly coming to the conclusion that it would take a locksmith.

"Didn't any of those kids at your school teach you how to do this?" Titus asked as he worked a stylus into the slot.

Harris took a drag on his cigarette. "I can crack a safe, Titus. I can't pick locks."

Grinning, Titus looked up. "The least you could do if you're going to smoke those things is offer me one." He stopped fussing with the handcuff and lit a smoke from the glowing tip of Harris's. "What're you going to do if you can't find your accountant, Harris? You know, the big guys could have come in with the warrants already."

Turning his attention to Summer, Harris replied, "That would be a raincloud on my picnic, Titus."

The black man musingly picked up the path of Harris's stare. Presently, he said, "You've heard the cliché about a silver lining in every cloud?"

Harris chuckled grimly. Summer was as untouchable as ever. He'd hurt her with his damnable pride. "I've always been more into the blessings in disguise, myself."

"Well, you can call *that*—" Titus inclined his head to Summer as she laughed at something Anita had said, "—one of the most disguised."

Looking up, Harris blinked. "Sorry, my mind wandered. What did you say?"

"That you should never underestimate her."

"Me? Underestimate the Assistant Prosecuting Attorney of Dade County?"

"I was talking more about just plain Summer Mac-Lean."

"Ah, yes." Harris sighed. "I do know what you mean."

Titus grinned. "I kind'a thought you would."

Off the kitchen of the Little ranch was a small niche that could be entered either from the outside or from the inside. There Anita had her washer and dryer set up. She had insisted on it being that way. She wasn't living in the same house with piled-up laundry for six people.

The dryer had just finished its cycle, and she was there now, motioning Summer over as she emptied a load and picked out Harris's black T-shirt and Summer's jeans and top.

Summer smiled as she folded the clothes, pausing for a moment to place her palm upon their warmth. There was something mysteriously pleasant about handling a man's clean laundry, something more intimate in its way than sex.

She unexpectedly wanted to be near Harris. She'd been unreasonable before. She wanted to apologize. Smiling at Anita, she turned to walk over to where the two men stood. They were watching her and smiling.

Unfortunately, Summer's turn coincided with two other events, one of them being the precise moment when a red wasp returned to search for his nest from which he had been so rudely evicted, and the other being the return of Titus's three daughters.

They bounded up the back steps, whooping and yelling and drowning out Anita's motherly scolding. The wasp stung Summer on the side of her neck, poison as painfully injected as if by a needle and, to her, just as lethal. Summer whirled around, not knowing what had happened and slapped automatically at the back of her neck.

"Oh!" she said and connected with the wasp again.

This time he stung her on the hand and left his stinger there. Before she thought, she scraped it out and sent a triple injection of poison into her arm.

Anita turned to Summer to make some disparaging mother's remark as she shooed at the girls. Summer was stumbling back against the wall, flailing to keep from falling.

"Titus!" screamed Anita, knowing at once what had happened. She ran as fast as her clumsy weight would allow her to. "Oh, no! I've told you, Titus, and you just never listen. Over and over I've told you . . ."

Titus had already tuned out his wife's familiar railing. He gaped at Summer.

The children, also gaping, turned to their father and chimed, "Daddy, come quick."

The changes going on around Summer were split-second. She was only vaguely aware of them. She saw Harris's start and the raw, haggard fear that swept over him as he threw his cigarette to the ground and started toward her.

His long legs took the distance, and he reached her almost before she slid down to the floor of the veranda. Then he was sweeping her up into his arms.

"In the house," Anita directed like a general used to emergencies. She snatched Harris's T-shirt from Summer's trailing fingertips and hurried toward the door to hold it open.

"I'll get ice!" Titus shouted, then to the children, "Stay out of the way. I mean it."

Not since she was ten years old had this happened to Summer. Then she'd nearly died, but she supposed she'd outgrown it. With her head draped back over Harris's arm and her legs dangling against him, her shoes swinging from her toes, she wanted to tell him lies—that everything was all right, that it wasn't as bad as it looked. He mustn't think of her now. For once, he must put himself first.

But he was sitting down with her, and someone was placing cloths wrung out in ice water on her throat. She tried to lift her hand to show them, but it weighed too many pounds.

"There's another sting on her hand," Harris said, his voice brittle and scared.

Summer was floating. Pinpricks needled all over her. She could hardly breathe. Harris was shaking her.

"Summer. Oh, God, Summer, do you have anything you can take?" he was asking, shaking her, keeping her lucid in spite of herself.

Go after your books! We've come so far! She gestured to her throat. "I . . . can't—"

"I know, darling," Harris said with terror-stricken eyes. Then to Titus, from the end of a long tunnel, "We've got to get her to a hospital."

Before Titus could make a suggestion, Harris lunged to his feet. On his face was the crazed glaze of desperation. "I'm taking the truck to the hospital, Titus."

Titus caught Harris at the door. "Hey, Harris." He shook the frightened man's arm, but Harris appeared to be in a private world of misery. "I'll take her, Harris. Let me take her, man. Put her in the front seat. Nita, you can go with me."

Harris kept doggedly striding toward Titus's garage. Titus found himself walking sideways and backward in an attempt to reason with him. "Harris? Hey, man, listen to me. You'll be spotted, Harris. You hear what I'm telling you? Listen, you show your face in West Palm, you can kiss those records goodbye."

"Get out of my way, Titus."

From her upside-down world, Summer was dazedly attempting to focus her eyes. A topsy-turvy pickup door was opening. She saw a dashboard in reverse.

Titus placed his hand upon the door handle to try to reach Harris one more time. "I think I have the right to call you friend now, Harris. I'm being honest with you. You're making a mistake."

When Harris wrenched his head around, bright tears clung to the tips of his lashes. "Do you think I care about mistakes, Titus? Don't you see that nothing matters if something happens to this woman?"

The black man knew what Harris was feeling. Love, when it came, was often without warning. It knew no mercy. It made fools of everyone.

"Get in," he said. "And hang on."

By the time Titus swung the 4X4 beneath the emergency ramp of The Hospital of the Palms, Summer's blood pressure was hovering at twenty. Harris's whole life had passed before his eyes as he'd held Summer in his arms and silently wished that Titus could drive faster, though the speedometer needle trembled between eighty and ninety miles an hour on the dusty roads.

The moment the brakes screamed on the asphalt, Harris was bounding out of the truck. His feet struck the pavement with a thud, and he took a fresh grip upon Summer and dashed for the rear doors. His back and arms burned with strain.

He kicked savagely at one of the doors. "Get this thing open!" he yelled to the orderly on the opposite side of the Plexiglas.

Titus parked the truck and headed for the doors himself.

Orderlies and waiting patients scrambled out of the way as Harris ran down the hall with Summer. The nurse who ducked out of a room cried out, "Where are you going?"

"Wasp stings!" Harris choked on the words.

"Put her on that table." The nurse, who was a good nurse and skilled at remembering people, instantly recognized the tall man's face she'd seen on television, even beneath the newly sprouting beard. She saw the broken handcuff on his wrist, and one on the patient's. She also saw the huge black man who came to wait in the doorway.

Stepping outside, she dialed an extension and received the order to fill a syringe. Returning, she ordered Harris out of the way. As he went to stand by the black man, she placed an oxygen mask over Summer's face and told another nurse to stay close and watch the vital signs. Then she walked into the office next door and called the police.

The man who answered the call was Pete Cavassas. The moment the dispatcher buzzed him, he was the man on the case. Harris Chandler was responsible for his friend's death.

"Is Harris Chandler still here?" he asked one of the nurses outside before he even walked into the emergency room.

By now, all of the staff was aware of who the man was who'd brought in the allergy case. The nurse pointed to the room where Summer was slowly responding to the injection. "He's in there."

"All right," Pete said. "Please keep this area clear."

Motioning to his partner, Pete flipped open the strap that held his .38 in place, but he didn't draw it. He wanted this collar to be as neat as pie. His instincts told him that Harris Chandler would come quietly, anyway.

Upon entering the emergency room, he officiously announced, "I'm with the Palm Beach County sheriff's department, Mr. Chandler. Would you please stand exactly where you are? Don't even so much as blink, or I'm going to do to you what you did to Hank Delaney."

As he stood holding Summer's hand, Harris was aware of his own breathing, of the pulse pounding in his ear. His rage began in the hollows of his knees and moved through him like fire, but by the time it reached his face and his fists, he had already clamped down upon it with a control that was perfectly deadly, perfectly cold-blooded.

He exchanged a look with Titus, warning him to stay out of this. To Pete Cavassas, he said, "I'll come with you in a few minutes. Not now."

Pete relished bringing Chandler down. He moved nearer, stared straight into the strong features of the man: the hard planes of forehead and cheek, the broken nose, the long, shapely mouth that was presently curved with a malicious twist—not quite a sneer. His bare-chested body was strung tightly upon some private torment.

"I'm afraid I'm in a bit of a hurry, Mr. Chandler," he said.

The man's eyes narrowed until they were blue slits. They glittered keenly. Without moving a muscle, he conveyed a sense of violence. Between his teeth, he said, "Get out of my face."

Pete saw small muscles twitching convulsively beneath the man's skin. Unwittingly he stepped back.

Struggling with the swirls from the medication they had given her, Summer wet her lips. She saw Pete Cavassas and thought for a moment it was Hank. But Harris was bending over her. Smiling unhappily, kissing her forehead, he smoothed the flyaway hair back from her face and shut out the room with his back.

"Summer," he whispered as he blinked rapidly, "I'm going to have to leave you for a little while, sweetheart."

Unable to speak, she nodded. She knew that already.

Harris thought his throbbing heart would burst. He hardly cared if it did. Part of it moved up into his throat and threatened to burst that, too. "I never thought... In all those years, I never thought—"

There were no words. They didn't need any. Summoning every shred of strength left in her body, Summer squeezed hard upon the rough, calloused hand holding hers. Their handcuffs clinked against the other.

Trying to smile, she fumbled with the broken chain and held it back together the way it had been. But it was broken, and she couldn't fix it. Her lips quivered uncontrollably.

"Mr. Chandler." Pete Cavassas touched the back of Harris's arm.

Jerking back, the wild look Harris flicked the man was capable of terrible things. He saw fear in Cavassas's dropping jaw, but Harris knew the inevitability of his position.

Bending, he kissed Summer's lips for a final time and licked the salt of her tears. For a moment he held the dangling chain she'd tried to make fit.

"What's here," he touched his breast over his heart, "is stronger than steel."

She compressed her lips tightly.

Moving to her ear, he whispered, "I love you, Summer." He wheeled hard on his heel, then, and walked out of the room with Pete Cavassas a few steps behind him.

Any good dictionary defined histamines and antihistamines: histamine—an organic substance that is released from the tissues during conditions of stress, inflammation and allergy; antihistamines—a group of synthetic drugs, counteracting the effects of histamine by competing with the latter at its sites of action.

A decent medical encyclopedia informed any lay person that, used in sufficiently large doses, nearly all antihistamines produced undesirable side effects. The most common in adults was drowsiness.

The shot the doctor gave Summer knocked her out for four hours. During that time, Titus Little never left her side.

At three o'clock in the afternoon, Pat and Arthur rushed into Summer's room and found her sleeping. Pat looked at the black man with affront, then dismissed him. Arthur introduced himself.

"What did they give her?" Pat demanded of the nurse.

The nurse smiled the universal smile of medical people. "You'll have to ask the doctor. I'm not allowed to give out that information." She did, however, oblige the MacLeans by taking a short break while they were in the room.

What Arthur and Pat could not know, however, nor the nurse, nor Titus, was that only Summer's face was asleep; her brain was bravely fighting its way up from the injection. She wanted to lift her hand and tell Pat that she knew they were in the room. She wanted to ask how Tom was. She wanted to find out what they knew about Harris.

"A dreadful business," Arthur said to Titus Little and stood before the window with him, not realizing what an incongruous pair they made—he in his neat three-piece suit and neatly rimmed glasses, Titus in wrinkled jeans and his bright orange shirt. "You know, I don't think I truly appreciated my daughter-in-law until this happened."

"She looks so innocent lying there," Pat said to her husband's back. "Do you remember how we used to stand over Martin when he was little? Worried over him? Fretted."

Arthur came to stand beside his wife. "Tom looks just like her. Never did favor his daddy."

Perhaps it was the mention of her most dreaded subject that gave Summer the final surge of strength to throw off her stupor. Moaning, she pulled up onto her pillow and lay with her eyes closed.

Before Pat could do more than take Summer's hand, a tap sounded on the door. A woman poked a homely face inside the room, took a look around and spotted Summer. "Is she awake?"

All three heads turned to the woman as if to ask, "Who are you?"

Stepping inside, the woman smiled. "I'm Lila Dean. It's taken me all day to find Mrs. MacLean."

For the next half hour, Summer lay with her eyes closed and listened to a strangely mixed conversation about Harris Chandler and herself. Titus explained to the reporter everything that had happened. Lila interviewed the Mac-Leans, and Summer was shocked to hear Arthur calling her Summer and capitulating with Titus's sympathy for Harris; Arthur was the last person she would expect to understand a man like Harris Chandler.

When Lila picked all their brains about Harris's school, it seemed clear to Summer that Lila was catching the same glimpse of Harris that she had caught herself: Harris's odd brand of integrity and far-reaching dignity.

"Lila," she said groggily, "I'm sorry I didn't make it to Miami when I said."

"Hey." The reporter came to stand beside the bed. "You're awake. Listen, I understand. I've found something of a story in Mr. Little, here. In fact, I'm coming to the conclusion that he and Harris Chandler are a matched pair."

"Lila," Summer said and reached out her hand, "there's something I wish you'd do for me."

"Name it."

"Bail Harris out of jail."

Titus made an unintelligible sound as he moved to interrupt. "Uh, I was going to do that myself. The minute you waked up."

Lila waved him away. "Nonsense. I've got one of my friends at the television station out at the airport. To tell you the truth, we 'borrowed' their helicopter. I'll be back in Miami before you can sneeze."

"I'll come with you."

"I don't care who does it," Summer said and waved limply in the direction of the utility closet. "Pat, would you bring... My bag! I don't have my bag."

"It's at the ranch," Titus reminded her.

Dropping back to her pillow in thwarted hope, she scoured her cheeks. They still felt dead. "I need my checkbook."

Arthur was already pulling out his own checkbook. "I'll foot the bail," he quietly offered, "if Mr. Little will take it."

"Arthur!" Pat exclaimed.

The older woman's protest sliced through the room like an out-of-tune note in an important performance. Everyone looked at the other, but no one said anything.

Feeling compelled to go through with her explanation now, Pat drew her husband aside and argued. "You don't even know this man, Arthur. I've never known you to be so irresponsible. You have to tell them you were mistaken. I won't have you getting our names linked with a convict."

Arthur felt as if he were waking up after a long sleep. For a year now he had wallowed around in his self-pity. He blamed Summer for something that no one was to blame for. She had gone on with her life, keeping up with the routine, marking time but doing it diligently, and he had faulted her for it. His son was dead. But Summer was not, and Martin had loved her. Tom was alive. And this Harris Chandler with his son's face—if Summer believed in this man Chandler, it was good enough for him. Or perhaps it was good enough simply because he wanted it to be good enough.

Leaning over, he placed a perfunctory kiss upon his wife's cheek. "For the first time in my life, my dear, I'm going to tell you no." Without waiting to see her reaction, he scrawled his name across a check and handed it to Titus Little. He said, "You don't have to make a big deal with Mr. Chandler about who paid this."

The huge man stood with thoughtfully puckered lips. When this was all over, Arthur MacLean was a man he wanted to come to know.

"Cool, Mr. MacLean," he said with a wide grin. "Real cool." He walked over to Summer's bed and kissed her forehead. "I'll take care of him real good, Mrs. MacLean."

Summer sighed with relief. She didn't care that tears shone in her eyes. "I know you will, Titus."

Pat was the only one left in the room who wasn't smiling when Lila Dean left with Titus.

When Angelica Santez whipped her bright red Volvo off Biscayne Boulevard, she was coming from her mother's house over on the side of Miami where high-crime street-lights washed all the color out of everything, and husks of men huddled in the doorways to dream of good liquor.

She pulled up beneath the canopy of the posh Olympic Hotel and, to her dismay, instantly recognized the valet. For one second her blood ran cold, and she considered whipping out of the drive and parking down the street and returning to the hotel on foot.

But it was too late. Tony had already seen her. Angelica threw back her head as he ran up wearing his valet's jacket. When he saw who she was, he stopped and shifted his weight to a jaunty hip. He ran his eyes over the car, whistled under his breath.

"Hey, Mama, check it out." He trailed a finger over the shiny paint job. "What'd you do, rob a bank? What're you doin' here, Angel? Slummin'?"

"You got a dirty mind, Tony," she snapped and jammed the gearshift into park.

He swept open her car door.

Angelica winced. She'd known Tony Domingue all her life. They'd grown up in the same building. Not the same exact building, but on their side of Miami the buildings were the same. She'd lost her virginity to Tony. An eternity ago. She'd moved up. Tony hadn't.

"Tsk, tsk, tsk. That's no way for an old friend to talk," Tony chided insultingly. "If that little rear of yours gets any more expensive, baby, you'll have the IRS on your back."

"I came here to visit a sick friend."

"Sick of what?"

Angelica whirled away.

Regretting his insults, for something deeply buried in his genes made him still care about her, Tony followed her and tried to restore communication. He patted the paper poking out of his back pocket. "Wish I had a cushy job over at the municipal building. What's the latest on your boss? Hey, Angel, come on."

Angelica made her black silk dress swirl haughtily as she faced him. A toss of her head sent her billowing hair afloat. "She's in a West Palm hospital." Angelica's fist found her hip. "Are you going to keep your mouth shut about seeing me here? Every time I go home my mother starts in on me about something your mother told her. Which, I suspect, came from you in the first place."

Tony held up his hands. "I've been your friend longer than you've been mine. 'Course," he eyed her legs and her chic spike heels, "I can be bribed to be a better friend."

Smirking because she knew it wasn't what he meant, Angelica slapped a five-dollar bill in his hand. As she clicked across the asphalt to the front steps, she threw over her shoulder, "Has anybody ever told you that you're crass, Tony?"

His laughter drifted after her. "Not anyone who looks like you, *Miss* Santez."

With a pretty smile for the doorman, Angelica breezed into the lobby of Miami's finest hotel. She strode quickly and boldly, aware that every male head in the place was turning for that second look and would liked to have made eye contact long enough to size up his chances.

"Yes, madam," the man at the registration desk said as he took one look at her and knew what she'd come for. "What may I do for you?"

"Santez. Any messages for me?"

The man looked over his shoulder into the slot beneath the S. He drew out an envelope. Without feeling it, he knew there was a room key inside, but his smile was flawless as he read the name on the outside.

"Yes, madam, I believe we do."

"Thank you."

Only when she was alone in the elevator did Angelica allow her nerves to show. Slumping back against the wall, she looked more like the little girl back in that two-room walkup.

She tore open the envelope and read the number on the key, then she pushed the button to the fourth floor and waited patiently for the conveyance to hum its way up. Stepping outside, she glanced at the numbers and turned left. When she came to 412, she slipped the key into the lock and turned.

"Neil?" she called softly as she walked in and let the door shut.

The room was almost dark, and the drapes were drawn. The tall shadow before the window moved, walked across the plush carpet. The smell of rum was strong on Neil's breath.

"Baby, am I glad you're here," he said and crushed her in his arms. "This thing with Summer's had me going crazy all day."

"When you called, I was surprised." She circled his head and pulled his mouth down to her for a kiss. "Don't get me wrong, I'm glad you called. So glad."

Neil held the kiss longer than he wanted to. Removing Angelica's arms from around his neck then, he returned to the bar and poured himself another drink. He gestured with it to her.

"Don't let me have too many of these. They make me a little crazy." Sipping, he let the blissful feeling take him. Then he said, "Have you heard anything? Is she still in the hospital?"

Angelica poured herself something to drink and shook her head. "I don't know."

"You'll tell me if she calls."

She shot him a surprised glance. "Of course, but you'll hear, Neil. You'll hear before I do."

He swiveled around to the window and stood contemplating the liquor in his glass. "I was the one who had her sign the damn warrant. She's mad at me. Hell..."

He rolled the glass on his forehead, and Angelica walked up behind him, circled his waist and pressed herself to his buttocks.

"Neil, it's all a fluke. No one in their right mind could have foreseen a thing like this. Chandler and her on the same train...that deputy handcuffing them together like that."

Neil clasped Angelica's arms tighter around him so that he could feel the high firmness of her breasts against his back. "She doesn't have any idea about us, does she?"

Stunned, Angelica jerked away. She had half a mind to walk out on him. Honestly! But, letting her shoulders droop prettily, she knew she wouldn't. "Of course, not. Didn't I give you my word?"

He crossed the room to her, circled her with both arms and clasped his hands behind her back. "Sorry. That was low. I just don't want any office gossip, Angel. And I'm going to pay Summer back for all this mess. I'm going to get her elected, you mark my words. But everything has to be clean there. No talk, no nothing. You'll protect us both, won't you, Angel? You'll warn me if there's any talk? I mean, *any* talk?"

He was drunk, Angelica knew. But at least he was a sweet drunk. She took the glass out of his hand and walked him to bed and pushed him gently down onto it. As he watched, she began taking off her dress.

"Of course I'll protect you, you pussycat. But there's not going to be any talk. Summer will come back safe and sound, and whatever will happen, will happen."

"I know." Neil buried his face into Angelica's stomach. "Just promise me, sweet Angel. Sweet, sweet Angel."

Angel let her head tip back as Neil assaulted her. Her whole future could lie with this man. Who would have thought that she, a little Puerto Rican girl, one of seven, could be making it with the state prosecutor? She couldn't blow her chance with Neil. This would be the only one she would ever get.

Chapter Eleven

The day Summer returned to Miami, Pinnacle State Bank made front-page headlines.

Along with pictures of Rex Jernigan and one of Harris. Rex was out on bail. For a reason that Summer suspected had something to do with Herschel Starky, Harris's release had been delayed.

With Tom still at his grandparents', Summer's first outraged thought was go to the county jail and cause a scene, but Harris would never forgive her for that. If the positions were reversed, what would Harris do for her?

She waited quietly at home and sat on her hands to keep from chewing her nails. For almost an entire day with her career on hold, her life on hold, her heart on hold. When Lila Dean called and said her piece on Harris was ready to go to press, she begged her to wait until Harris could look at it himself.

"People are going to eat 'im up, Summer," Lila promised. "A reluctant hero? In this age? You know, when I was writing about him I thought of Gary Cooper, or those heroes Gregory Peck used to play. Strong, silent. You know what I mean?"

In the protection of her living room, Summer buried her face in her hand. Yes, she knew. She swallowed. "Would you hold off just one more day, Lila?"

"Why, for crying out loud?"

"Just . . . will you do that for me? I'll never ask another thing of you, I swear. Just this once."

Lila reluctantly agreed to hold the piece.

When the phone rang again, Summer started with a gasp. She snatched it up. "What!"

"Will you meet me?"

His voice was heartbreakingly weary. Summer asked only one word, "Where?"

They were both too fragile to brave the realities of home or telephones. They went to a quiet motel. Once the door was shut on the world, they went into each other's arms for long, long moments.

Teary-eyed but made happy by the warmth and the unquestioning sense of safety they found in each other, they kissed endlessly. All they could say was the name of the other and taste the honeyed boundaries. Soon, however, as if moved by the same necessities—Summer had taken precautions against pregnancy this time—they showered. They kissed again. They burrowed into each other's arms. Then they pulled away. There was still too much. Too many complex problems. Summer guessed she could have spared herself the precautions.

Presently, with the moments drifting into history like sand filtering through an hour glass, even the words slowed down. Undressed, they lay beneath the sheets. Looks were their words. Then, with casual, careless touches, they gradually began to talk.

They talked. And talked. And talked. They talked legal strategy and Starky's guilt, Titus and Anita Little, Tom, Martin, Bud. They called out for food and let it stand without tasting it. They talked pride and humility. They talked until they were empty of talking.

Hours later, Harris finished a cigarette. Summer lay upon his chest, her cheek pressed into the scar.

"Tell me about this," she said, kissing it.

"Not much to tell. Some of the boys and myself were picking apples in Michigan. A couple of us got caught without a ladder over a chainlink fence. We jumped. He missed the fence. I didn't."

"I love your flair for detail, Harris."

"Turn over. I'll rub your back."

It was heaven being at the mercy of Harris's strong, rough hands. Summer sighed with bliss as some of the strain filtered out of her aching limbs.

"Don't try to seduce me," she teased lightly. "All my body processes died at ten o'clock."

"Do you think you're dealing with a charged battery here?" he countered, laughing. "Hell, Summer, I'm getting too old for this."

"Maybe I'd better run out and get a magazine that tells us how to do it."

They laughed. Then they laughed because they didn't know what to laugh about. Summer was more comfortable with Harris than she'd ever been, but she felt vulnerable, too. A woman without secrets was a target for any man, even Harris Chandler.

Without warning, he pulled the sheet completely off her and she reached back to claw for it. He said, "Don't do that."

Unable to forget the sight of herself standing before the mirror examining her thirty-four-year-old behind, Summer realized with a flush that she wasn't quite as comfortable with Harris as she'd thought. She reached for the lamp beside the bed.

He refused her that, too. "Uh-huh. You're all right."

"Oh, God."

Summer squeezed her eyes tightly shut and steeled herself to endure his lingering kisses from the top of her head to the soles of her feet. But when he started licking her, her limbs trembled uncontrollably. There was no skilled technique to it, he was simply doing what brought him pleasure, and by the time he had made an exploratory tour all over her back, dampness had welled between Summer's legs.

She felt at once a tremendous power and a total helplessness. "Harris?" she whimpered as he reached under her waist and pulled her back up to him.

"Shh," he whispered and slid his tongue down the relief of her spine and into the silky furrow.

In all of her fantasies, Summer had not known that so many sensations lay yet untapped within her woman's body, or that they would be sharpened to such a breathtaking edge. Harris's huge pleasure in what he was doing made her feel disembodied.

But such rapture was not to be borne more than a few moments. When he finally did enter her, Summer was more ready than before. There was no pain, though he was remarkably aroused and she could feel all the hard and soft places, all the hooded mysteries. They communicated with stops and starts that were enormously private and tender.

A murmur: "How do you feel?"

"Wonderful."

"Does it hurt?"

"I want it to last forever. Touch me here."

"Here?"

"And there."

"I've always wondered how good it would be."

"No one can make you feel like this."

"I don't want anyone to make me feel like this but you."

Harris lost himself, lost all of the pride he had cherished for so long. He gave Summer everything. He didn't care; he had nothing to prove with this woman. He knew she would never judge him on this level, so he didn't think in terms of endurance or technique. What he lacked, she would make up for, just as he would make up for what she lacked.

His energy seemed to respond to her hands and her mouth and her whispered words and her kisses as she reciprocated. Her nipples were aroused and tender, and she licked her finger and touched them.

Just watching her was enough to make him insane, Harris thought. But he wanted her to make more demands. He wanted to touch the very core of her dreams. He let her turn him onto his stomach, and when she kissed *him* from the top of his head to the soles of his feet, he let her know that he adored it.

She made further demands, knowing that he liked them. She turned him over and climbed upon his waist. When he wanted to thrust up inside her, she refused him. She sold herself to him with a look and arched herself higher so that he laughed and tasted of her while she pulled his hair.

She demanded the whole of his body then, and he refused. It became a test of enormous proportions. She took him in both hands and engulfed him, and she was no longer gentle. She ran her nails down the inside of his legs and virtually drew pain from the very marrow of his bones.

Harris was stunned, and ecstatic and enraged. She made him feel as if a steel rod was driving upward through his body to the top of his head. She refused to stop but forced him nearer and nearer the brink, threatening him if he went over. By the time Harris fought himself loose from her, he was aching and vibrating. He threw her to her back and she reached up for him, but he was too quick.

Her mouth was open when he plunged into her. Her hair was a swirling cloud. She didn't want his kisses, she wanted only the savage thrusting, thrusting.

"Damnation," he groaned, bending over her like some driven beast, bent on destroying her.

"Just do it," she demanded and pushed her breasts against him.

Through viciously clenched teeth, he hissed, "I can't stand this." He thought that he would surely have a heart attack trying to please this woman.

"More."

"Summer—"

"More."

She shuddered over and over with release, until Harris began to hate her for it. Then, feeling as if he were sliding over that threshold into a pit of flames, he found his own, and it was a mixture of pain and pleasure that he had never experienced before.

"Jesus, lady," he mumbled when he lay upon her, crushing her but too exhausted to move. "Are you trying to kill me?"

Her eyes were still closed. She still couldn't breathe. She felt poured upon the ground. "If you so much as touch me again, Harris Chandler, I think I really will kill you."

Before they went to sleep, Harris hoped that she would say she loved him, for he knew in his heart that she did. But she didn't say the words, and he wasn't sure, when he thought back upon it, that she remembered when he had said them to her.

As Summer strode down the hall toward Judge Starky's chambers on her first day back at work, she dreaded facing the man.

Herschel Starky's private chambers looked like the back room of a Georgia grocery store during the great Depression. Summer had always suspected that if a person looked long enough they could find an old Studebaker hubcap. Or perhaps one of Huey P. Long's old hats.

The judge himself could usually be found back of the jars and boxes of books and papers and stacks of folders and old campaign handbills on his desk—sitting as near to the dusty chaos as his girth and emphysema would allow.

Few people invaded the inner sanctum, however, for few got past the arsenal of beautiful, red-lipped secretaries with whom Starky adorned his front office. The good judge had been known to adorn his arm with one of them upon occasion, but Summer didn't believe there was any truth to the rumor that the Florida judge cheated on his wife. She didn't think Starky had the nerve.

When Summer walked into his outer office and slammed the door behind her—no one, not even a circuit judge, could hang up on her and get away with it—three gorgeous creatures glanced up from their IBMs.

What Summer could not know was how much Harris Chandler had changed her. The secretaries were stunned. Instead of being in its customary bun at her nape, Summer's hair poufed loosely on the top of her head in a doughnut with a shiny knot atop it. Most of the sun she'd gotten in West Palm Beach County had turned into a very respectable tan, and she was wearing a pair of loose indigo linen slacks.

Never, in the seven years that Summer had worked for the State of Florida, could any of the secretaries remember Summer wearing pants to work, much less with a knit top and a flowing fuchsia shirt worn outside with the tails softly looped in front. Plain silver hoops hung from her ears, but her eyes were silkily and subtly shadowed so that the brown of her irises had come alive, and her lashes were velvety thick. Her nails weren't painted, but they were immaculately manicured and buffed. On her wrist was a simple but extremely expensive wristwatch.

"My God," muttered Lindy Sedita as she chipped a lacquered nail on her space bar but continued to smile and speak from the corner of her mouth. "Will you get a load of this?"

"Palm Beach County fried her brain," Carol Hollis murmured and rose to her feet, leaving her hand discreetly poised on her intercom buzzer.

"Maybe it was the ex-con." The third secretary, Ellen Pride leaned back in her chair and drawled, "Why, don't you look lovely, Mrs. MacLean? I declare, all of us were worried right out of our heads. What with that write-up of Lila Dean's on the front page about you wanderin' around in th' desert with a hardened criminal. And then havin' to go to th' hospital and ever'thing."

Summer stopped stone still in the office and looked at them all with dispassion. She had changed clothes four times before coming back to work. Did it show?

"Thank you, Ellen, for your sweet concern," she said with her reliable courtroom smile. "Lindy, it's good to see you again. Carol, I'd take it as a personal favor if you'd remove your hand from off that buzzer. Is His Honor in?"

Lindy, privately green with envy of Summer's overnight popularity, walked around her desk in her two-hundred-dollar Gucci's and gave the attorney an appraisal that would have intimidated Hitler. "Well, actually yes and no, Mrs. MacLean. The fact is—"

Summer's smile was enough to stop the younger woman dead in her tracks. "Don't bother to announce me, dear."

"But Mrs. MacLean—"

"You can't go in there," blurted Carol. "The judge gave strict orders that he doesn't wish to be disturbed."

Like hell I can't, Summer thought, and strode across the room before their three open mouths.

"That's too bad," she said and thrust open Starky's door without knocking.

When Summer stepped into the office, she found Herschel Starky leaning back against the wall in his swivel chair with his wing-tipped shoes balanced on the edge of his desk and his fat fingers laced over his swelling middle. He lunged forward in his chair as Carol followed Summer into the office.

"I'm very sorry about this, Your Honor," she said, nonplussed as she faced the other occupant of the room whom Summer was gaping at. "Mr. Jarvis. I . . ."

Summer's temperature dropped several degrees when she saw Neil. With a small inclination of her head, she smiled tactfully to her own boss and bent more respectfully to the judge.

"This is not Carol's fault," she said as she waved Neil back down into his chair. "I made her an offer she couldn't refuse."

Her attempt at humor was disgracefully bad. Neil came to his feet anyway and smoothly maneuvered himself around to the lovely blond secretary. He lifted her hand and placed it upon his arm and, escorting her to the door, gave the hand a pat.

"Don't give it a second thought, Carol," he cooed. "You didn't stand a chance with Summer. How do you think I became state prosecutor?"

Not even Neil's flattery could turn Carol's smile into anything more than a sick grimace. The woman sent Summer a you-haven't-heard-the-last-of-this look, and, with a final plea of forbearance from Judge Starky and a smoothing of her skirt over her hips that wasn't lost on the state prosecutor, she shut the door behind her.

The moment the door clicked shut, Neil let his hand drop from the brass knob. He spun around to face Summer, his usual composure marred.

He hissed through his teeth, "Have you taken leave of your senses?"

Summer guessed that she had, but she strode to the pile of disorganization that passed for Starky's desk. She didn't flinch as he fixed his drilling, gray-eyed look upon her that had been known to fell legal giants.

"You hung up on me," she said.

"That should have told you something," he said calmly.

She knew she must keep her anger from sounding like self-pity. "What it tells me, Your Honor, is that you have an inordinate interest in Harris Chandler's case before it's even come to trial."

The casters of Starky's chair squealed as he shot back to the wall and pried his bulk from the chair. His brows, fiercely black in comparison to his snow-white hair, seemed Satanic as they beetled together.

"Summer!" hissed Neil.

Starky's lips curled. "Watch yourself, girl. Don't do something you'll wish later that you hadn't."

A tremor of fear passed through Summer. She felt as if she'd just wired up a series of explosives to the bridges of her life and was about to push down the plunger on the detonator.

She shook her head and struggled to sound respectful. "Perhaps if I understood why, Your Honor. Harris Chandler is innocent. I can assure you that with every ounce of my life's blood."

Starky waved her away as if she were a whining child. "Don't speak to me about guilt or innocence. You're out of line here, counselor."

"Your Honor, I'm not prosecuting this case."

"I know. Dardis is."

Summer's breath was gone. She felt herself strangling on the loose ends of her good intentions and slammed her fist down upon a stack of papers and the dust swirled up in a maelstrom.

"Dardis is a piranha, sir."

Starky's expression was a dismissal. "It's decided."

"I don't think that's all that's been decided. The stench of this rot reeks to high heaven."

"Hold your tongue, girl!" Herschel Starky roared, then gagged with coughs, both from the settling dust and the exertion on his ailing lungs. He fished a handkerchief from his pockets and slapped aside Neil Jarvis's attempt to help.

"Get away, get away," he bellowed and reached out his other hand to point a finger at Summer. "And you, girl, if you say one more word, I'll have you thrown out the next time you darken the door of my courtroom."

Summer had a desperate, insane impulse to run and hide behind the first large object she could find. She was also offended and insulted, and she wanted to throw both back in the judge's face. But if she stood up for herself now, what would happen to Harris? Without her, he was doomed.

She had made a terrible mistake in pushing Starky. But it confirmed all her suspicions about him. A door opened behind her, and she didn't have to turn around to see Ellen.

A cruel smile of triumph curled Starky's face, and Summer knew that he had her. She had exposed herself. She was embarrassed.

Laughing, Starky waved negligently to his secretary. "Ellen, please show Ms. MacLean to the door. I think she came to fight a war and has just realized that she's lost her gun."

Starky's dismissal was a profanity. Summer felt it spilling her life's blood. She wanted to rush out, to go wash herself, to bind up her wounds. She wanted Harris.

But she had the length of that feminine domain to cross, and she tried to lift her head the way Harris had thrown his back in the face of the authorities. *I made my decision by choice,* she told herself. *Harris is innocent. I'm standing by him.*

But it hurt like hell, and she didn't know how she could bear it. She knew then what Harris had experienced when he'd crossed the system. It was the most awful aloneness she could imagine.

As she passed Angelica's booth, her friend spoke to her. "What's up, counselor?"

Either not hearing or with something inside her disabling her answer, Summer returned to her office. When Angelica walked in, Summer was turning a ceramic pencil holder in her hands, absently running her fingers over the glazed knobs.

"Summer?"

Rearing back, Summer threw it against her wall as hard as she could, and the sound of shattering glass seemed to echo forever. Angelica shut the inner door.

Summer stood looking at her, then blurted, "I'm going to have them both," she said with deadly intensity. "And I don't know who I want the worst, Starky or Neil."

"Ladies and gentlemen," Angelica announced in a sassy voice as she breezed into Summer's office with her arms laden with Chinese food. She kicked the door shut with a neat backward thrust of her spike heel, walked to Summer's desk in a swirl of royal blue jersey, and plunked down four white sacks.

"Ladies and gentle*man*. Angel," Tricia Reed, Summer's pretty blond assistant of twenty, corrected. She rose from her chair and locked the door behind the receptionist.

Angelica puckered her perfect mouth and leveled her look upon the only man in the room. His prematurely bald head was shining above a clipboard.

"Ahem!" Lowering the clipboard, Melvin Holland bared a mouthful of widely spaced teeth.

Melvin's one really great asset, besides a mind that was well nigh photographic, was a homely face that could go anywhere and never be seen. He was Summer's legman. People had a way of unconsciously baring their souls to him. Summer had lost count of the cases Melvin's face had won for her.

"I heard that," he said to Angelica in an unthreatening effeminate voice.

"Shut up, scrub," Tricia said. "What do you know?"

Angelica envied them all their camaraderie. She held up both her hands.

"Will you let me finish?" She poked her nose into the sacks on the desk. "Where was I? Oh, yes. Here you have, ladies and man, your sweet-and-sour chicken. You have your egg rolls, your noodles, and your cold-and-sticky white rice with all the vitamins removed. Plus your fortune cookies."

"Good grief, Angelica!" Summer exclaimed, lifting her head from a file with a laugh.

Angelica shrugged at her best friend. "Doesn't anyone eat tacos anymore?"

Mugging, Summer closed the file and tossed it to a stack of them. She pushed her chair back from her desk. "I'll get some paper plates. Never let it be said that a working lunch in this office isn't first class."

Melvin searched through the sacks. "I gave you a ten dollar bill, Angel. I hope you brought back the right change."

A fierce glare replaced Angelica's whimsical smile. "You've got to be kidding." This to Summer as she groped in her bag for Melvin's mismatched change, "How's it coming?"

Summer had stooped before a rank of floor-level shelves. She looked over her shoulder. "Which one? The tacky case Neil assigned us or Harris's?"

"Either one's a bust," Tricia cheerfully supplied as she swept aside all the newspaper clippings on the Pinnacle State Bank scandal.

Angelica questioned Summer with a disappointed look. "I thought you said it was coming along."

As Summer laid the paper plates on the desk and watched Melvin spooning rice, brown nausea rose up in her throat. She arranged a smile on her face. "I think we can raise reasonable doubt. But Harris is a purist. He wants vindication or nothing at all."

"If the accountant hadn't disappeared from the face of the earth with the alleged records, we might be okay," Melvin said and poked around in the sweet-and-sour chicken.

"They are *not* alleged records."

Summer's tone was so killingly meaningful that the two assistants exchanged a look with each other and sent Angelica a warning not to pursue the subject of Harris Chandler if she knew what was good for her. The assistant prosecutor had been extremely touchy ever since her run-in with Starky. The whole municipal building was buzzing about it.

Realizing that she was taking out her nerves on the people who were the most loyal, Summer busied herself with tidying up the desk even before they finished eating, which was an even worse giveaway.

Heaving a dreary sigh, she walked to the window and stared down at the patrolmen heading out to lunch.

Tricia sighed. Then Melvin sighed. Angelica, sliding from the side of the desk where she'd perched to cross her legs, walked over to slip her arm around Summer's waist.

"I'm sorry, Summer. I know it's a drag. But everybody around here thinks Chandler is innocent. It'll all work out, you'll see."

"Yeah," Tricia agreed, her mouth full.

The room took on an air of dejection.

Enough of that! Turning, Summer walked back to the desk with a directness that placed a spring in her step. She didn't bother to hide the angry mist glistening in her eyes. "I'm not taking any more of Neil's smirks, damn it, or Starky's nasty threats. All my life I've played by the rules. Sometimes they don't apply. It's time to get dirty."

"Yeah!" yelled Tricia.

"Right on!" crowed Angelica.

Melvin swallowed a mouthful without chewing it and smiled his goofy, space-toothed smile.

Tricia started boxing up the leftovers. "What's first?"

"I'll do that." Angelica took everything out of the junior assistant's hands. "Since I can't do anything else to help."

As if she were preparing to pray—and it occurred to Summer that praying wouldn't be such a bad idea, for what she was doing, if it wasn't downright illegal, could get her professional head lopped off—Summer pointed her finger at Melvin.

"I want you, Melvin, to find out if Judge Starky has an account at Pinnacle. Had an account, I should say. I don't care how you find out, and I don't want to know. Just do it."

Tricia stopped lipsticking her mouth to whistle. "God, Summer, you're really going after the man!"

Summer scratched at the center of her upper lip. "It's just not reasonable that he should be so rabid. Anyway, what can it hurt to find out? When we know, we'll go from there."

"But to where?" Tricia mumbled under her breath. "Hell?"

Hearing, Summer said with uncharacteristic bitterness, "Harris Chandler has been there and back. He deserves better."

When the telephone buzzed, Summer automatically picked up the receiver, pinched it between her shoulder and chin and motioned for Tricia to bring her the files stacked on her desk. She opened the first one and leafed through several pages.

She froze as she was, the sheet of paper extended. "What? *What?* Who is this? Will you speak louder, please?"

A hush spread over the room, and Tricia waved for Angelica to stop rustling the paper sacks.

"Yes, this is Mrs. MacLean," Summer said, changing ears. "Who? Sib? For crying out loud, man, where have you been...? Yes, I certainly do want them. Do you have them with you...? I see. Well, tell me where you are, and I'll come get them myself."

Summer waved a frantic hand to Melvin, and he slapped a pad in front of her. As Summer talked, she wrote down the accountant's location. "Key West? Yes, I know where the Conch Train is... All right. It'll take me a little while to get there, you understand. You stay put, hear...? Hey, wait a minute, wait a minute. How will you be dressed...? I know Harris will recognize you, but what do you have on...? Okay, I'll see you as soon as I can make it."

Hanging up, Summer threw her pencil happily at Angelica and tipped back her head with a merry giggle. Her hairdo fell to one side. Reaching back, she yanked out the pins that held it and shook it free.

"She's letting her hair down, ladies and man," Angelica announced with a smile.

Summer ran her fingers through the long locks and hurriedly began cramming things into her bag. "Angelica, take all my calls from the switchboard. We're back in the ball game."

"I'm sorry," Harris's deep voice came over the answering machine after everyone had cleared out of Summer's office and she dialed his house. "I'm not able to come to the phone right now. Summer, if that's you, I'm doing a job at Flagler and First. If it's someone else, the house is locked so don't bother."

"Damn!" Summer muttered to herself. "What am I going to do now?"

She thought of Sib out at Key West, waiting, then giving up and going home. She debated about catching the MetroRail and going back uptown and hunting for Harris. But by the time she found him and they got to her house and into her car, she could be halfway to Key West.

So now what? Drive the Bentley herself?

Summer felt fear unraveling in her throat. She had always known this day would come. She had imagined all the reasons why she would do it. None of them involved Harris, and now his future could crazily hinge upon whether she could overcome a phobia that had dogged her heels for months.

It was then, she guessed, that she knew the simplicity of the truth. Nothing but love for Harris could compel her to take her fear by the horns and conquer it.

Grabbing up her bag, she walked out of the municipal building.

All the way home on the MetroRail, she could hardly think about Sib for going over and over the facts; she was in love with a man who would never bend. Harris would never give her the edge that Martin had. Harris would go first, yes, but in doing that, he would be more his own man than ever.

By the time Summer reached home and read Tom's note saying that the MacLeans had brought him home and that they were shopping, sweat was collecting on her back. There was nothing whatsoever romantic about this aspect of love.

Flicking the key off the rack that perched above the kitchen stove, she studied it lying in her palm. She walked firmly into the garage and eyed the deep green automobile with mistrust.

Could she do this? She got into the car and carefully shut the door. She had been a good driver. It was just that the memories. . . .

The key turned easily in the lock, and the motor purred. Summer gently worked the gear. It moved like a charm. She closed her eyes for a moment and took a grip on herself. Then, looking over her shoulder, her heart pounding frightfully in her ears, she backed out into the street.

She miscalculated and jammed into the curb.

Oh, God! Coming forward, she sat with her head resting upon the steering wheel and sweat streaming down her sides and her stomach churning with a thousand butterflies and thought, *Harris, I don't know if I can do this, even for you.*

She had to. She simply had to.

By a process that she would really never remember, Summer managed, with a lot of overcompensating, a lot of slowing down blocks before an intersection, and a few dirty looks from other drivers, to reach Rickenback Causeway.

Jet planes were screaming over the vast expanse of water as Summer drove. She knew the highway. She and Martin had spent their honeymoon on Key West.

By the time she got the Bentley into a parking space at the tour train with its advertisement to see picturesque Key West and Hemingway's and Audubon's houses by way of tropical foliage and on Conch architecture, Summer had begun to worry that Sib would have given up on her.

After locking the car, she tried to see around the crowds of tourists to the pay booth where lines were already forming. Sib had said he would be by the concession stand and would be wearing a bright red knit shirt.

She glanced at her wristwatch. A quarter of two. There was an abundance of brightly colored shirts, some red-and-white stripes, some red-and-blue check. No solid red shirt anywhere.

She paced. For five more minutes, she watched men go in and out of the men's room. No red shirt. Maybe he'd gone home. Maybe he'd gotten scared. Maybe....

She checked at the concession stand. "Did a man leave a message for Mrs. MacLean? He would've been wearing a red shirt."

The lady behind the ticket dispenser took a quick, unsmiling look. "Sorry, lady. No messages."

Summer strolled over to the nearest restroom, making sure she kept visible, her eyes constantly assessing, searching, flicking back and forth.

Finally she stopped a man preparing to enter. "I'm sorry," she said. "I'm trying to find someone. I'm afraid maybe he got sick. Do you think you could look inside and see if a man in a red shirt is there?"

The man looked at her as if she were some kind of freak. "Sure, I guess so."

Hardly caring what anyone thought at this point, Summer leaned against the cement wall and strained her ears to hear. When she heard a voice mutter, "Jesus Christ!" she lunged forward.

Ignoring the men who tried to stop her and tell her she was going into the wrong restroom, she charged in anyway. There, hunched against a wall, huddled a small, thin man dabbing at his face with a wadded-up wet paper towel. The man she'd spoken too was squatting before him asking if there wasn't something he could do to help, mister.

Summer pushed him aside. She knelt down on the dirty floor. "Sib," she said, "I'm Mrs. MacLean. Come on, I'll help you up. What happened to you?"

What happened was that Sib had waited beside the concession as he'd told her he would. Someone had come up from behind and struck him to the ground. Then, grabbing him by the back of the hair, they had slammed his face against the asphalt, shattering his glasses.

He was virtually blind without them. Summer picked up what she could of the ruined spectacles.

A man rushed in, looked at her and blurted, "You're in the wrong place, lady."

She smirked at him. "No, you are. Can't you read?"

While he went back out to check, she helped Sib walk out. The drive back to Miami was accomplished without a bobble. She kept up a cheery monologue all the way home, but privately she was planning to call Jerry Haywood, one of her favorite detectives. Someone had tapped her telephone line. She wasn't taking one more phone call before it was debugged.

But first, she must find Harris, and they must take Sib to somewhere safe.

From the first moment he laid eyes on it, Harris despised Summer's house.

It was a private, tree-lined street. Here homes maintained their own private sanitation service, a staff of gardeners and a force of security guards. Many of the homes were even more lavish than hers, set back among trees and velvet lawns and hedges and twisting brick pathways.

Summer's was a soaring, columned affair with rows upon rows of high windows, having twelve baths and a half acre of sculpted lawn—a realtor's dream and a cleaning woman's nightmare. Just after World War II, Arthur had built the house for Pat. When the MacLeans retired and moved up to West Palm, it had been passed down to Martin as a wedding present.

By default, it was passed down to Summer, though she could no more afford to keep the gargantuan place heated and cooled than she could keep up with the buttressing, scraping, and painting. To say nothing of the treatment for termites, repairs from the wind, upkeep from the rain and the gardening. Plus the critical eye of her in-laws who insisted on "helping out" with money when things began looking a little shabby.

Harris pulled the Bentley into the two-car garage and thought dourly of his ten-year-old Ford pickup still parked at the development in West Palm Beach.

"I know," Summer murmured, reading his thoughts as she swung out and led the way to the rear entrance. She fumbled through her bag for the key to the back door.

"Arthur bought us the Bentley, and three-fourths of the house is closed off. All this is nothing but a front, and if the MacLeans wouldn't have a stroke, I'd move tomorrow. Try to ignore it all."

"You can ignore acid rock," Harris mumbled unenthusiastically as he trailed along behind her. "You can even ignore Godzilla. You don't ignore a Bentley or this house."

Laughing, Summer turned the key in the lock. "Godzilla."

Tom swung open the heavy oak door before his mother could push it open and stood with his arms full of a huge Persian cat. He peered up in all his wonderful innocence, his thin face beatific with smiles. "Hi, Mom."

It had been Summer's plan to talk to Tom before he actually met Harris, to sort of prepare him for the man whose name was smeared all over the media along with Rex Jernigan's. More than anything, she wanted them to get off to a good start.

Now she blinked at her son and gasped, "You're back."

Tom's face fell. "Gran'Pat brought me. You said you wanted me to come home early."

"Of course I did, darling. I've missed you like crazy."

Summer wrapped her arms around him and swung him in a circle and kissed him until he blushed and the cat, yowling his dislike, jumped to the floor and darted behind the grandfather clock. Then it dawned on her what Tom had said.

Releasing him, Summer glanced around the large den and whispered, "Your grandmother! Oh, Lord. Is she here now?"

Tom mutely nodded his head up and down.

"Where's the Seville?" Summer demanded, her voice rising to a shrill stage whisper. "I didn't see it."

"Grandpa's gone to the store." Tom gave a sidelong glance up at Harris.

Summer rolled her eyes at the ceiling, having forgotten Harris in the momentary dilemma. Harris was wearing jeans, neatly starched but faded, and a T-shirt and sport jacket. His boots were a bit scuffed, and he was letting his beard grow. He was tired of reminding her of Martin MacLean, he'd said.

"Hello, Tom," Harris said and extended his hand as if they had always known each other and this were a mere formality after a brief absence. "I'm Harris Chandler."

Summer waited, as if she expected the roof to start leaking.

"I know." Tom extended his own small paw and peered up, wide-eyed. "We saw you on television."

"Yeah."

No apologies? Summer wanted to take Tom by the shoulders and say, "But everything you saw on television was misrepresented. Harris isn't really like that."

Releasing the boy's hand, Harris stepped out into the minutely appointed kitchen and gazed around, as if he were a twelve-year-old boy himself. Good going, Harris, she thought, you really know how to impress kids.

"Some kitchen," Harris said as if he would just as soon face a Coleman cook-out stove and a can of baked beans. "You eat in here?"

"Nah," Tom said and followed the tall man, matching him step for step. "We eat in the dining room."

Harris shot Tom a suspicious, squint-eyed look. "No butler, though. Right? Always pushin' the hot dogs to the back of the refrigerator where you can never find 'em?"

Tom tried to hide a smile, but it popped through. "But Mom does. Too many food additives, she says."

"She makes you eat granola bars."

The boy laughed out loud. "And whole-wheat spaghetti."

"Yeah. Who wants to live to old age anyway?"

Tom giggled. Before he could reply, Harris said gently, "They say I look like your dad."

"Harris—" Summer started to interrupt. What did Harris think he was doing?

But Tom had turned down one side of his mouth. "Maybe. A little at first. You don't act like him, though." The room grew still and very, very quiet. Tom added, as if Summer were not anywhere around, "My dad's dead."

Without looking, Summer groped behind her for something to sit upon. In the doorway beyond them stood Pat, and at Tom's point-blank utterance of the word "dead," she lifted her hand to her mouth. Death, like blame, was a word no one said out loud around the MacLeans.

If Harris noticed Pat's presence, he gave no indication of it. He walked over to a gadget hanging on one of the circular racks above the butcher-block island in the center of the kitchen. Without turning around, he said, "Your brother's dead, too."

Tom shrugged, but to Summer's astonishment he didn't seem overwhelmed by the bizzare discussion he and Harris were having. Then Summer realized that it wasn't the discussion Harris and Tom were having that had turned Pat to the shade of a sheet; it was Harris's resemblance to Martin.

"Are you a criminal?" Tom asked as calmly as if he were inquiring about Harris's suntan.

Pat reared back, aghast, but Summer, as she glimpsed Harris's grave consideration of the question, began to understand several things. Harris wasn't the brash man who had dealt with Emilio. He was treating Tom as an equal, and he was neither shy about discussing death nor alarmed at answering personal questions about himself.

"I've often wondered about that, myself," Harris said. "I think I've done some criminal things. Have you?"

Tom ran his thin fingers through his hair as he pondered. "I don't know."

"Well," Harris said, walking over and rearranging the hair that Tom had mussed, "I've been in jail, and some people say that's proof I'm a criminal. To my mind there's just one basic law, and that is to look out after the next fellow. I don't want to steal from him, and I certainly don't want to kill him. I guess I don't want to hurt him at all. Maybe I'm not a criminal."

Laughter bubbled up from Tom's throat. "I guess I'm not either."

Harris flabbergasted Summer by bowing from the waist before Pat, who still waited in the doorway with her mouth open. "Mrs. MacLean? I want to apologize for any worry I might have caused you and your husband. I'm sure that

Summer's explained everything. I want to add my regrets to that."

Pat appeared in a state of shock.

Tom shyly tapped the tall man's arm, and Harris, without waiting for Pat MacLean's reply, grinned down at him. "What?"

"Did you really get found by Titus Little like they said on TV?"

Harris laughed. "Maybe I should tell you about that."

"Come on!" the boy shouted. "We'll be in the living room, Mom. Call when dinner's ready."

The insult to Harris came with the flickering of an eyelid. In fact, it was the lowering of Pat MacLean's lashes that wielded it. Harris saw horror pass over the woman's face as she envisioned him sitting upon Martin MacLean's priceless furniture.

"Ah—" Hesitating, Harris removed Tom's hand from his arm. "Maybe we'd better make that some other time, Tom. I really need to be getting home. We'll take a rain check. Okay?"

Summer was furious. Tom was embarrassed without knowing the reason why.

Harris swiveled on his heel and met Summer's infuriated eyes. "I guess I'll have to ask you to drive me home."

"Summer doesn't drive," Pat said. "I can take you."

Through a terrible smile, Summer said, "I'll take care of it, Pat. Thank you."

Tom bounced back with typical boyish enthusiasm. "Can I come?"

"Sure," Harris said.

"No," Pat said at the same time.

The declarations of war. Summer realized now that if she wanted Harris, she would have him at the disapproval of Tom's grandmother. Her smile was a torture.

"It's all right, Pat," she said. "Tom can come."

The crests of Pat's cheeks spotted with crimson. She compressed her lips.

"I'll be right back," Tom said happily. "I want to get my football."

"Football?"

"I want Harris to get Titus Little to autograph it."

"We'll wait for you in the car," Summer called feebly after her scampering son.

"Well," Pat said at last, lifting her silver brows and drawing in her breath, smoothing her throat with her diamond-studded hand. "I think I hear Arthur at the door. Don't bother to see me out, Summer, darling. If you remember, I lived in this house before you and—this man— were even born."

An icy hand closed around Summer's heart. *Go*, she thought. *Go, Pat, before you do irreparable damage*.

As Pat was leaving, she turned back, her condescension cold and generations old. "If you move in, Mr. Chandler, I do hope you don't ever sell the house. If you ever need money that badly, please come to me. After all, it was Arthur who got you out of jail this time. I'm sure we'll be used to it by then."

When Summer looked at the stony, monumental face of Harris as he stood with his eyelids closed, only a flicker of movement beneath them, she knew she was losing him.

Chapter Twelve

Everything was hideously wrong.

When Summer stormed out the back of the MacLean mansion, she took one look at Martin's Bentley and wished wretchedly that it was a Volkswagen. She wished the mansion was a tepee. She wished she were a two-bit legal aide working out of an insurance office. She wished...that things were any way except the way they were.

No one spoke as Harris drove out onto Highway One and headed north. Summer stared mutely at the MetroRail. Tom pressed his nose against the window and blew vapor mists and wrote his name in them.

Summer glanced over at Harris's stern, silent profile. What did she say? *I'm sorry that Pat thinks you're beneath us, Harris.* Or, *Pay no attention to Pat. She's just prejudiced against ex-convicts.*

As Harris turned and followed the Miami River, the residential districts grew more and more old, the streets more narrow. Summer pressed the bridge of her nose. Her head was hurting. Her head? Her heart was breaking.

The lane Harris switched onto was narrow and winding, and the purr of the car was like a sleek cat prowling in the night with its eyes flicking out in a brilliant arc against thick borders of fir trees and small expanses of turf here and there.

The large stone house—what she could see of it for the secretive shrubbery—rather resembled a Norman castle with its tower jutting into the clouds like a needle. Summer was surprised. Harris had spoken of his home so modestly.

"This is yours?" she said.

The curl of his lips said he had read her mind. "Don't get your hopes up, Summer. Only the tower is mine, and I don't own it."

She cursed her tactlessness and stared hard into the darkness. The drive twisted again until all that remained in the headlights was the tower flanked on both sides by old, lofty firs. Ivy dripped off the stones. The gardening was painfully neat.

At the base of the tower, a buff clump of color came to its feet. Harris rolled down the window and called out to Shag, and the dog, eagerness transforming his ugly face, dashed ahead to welcome them.

Once the engine died, they all sat for a moment in the car. Breathing was awkward. Everything was awkward. Summer looked over at Harris and reached out to touch his hand, which was flexing around the steering wheel.

Please don't hurt, she begged him with a look.

He caressed her face with his eyes. *Now do you see what we face?*

From the back seat, Tom's voice came in a strained, tearful whisper. "I'm sorry, Harris."

All it took was a child's tears.

Summer wanted to cry herself as she swiveled on the seat and reached back to wrap her arms around her son's bent head. When Harris's big, capable arms encompassed them all, she went limp with gratitude for his strength.

"Hey, now," he said, gruff with emotion, "your grandmother was doing the most natural thing in the world, Tom. She loves you, and she wants to protect you from anything that could hurt."

Tom's head lifted. The streaks of his tears glistened in the glow of the dashboard. "You won't stop coming to see us, will you?"

Harris ruffled his hair. "No, I won't stop coming."

The boy shrugged shyly. "I just thought that maybe you and Mom..." Realizing the awkward ground he had just ventured upon, he ducked his head. "Oh, I don't know what I meant. Can I get out and play with the dog now?"

Once they were alone, the barrier that lay on the seat between Harris and Summer was as real as the stones that threw the headlight glare back into their faces. Wasn't it stupid? she thought, that they couldn't just say, "To hell with it"?

She wanted to reach across the barrier. He wanted to reach across it. But all they could do was look at each other with agony in their eyes.

They cooked dinner in the yard. The dreadful food spared them a discomfort neither of them could bear.

Harris found frozen wieners in the top of his refrigerator. Tom happily began singing a television commercial while Summer filled her arms with mustard, mayonnaise, relish, knives, napkins and paper plates and stumbled outside with them.

Harris set up the grill only to discover that Shag had ripped open the briquettes, and they had to use the microwave instead. After eating, they inspected Harris's shrubbery by flashlight. Harris knew his landscaping, Summer discovered, and was lost in all the talk about Pittosporums and *Choisya ternata* and *Thuja Occidentalis*.

"Can I go watch *Star Trek* reruns?" Tom asked as he tired quickly of the gardening.

Summer hid her smile.

"Take Shag with you," Harris called after him and mumbled under his breath, "that dog has a thing going with Shatner."

Shaking her head, Summer laughed for the first time. "I don't blame him. I kind of have a thing going myself."

Her laughter captured the yearning mood as surely as a net thrown out to gather in their history. The night smelled of freshly watered blooms and still-warm trees. They walked hand in hand.

She asked him, "Do you rent this place, Harris?"

"Not exactly," he said.

"There doesn't seem to be anyone at home in the castle."

"They generally go to Colorado when it's hot. I did them a favor once. They just let me live here whenever I need to."

Summer leaned her weight on his arm and felt the memories rolling in on him in waves. "You don't have to tell me any more if you don't want to."

He laughed. "Which means I'd better if I don't want a thirty-minute sulk on my hands."

"Nonsense."

"I know you pretty well by now."

"I wonder." She dipped her head, leaving him for a moment in her own memories.

Their breaths were lost in the night's soft focus of birds settling down for sleep and crickets rousing so they could go crazy in the damp summer flowers. When Harris spoke, it was with the gentleness of someone who has been reading poetry.

"These people once had a son. By the time he was fourteen, he was a junkie. Mainlining heroin. They knew something about who I was, and they said they would pay me whatever I wanted if I would straighten him out."

Summer stopped walking to study the curious light in his eyes. He seemed able to see in the dark. He seemed able to read the secrets of every man, and it frightened her. He would always know more about her than she would know about him.

"Go on," she prompted him.

He flicked the ball of his thumb against his thickening mustache. "I moved in here. Into the tower. It took me weeks of working with him. There were times when I thought he'd never make it. Every time I got him on his feet, he'd go right back."

"What happened?"

"He stole some money from me once to make a connection. It sent me over the line. I beat him within an inch of his life and said I was through with him. I don't know, something kind of clicked in him. He didn't have anyone left by that time but me."

"Did he make it?"

Harris patted his pockets for a cigarette, then realized that he had left them inside.

"You don't need a cigarette to tell me this," she chided tenderly.

He smiled. "He moved back in with his parents. To my knowledge he never put a needle in his arms again."

Summer hugged him. "Happily ever after."

"Not quite. The draft got him. He never came home."

Christ! With compassion welling up into her throat until it threatened to strangle her, Summer walked away from him and turned her back. Whoever said that loving another person was wonderful. It ripped the heart out of you. It made you hurt in ways you couldn't imagine.

Softly, almost inaudibly, as if she didn't really want to know the answer, she said, "You aren't ever going to marry me, are you, Harris?"

It was as if everything were suddenly mislaid—the mellow night clouds that hung like lace curtains above them, the breeze flinging them back with no apologies.

Harris stepped up behind her and wrapped his arms around her and buried his face in her hair. She felt the indestructible strength in him and despised it.

"Ever is a long time, Summer."

What could she possibly say to that?

At home in her own bed when the telephone rang, Summer didn't think she'd ever been asleep. She'd been lying there, torturing herself over Harris. She groped for the receiver, dropped it, found it again. "Yes?"

The silence was not that of a disconnection. Far in the distance blared ZZ Top.

"Who is this?" she demanded. "Who did you want to talk to?"

"Is this Mrs. MacLean?"

"Yes." Summer thought she detected an accent of some sort. Dragging herself up onto the pillow, she fumbled for the lamp switch and tried to clear her head. "It's all right. You can talk to me."

"Would you be interested in some information?"

"For real?"

"Sure, for real."

"Will you tell me your name first? I'm not interested if you don't tell me your name."

"Tony Domingue. I work here at the Olympic. I just saw something I thought you might be interested in. It has to do with the man in the paper."

"Who?"

"That bank guy. I read where you weren't going to prosecute the case, but anyway, I—"

Summer was already out of bed, scrambling for her shoes, dancing around on one foot and trying to keep the receiver pinched between her jaw and her shoulder.

"You work at the Olympic?"

"Yes, ma'am."

"You know where Arthur's is?"

"Yep."

"I'll meet you there in about a half hour. Hey, Tony?"

"Ma'am."

"Don't you stand me up. I'll pay well for anything you've got."

"I ain't doing it for the money, Mrs. MacLean."

For what then? she wondered as she flew to the closet and snatched out a pair of jeans and a cotton knit top.

She had no difficulty spotting Tony Domingue once she got to Arthur's. She'd been right. He was Puerto Rican, and he appeared still to be wearing his working clothes with the jacket removed.

He looked up from the table where he'd been drinking coffee and smoking. When he extended his hand, she smiled. "Thank you for being here. So many times people get cold feet."

"I thought about it for a little while before I called."

Summer made small talk until her coffee arrived, and she sized up Tony while he told her shyly about himself. He was about Angelica's age, she guessed, barely pushing thirty, not especially deprived but certainly not affluent. She had no reason to think he would lie to her.

"If you didn't do this for the money," she asked him, "why did you?"

He raked through his hair in a gesture that reminded her painfully of Harris.

"I'm doin' it for a friend," he said.

"What friend?"

Tony shook his head. "That don't matter. This is true. You can count on it."

Summer leaned back in her chair and crossed her legs. "Tell me then, Tony."

With difficulty, "This friend of mine, well, she's been havin' a little thing at the hotel with the state prosecutor."

Summer leaned forward, feeling as if she had just stepped out of the way of a truck that missed her by inches. But she compelled herself not to interrupt.

"Tonight it kind'a got out of hand," Tony was saying, "What the deal was, he wanted to kind of threesome-like, see, and my friend—well, she ain't into that. It made the big guy mad. Seems he owed this guy a big favor, and when she wouldn't cooperate . . . well, he scared her pretty bad."

"You mean he roughed her up?"

"Not bad, more mean drunk talk than anything else."

Summer could believe that, how she could believe that! Wetting her lips, wishing she could take notes but not daring to throw the young man off, she pleated her napkin. "You said this was about the bank man? Jernigan?"

Tony paused, drew a long, deep breath. "Well, I settled down my friend, see, and she gets in her car. But before she can get out of the place, this dude—the prosecutor, I mean—walks over and starts talking to her. I don't know what they said, more of the same, probably, 'cause she started cryin'. Anyway, after she left, the prosecutor gave me a twenty-dollar tip."

He fished the money out of his front pocket and laid it on the table. "When he went to his car, I was just standin' there watchin' him go. This other dude—he comes out of the hotel, then, and he gets into the car with the prosecutor. I got a good look at 'im. It was the man in the paper, all right. Jernigan. That's his name, ain't it?"

Summer sat covering her mouth with both hands, and she nodded without speaking. Her brain was seething. All this time she'd been after the wrong man! It wasn't Starky who had framed Harris to cover his tracks, it was Neil!

But what now? Did she have enough to turn the matter over to the police? Neil was clever, oh, was he ever clever. There was no telling what he'd promised Jernigan to protect him until the election. And what did this mean to Harris? Nothing, perhaps, if she couldn't prove it in court.

Wetting her lips, smiling at Tony, she asked, "If I ever needed you to, would you tell on a witness stand what you just told me?"

Tony dropped his head until his chin nearly touched his chest. "I knew you'd ask me that. My friend, I mean... I couldn't do her that way. They'd get her up there and make her tell all her private stuff. You know how that goes. I—"

Summer laid her hand over the boy's. "It's all right. At this point, I'm not sure I have a case anyway, Tony. Tell you what, I want you to take this, and I'll work on things from a different angle. You've been a wonderful help. Maybe I won't even need you."

Reaching into her bag and flipping through the bills in her wallet, Summer drew out two twenties. Folding them, she slipped then into the curl of his hand.

Tony looked up and shook his head, pushing the money back at her. "I mean it, Mrs. MacLean, I—"

"The money isn't for what you told me, Tony, it's for being the kind of young man who does what needs to be

done. I have a friend who's taught me just how rare a quality that is these days. Don't ever change. I have to go now."

He rose awkwardly with her. After waving once, Summer didn't look back. She had to get a little sleep. Tomorrow she was going to her detective friend, Jerry Haywood.
She was going to get down on her hands and knees and beg
him to wire her. Then, she was going to deal with Neil herself.

With all his faults, Harris had never been much of a
drinking man, but tonight he wanted to get so drunk that he
couldn't walk to bed. After searching the house, however,
he discovered to his dismay that the only bottle—and it
contained only one healthy shot, not nearly enough for his
purposes—had sat for several months minus a bottlecap.

Pulling on a shirt over his head, he took the flashlight and
made his way through the thick hedges and masses of shrubs
to the little-used back door of the Smith's empty house. The
key was where it always was, beneath a crusty pot with a
dead fern in it.

Fishing it out, he opened the door and ordered Shag to
remain outside. He walked down the clammy hall and
through the dank, dusty rooms. As his feet pressed into the
floor with splintery sighs, the house seemed to tremble. He
remembered where the liquor cabinet was, and he swept his
light over the clumps of dust covered furniture that stared
back at him like ghosts ordained to mark the nature of every
trespass in the owner's absence.

He found a bottle of old blended whiskey and broke the
seal on it. Twirling off the top and lifting the bottle in sa-
lute to the watching ghosts, he tipped back his head and let
the mellow liquor scald the lining out of his throat.

For a few moments he gasped and stood with his eyes
watering. *Oh, Summer, you're the first person who's ever*

shaken me down to my roots. But you did that. I thought I had it all worked out—all that self-sacrifice of mine, the dues I paid so I could hang on to that last shred of pride. But I can't have pride and you, Pat MacLean will see to that. And it's so hard to let it go. So damned hard.

Recapping the bottle, Harris took a final look at the phantoms and left them to their solitary vigil. He locked the back door and stood listening to the crickets and watching the moths discover his light. Dropping heavily down upon the back steps, he switched off the light and wished unhappily he could talk to Bud.

Sniffing his need to understand, Shag hobbled up and plopped down beside the feet of his master.

Harris chuckled bitterly and sluiced down another drink. "We're a couple of strays, eh, boy? You and me?"

Only the crickets cared, and one lonely owl.

"You know, Shag, I really don't understand why we put ourselves through things like this. But she makes me want to be good, isn't that a kick? All my life I've sworn I didn't want to fit in, and here she is, making me want to do it. And buy a station wagon, for crying out loud, and have kids." Another drink. "She even makes me want to be looked up to and respected by her friends and that witch of a mother-in-law. Hell, she makes me want to buy a suit."

Another drink. A sigh. "But some things just can't be dressed up, Shag—the color of a person's skin, scars, death . . . the past."

Even in front of the dog, Harris was embarrassed when his face twisted and the tears rushed hotly out of his eyes. He gagged for control over them, but they came anyway, running into his rough mustache, his mouth, into his beard.

Whining, Shag nuzzled and offered his sympathies. Draping his arms around the dear old friend who had seen almost as much of the desperation of man as he had, Harris wept as he had not wept since his mother died.

Jerry Haywood wired Summer for surveillance against his better judgment. It wasn't that he doubted the track her investigation was taking; he didn't think she was a match for the state prosecutor.

By the time Summer had all the necessary equipment explained to her, she knew the exact dress she would wear to coax Neil out into the open, a burgundy silk that was full-skirted and caught high at the point of a deep, plunging neckline. She would place the microphone in her bra and lean forward a lot.

She told Jerry she would set up a meeting with Neil at one of the clubs on Miami Beach. She would call him to confirm so that he could be prepared to monitor her from the outside. Until then, she was staying out of her office and away from her house.

Summer did, however, go home long enough to leave a note for Tom so he would find it when he returned from his friend's house later in the day. She put Jerry Haywood's number on it in case of emergency. If Tom decided to spend the night with his friend, he must put a message on the answering machine so she would know where he was.

Harris didn't actually become frantic to find Summer until around noon. He has awakened with a prodigious hangover, but by nine o'clock he was able to navigate passably well.

Work was out of the question. He couldn't do anything until he found Summer and settled everything between them. Did he propose marriage, he wondered dryly, or did he accept her proposal?

Yet, every attempt to locate Summer wound up in a dead end. At the end of his rope, Harris stormed into the municipal building and tried to get Summer's whereabouts out of Angelica. The young woman was so taken aback, she couldn't put two words together. She had no idea where Summer was, she said. Summer had just called and said she wouldn't be in.

That was when Harris called Lila Dean.

The reporter picked him up in front of the municipal building. The first thing Harris said to her as he poked the upper half of his body in through an open window was, "You wanna go with me to break into Summer's house?"

No, Lila did not want to break into Summer's house. But she drove Harris so he could.

"Jerry Haywood," she said in amazement when Harris sauntered out to the car after having read the note. "Well, he probably won't tell us anything, but I guess it won't hurt to try."

Jerry Haywood was a systematic man, swarthy with a thick black mustache that curled around the corners of his mouth and a short, thick neck coming out of his perfect collar and tie that reminded Harris of a turtle. His fingers were manicured, and his eyes, missing nothing, revealed nothing either.

Harris's shirt that he'd dragged out of the dryer and the tie he hadn't worn in years were slightly seedy in the face of the detective's meticulous neatness. He had, however, pulled on his newest jeans and his best shoes and topped it all off with a sport coat, which gave him, even if he was unaware of it, an off-beat charm that turned more than one thoughtful feminine head.

If Lila Dean hadn't been with him, though, Haywood wouldn't give him the time of day, and Harris knew it. Which was the point, really; it was five o'clock in the afternoon, and no one knew where Summer was.

But for once, fate favored Harris. Jerry Haywood received Summer's call as they all sat in his office. When he hung up the phone, Harris asked simply and eloquently, "How much will it take for you to allow Miss Dean and myself to come with you on this stake-out?"

Summer had decided that she would come closer to getting Neil drunk by trickery. She decided on the Konover Hotel on Miami Beach for several reasons, one being that it wasn't too far from where Neil lived, and the others having to do with style, live entertainment and the fact that she knew a bartender there.

Surprisingly enough, Neil was on time when he kept their date. He seemed to have no difficulty spotting her in the small, intimate cave that was lit with such intimacy that a person could get lost trying to find a table. From the bar where she was nursing a Bloody Mary that was, by prearrangement, only a Virgin Mary, she waved at him.

Neil was in fine fettle tonight. Summer watched his reflection in the mirrors behind the bartender's head as he weaved his way over between waiters and customers and a lovely female vocalist whose platinum hair looked as if it had exploded. Even Neil's reflection had finesse.

She had told him on the phone she wanted to make amends.

"I thought it was a joke," Neil confessed as he melted onto a plush stool and signaled the bartender. "It's about time, counselor."

"Now, Neil," Summer said, getting off to a bad start from the beginning by beginning to perspire, "would I joke about keeping my career from going down the tubes?"

He laughed. "Sweetie, the way you were going, you wouldn't have had a career. Rum and Coke, bartender. Summer, you want to get a booth?"

Shrugging, Summer gave the bartender a warning that whatever happened, he was to keep the booze out of her drinks. "Sure," she said and self-consciously touched the dip of her neckline.

He noticed. "Great dress," he said and headed for the other side of the lounge where the decibel level was a little less acute.

"Thanks."

"A little on the brave side for you, isn't it?"

"Well, you know what they say, Neil."

"No, what?"

Summer laughed. "I was hoping you knew."

Neil laughed promisingly, and Summer thought that perhaps this was all going to turn out well, after all. The tape recorder was a lump at the base of her spine, however; if Neil asked her to dance, she was in trouble. *Jerry? Are you out there?*

Yes, Jerry was out there, and not alone. For over an hour after Neil arrived, the trio of listeners waited in the drab, chromeless car on the parking lot of the Konover.

"I don't think it's working," Lila Dean said. "He sounds very sober to me."

Jerry Haywood chewed the end of a cigar that was making Harris nauseous. "Give 'er time."

Harris said nothing. He had already gone through several lifetimes just listening to Summer's false bravado and knowing that she was doing it for him. If he'd known in time to stop her, no way would he have let her expose herself like this.

Haywood fiddled with some knobs on the monitoring device. Music blared in their ears, and he turned it down. Summer was heard saying nervously, "No, I don't wish I hadn't taken the defense, Neil. The whole thing stinks. Jernigan's lying through his teeth. He'll break on the stand, I tell you. All I have to do is allude—I mean, just *allude*—to his sexual habits, and I'll have him spilling everything."

"You're crazy," Neil said, his voice now showing the slur of drunkenness for the first time. "And what do you know about Rex's sexual habits? My God, Summer..."

The words faded. The detective jiggled a knob, and music faded in and out. Harris felt his blood pressure escalating. He exchanged a dreading look with Lila.

"Because," Summer returned, saying, "he made a spectacle of himself over at the Olympic the other night. Or haven't you heard?"

Suspicion was a thick layer upon Neil's voice now. "So, you've turned to spying now? Tacky, counselor, real tacky."

A confusing pause where the waiter was heard, and Neil ordering another drink.

"Do you think you should, Neil?" Summer was heard to say.

"Don't turn to mothering, too, Summer, it isn't attractive."

The three people in the car grew more tense. The state prosecutor was growing surly. Harris wiped over his beard and heaved a sigh. "I don't know how much more of this I can stand."

"You wanted to come," Jerry Haywood loftily reminded.

Harris mumbled an oath.

"Shh!" The detective leaned nearer, listening hard. They were quarreling now, and Summer was leveling questions at Neil, whose brain was becoming too befuddled to fend them off: questions about who could have assaulted Sib and stolen Harris's records; questions about Starky's possibly protecting a prominent figure who had desperately set up a frame using Harris.

Neil haughtily accused Summer of treating him like the accused and said he was leaving.

Summer said he could leave if he wanted to. "But there's one thing I'd better tell you before you go, Neil," she warned so quietly the microphone hardly picked it up. "Get yourself a lawyer, Neil. Right away. You're going to need one."

"What're you talkin' about, you bitch?" he hissed at her.

Loud scraping blared over the monitor that made Harris steel himself and grip the door handle.

Lila grabbed his hand, held it tightly and shook her head. "She knows what she's doing, Harris."

Harris took several breaths and pressed his eyelids.

"I'm talking about grand larceny, Neil," Summer said in the same quiet voice. "I know it was you who made the deal with Jernigan, Neil. I know about your affair. I know about the little kinky things you and Jernigan do. How long has that been going on, Neil?"

Neil was wasted. His brain couldn't keep up. "What?"

"I've got everything on you, Neil," Summer bluffed. "The audit didn't go like you expected it to, did it? How much was it you borrowed at Pinnacle?"

"That audit won't show a thing against me! Damn it, Summer, that was an invasion—"

"Wow," breathed Jerry Haywood.

"And the man you sent to get Sib?" Summer's questions were razored now, firing quickly and driving Neil back and back and back.

"How did you know that?"

Lila Dean blew out her breath. "Oh, brother."

"He'll testify against you, Neil."

"He will not. He owes me, by God. He will not testify against me. An' I tell you what, Miss High Pockets, Miss Tight Ass, I wouldn't be throwing around all that talk about kink if I were you—you, who had t'get impregnated out of a bottle.''

Summer felt as if someone had struck her across the shoulderblades with a poker. Only one person besides Harris knew about that. Angelica, her best friend. *She* was the woman Tony Domingue was protecting. She was one who... Good Lord, she had been feeding Neil information.

With a flash of memory as clear as a bolt of lightning, she saw Angelica cleaning up the office the day Sib had called and told her about the record books.

Summer didn't totally understand the rage that sent her lunging to her feet and leaning over the table until her finger shook in Neil's face. "You went too far with Angelica, Neil. She'll turn state's evidence. Even if you're not convicted on at least a half dozen charges that I could file against you tonight, you won't be able to get ten votes in this state by tomorrow noon. By the time I'm through with you—"

Neil's roar was like that of a bull. Out in the car, Harris thought he could have heard the man raging even without the microphone attached to Summer. It was followed by a terrible crash of breaking glass and people's abrupt yells and confusion.

In the time it took looks to exchange, three doors flew open on the surveillance vehicle, and all three of them raced for the door of the lounge. Jerry Haywood reached there first, but Harris pushed in front of him, shoved through the door with a thrust of his shoulder.

In the melee, Summer truly didn't know exactly what happened. She knew that she was crying and trying to escape Neil's drunken rage as he grabbed at her dress and ripped one side of it down to the waist, exposing her breast, the microphone, the wires.

Once Neil saw that, he was a wild man. Summer clutched her clothes and tried to dodge him, but someone at a neighboring table stumbled into her and knocked her right back into him again. Neil swung at her, caught her in the stomach with a doubled fist.

She gagged and folded to her knees. But not before she saw Harris in the blur of her shock.

Harris lifted Neil completely off the floor by the front of his Ralph Lauren suit. Knocking over two more tables, he drove Neil into the nearest wall. He buried one fist into Neil's belly, then threw another to the side of his head.

Neil sprawled across the floor and struggled to his knees. Women screamed, more broken glass. The floor bouncers were fighting their way through as the vocalist yelped an obscenity over her microphone.

The manager grabbed the mike and began shouting. "Keep calm, everyone. Keep calm. It's just a little scuffle. Stay back, please. Eddy, will you grab the big guy, for Chris'sake? And somebody call the police."

Again Harris went at Neil, hit him, and Neil crashed against a railing and gasped loudly. Harris's heart was pounding madly in his breast now. Neil's face was bleeding.

"That was for the woman I'm going to marry, you animal," Harris growled. And with the last thudding punch before Jerry grabbed his arms and dragged him off, "And this one's for me."

Perhaps the last blow was the most potent, for Neil crumbled to the floor and didn't get up. Harris, not caring anymore, shook the detective's hands off him and swept over the crowd for Summer.

He found her standing beside Lila Dean, shaking, crying, trying to hold her dress together. His eyes overflowed, and he could not speak. What she had done, she'd done for him, and what he had done, he'd done for her. What more tribute did love exact?

He saw the answer in the lovely sparkle of Summer's eyes—Sensible Summer MacLean who knew him so well now. In her, he would find the best of himself. The past was immutable. But the future? Ah, it was for them together.

Her arms went around him naturally as he held her close, then led her through the streams of people who parted like walls and watched them go with voices, gestures, returning laughter, the jingle of coins and the clink of glass.

Intense pleasure filled Harris as he stepped with Summer into the warm night. Without caring who saw or how they looked, he kissed her. He gazed down into her face that was misty with love for him.

"I once told you," he said hoarsely, "that I was alone and empty, with nowhere to go."

Tenderness laced her smile. "I know."

"There is somewhere I want to go."

Summer reached up to hold his beard in her hands, her heart brimming. "Where, my lovely man?"

"Wherever you are."

"Harris, do we even know where that will be?"

"Does it matter?"

"No." Lifting up on her toes, she touched his lips with hers. "I think a lot of strain is going to be placed upon my first thoracic vertebra."

He smiled. "Infinitely."

She leaned back in his arms, her eyes narrowing with her best courtroom drill. "You do love me, don't you?"

Setting her on her feet, Harris took her gravely by the shoulders. "Summer, it's a hard and lonely job, but someone's got to do it."

Laughing, they walked hand in hand to Jerry Haywood's car. Life would be different now. They would not resist.

Silhouette Special Edition

COMING NEXT MONTH

THE ARISTOCRAT—Catherine Coulter
An arranged marriage in this day and age? There was no way Lord Brant Asher
was going to marry Daphne, the ugly duckling. Until he found that the ugly
duckling had grown into a beautiful swan.

A SLICE OF HEAVEN—Carole McElhaney
Lamont Cosmetics *had* to have Dr. Alex Harrison launch their new line. So
Cass Mulcahy went to Texas to reason with him—and instead found herself
losing all reason.

LINDSEY'S RAINBOW—Curtiss Ann Matlock
The Ingraham heiress suddenly found herself fighting for control of the family
business. How dared Michael Garrity try to take it from her! Then Lindsey and
Michael came face-to-face—and heart to heart.

FOREVER AND A DAY—Pamela Wallace
Stephen Kramer didn't want novelist Marina Turner to write her own
screenplay. But she refused to let him turn her novel into a trashy teen flick.
How could she prove to him that a collaboration would be profitable to both of
them?

RETURN TO SUMMER—Barbara Faith
Fifteen years earlier Sarah had fled Mexico in shame. Now she was back, and
history threatened to repeat itself. Was their future doomed by the past, or
would it survive the dark secret she kept hidden from the man she loved?

YESTERDAY'S TOMORROW—Maggi Charles
Just one ride aboard *Alligator Annie* convinced Susan Bannister to stay in the
alligator-infested backwater that was Florida State Park. She needed a
distraction—and *Annie*'s silver-eyed captain filled the bill.

AVAILABLE NOW:

SOMETHING ABOUT SUMMER
Linda Shaw

EQUAL SHARES
Sondra Stanford

ALMOST FOREVER
Linda Howard

MATCHED PAIR
Carole Halston

SILVER THAW
Natalie Bishop

**EMERALD LOVE, SAPPHIRE
DREAMS**
Monica Barrie

**Enchanting love stories
that warm the hearts
of women everywhere.**

SIL-ROM-1RR

FOUR UNIQUE SERIES
FOR EVERY WOMAN YOU ARE...

Silhouette Romance

Heartwarming romances that will make you
laugh and cry as they bring you all the wonder
and magic of falling in love.

6 titles per month

Silhouette Special Edition

Expanded romances written with emotion and
heightened romantic tension to ensure
powerful stories. A rare blend of passion and
dramatic realism.

6 titles per month

Silhouette Desire

Believable, sensuous, compelling—and
above all, romantic—these stories deliver
the promise of love, the guarantee
of satisfaction.

6 titles per month

Silhouette Intimate Moments

Love stories that entice; longer, more
sensuous romances filled with adventure,
suspense, glamour and melodrama.

4 titles per month

SIL-GEN-1RR